Highlander's Ransom

Books by Emma Prince

The Sinclair Brothers Trilogy:

Highlander's Ransom (Book 1)

Highlander's Redemption (Book 2)

Highlander's Return (Bonus Novella, Book 2.5)

Highlander's Reckoning (Book 3)

Viking Lore Series:

Enthralled (Viking Lore, Book 1)

Other Books:

Wish upon a Winter Solstice (A Highland Novella)

Highlander's Ransom

The Sinclair Brothers Trilogy

Book One

By

Emma Prince

Highlander's Ransom (The Sinclair Brothers Trilogy, Book One)

Copyright © 2014 by Emma Prince
Print Edition

All rights reserved. No part of this publication may be reproduced, distributed, or transmitted in any form or by any means, or stored in a database or retrieval system, without the prior written permission of the author except in the case of brief quotations embodied in critical articles and reviews.

For more information, contact emmaprincebooks@gmail.com.

This is a work of fiction. Names, characters, organizations, places, events, and incidents are the products of the author's imagination or are used fictitiously. Any resemblance to actual events or persons, living or dead, is entirely coincidental.

For Scott. Always.

Chapter One

February 24, 1303
Roslin, Scottish Highlands

Robert Sinclair wiped his bloodied blade on the sleeve of a dead Englishman. As he returned his sword to its scabbard, he let his eyes scan over his lands. The brown grasses of winter were barely visible underneath the bodies; though some were Scottish, most wore the armor and colors of the English. His clan's men, along with the McKays and Sutherlands, had managed, after three bloody engagements, to defeat the English army sent by Edward I to steal their ancestral lands. While all the Scots present would celebrate this victory long into the night, Robert had a personal stake in the outcome. Roslin was *his* land, and as Laird of the Sinclairs, it was his duty above all to protect his people and their homes.

"You fought well, Robert," Burke said at Robert's side.

Robert's right-hand man and closest friend let his eyes survey the battlefield before facing Robert. The two clasped arms, glad to have survived the day, though it wasn't merely chance that had seen them through. Robert had heard whispers, then murmurs, then shouts rippling through the English army when the red Sinclair plaid was spotted. And a few English soldiers had actually turned tail and run when they recognized him at the front of his men. Apparently his reputation as one of the deadliest sword wielders in all the Highlands had reached the English. The years of training, fighting with his brothers, and eventually the enemy were paying off. He hadn't been a boy for a long time, but he felt like more than a man today—like a true Laird.

"Aye, we did well for our people," Robert replied.

After a pause, Burke asked with a shadow of hesitation, "And what of Warren?"

Robert clenched his fists at his sides, feeling the heat of battle rise in him once more despite the icy breeze rippling his kilt. Only one man had eluded the death he brought down upon his enemies—Raef Warren. "Escaped. He ran like the coward he is," he rasped through gritted teeth.

Just as the English had heard rumors of Robert and the Sinclairs' lethal skill, Warren's reputation for cruelty and trickery preceded him on the battlefield; Robert had come across the snake a year earlier during one of many tense negotiations between several Scottish clans and the English nobles who sought to control them. Though a capable fighter, Warren preferred subterfuge over direct confrontation. He had been a key player in the breakdown of negotiations between the Scots and the English, counterfeiting missives between clan chiefs that hinted at a surprise attack. Those forged missives had nearly drawn blood that day in negotiations, and they certainly had led to the bloodshed at Robert's feet on this bleak afternoon. Robert had caught a glimpse of the man in the conflict that had ended just an hour ago, but Warren had slipped away.

"His time will come," Burke said, just as much anger in his voice as was in his Laird's.

Robert spat on the ground in frustration, then inhaled a lungful of the crisp February air to cool his nerves. The fighting was done for now, but he was sure Warren would cause trouble again. Next time, Robert vowed silently, he wouldn't let the man escape. Warren had helped bring this battle right to Robert's doorstep, endangering his people and lands. The Scots were victorious, but Robert would only consider victory secured when that weasel Warren could no longer poison England and Scotland with his lies. It seemed as though the real battle had only just begun.

Chapter Two

January 1, 1307

Alwin attempted for the hundredth time to shift to a more comfortable position, and for the hundredth time found none. Despite the fact that her heavy fur-lined cloak cut some of the chill and dampness from the air, it did little to cushion her bottom from jostling about on the hard wooden floor of the canvas-covered supply cart she rode in. Thank goodness this journey was only a long day's worth of travel. If she had to do this again tomorrow, she was sure her teeth would rattle right out of her head, her brain would turn to jelly inside her skull, and her bottom would be blue and purple with bruises.

She sighed, guessing that it had only been about four hours since she'd left her father's manor. She didn't even think of it as her home. No, Lord Henry Hewett saw her as more of a guest than his daughter, and an unwelcome guest at that. She knew she had never pleased him. Such thoughts no longer made her heart burn with shame and sadness anymore. Years of his criticisms and coldness had granted her the opportunity to practice thinking about him analytically rather than with the rage or heartache that characterized her relationship with the man. So far today, she had kept her thoughts cool, but another jolt of the cart had her biting back an oath.

Her first offense against Lord Hewett was the fact that she had been born a girl. After that, her very nature seemed to grate him. She simply couldn't bear to sit quietly with her hands in her lap and let the man control her life. She was always earning his ire, normally for sneaking into his study to read any of the precious few dusty volumes on his bookshelves. Her mother had done her best to encourage Alwin's "spirit," as she had called it, but after her death five years ago, Alwin was left alone with her brusque father. She knew he now only saw her as a bargaining chip, a tool that could secure alliances, greater wealth, and titles through a favorable marriage. He would reap the benefits of having a daughter after all, she thought with a lingering bitterness that surprised her. She was rid of him now, she reminded herself.

In a way, Alwin admitted, she could understand her father's motivations. They lived in the far north of England, and though her father's holding was considered rather wealthy, tensions had been running high of late. Her father needed more protection against the threat of invading Scots. With their location so close to the border, they were in danger of becoming easing pickings for the increasing number of bands of Scottish barbarians drifting southward in search of loot.

Lord Hewett needed to align himself with someone farther north than he was, so that he'd have a first line of defense. He also needed someone with more men-at-arms, weapons, and supplies to ward off invasion, or perhaps even take the battle to the Scots. And a nobleman with influence was necessary also—that way Lord Hewett could have a voice, albeit a muted one, with the power-players at court. All these criteria made his choice for his daughter's husband easy: Lord Raef Warren.

Warren held a castle just north of the border, on Scottish land. Although that often meant he had more raiders to deal with, he was also strategically positioned to have an ear to the ground for the first signs of Scottish rebellion. He had already participated in major negotiations and even some battles, and although the English had been bested a few years back, Warren had returned home with tales of Scottish weaknesses that could be exploited in the future—plus stories about his own fighting prowess.

It was a good match from Lord Hewett's perspective. He had probably even imagined he was getting the better end of the deal, Alwin thought with wry sadness. Normally, a man of Warren's standing wouldn't consider a marriage with a lady from such a comparatively smaller manor. Although they too were of nobility, albeit of a lower station, an alliance with her father did little to increase Warren's already-great wealth, prestige, and noble standing.

No, her father was trading on the rumors of her beauty to secure his own position. It didn't hurt, of course, that Lord Hewett had pulled together a sizable dowry for her as well, to be paid out after the wedding took place. Lord Warren had never laid eyes on her, but he must have believed what he had heard about Hewett's fair daughter and agreed to the union. Or perhaps her father's efforts to broadcast his wealth and her large dowry had caught Warren's ear. Lord Hewett was a proud man, who wanted all to know of his clever power play at securing Lord Warren as a son-in-law.

Of course, her father hadn't told her any of this directly. Alwin had had to piece the story together on her own, catching snatches of conversation, begging the messengers who shuttled missives between her father and Lord Warren to let a few words slip, and, when necessary, even eavesdropping on her father's study. At first she'd felt a little guilty about her actions, but her knowledge of the strategic union couldn't change matters, so what did it hurt? Alwin had no say in the matter. Her father had simply informed her last week—on Christmas, no less!—that she was to be wed to Lord Warren, and that she would depart on the first day of the new year. Yes, she could understand her father's reasoning and strategizing—when she ignored the fact that she was his daughter and not just another pawn in his power playing.

She fisted her hands in the soft brown material of

her dress, trying to suppress the anger rising in her yet again at the thought. She had tried to reason with her father that such an arrangement was ill-advised, and when that hadn't worked, she tried shouting, but to no avail. In fact, it only seemed to make things worse. Although her mother had seen the spark of fire in her as an advantage, her father had always hated it.

After the initial grief of her mother's death had passed, Alwin's home life had become unbearable as her father sought to break her of her sharp tongue and even sharper mind. At first, he only verbally admonished her for her unladylike behavior, but when that hadn't worked, he had resorted to locking her in her room for days at a time, not even allowing her loyal maid Betsy to check on her. The sharp pangs of hunger and thirst had only strengthened Alwin's determination to resist succumbing to his force of will. She knew she was smart, strong, and capable—why should she hide those traits under the guise of simpering submission or empty-headed daintiness? As she jostled in the back of the cart, her mind tugged toward memories of her mother, who had likely been the one to pass on such spiritedness to her, but from what Alwin could remember of her, her mother's spark seemed to have gone out. No doubt it was her father's iron will that had tamped it, she thought, the bitterness rising in her throat again. She would not allow that to happen to her.

And yet, she had no illusions that where she was

going would give her any reprieve from such treatment. Although she knew next to nothing about her intended husband, she imagined he too would demand her submission. From the skillet into the fire, she thought without joy. She would just have to be strong, even more so than before. She had survived her father's resentment, punishments, and anger for her entire life—a full twenty years of his disgust. Surely she could keep her spine straight and her chin up in a new setting and with a new overlord. Maybe her future husband would even welcome the fact that she could read, keep the household ledgers, and carry on an intelligent conversation. She swallowed the tears that threatened to choke her yet again. She hoped.

The canvas, which stretched over a wooden frame built several feet up from the floor of the cart, blocked the landscape from view, but she imagined they had crossed over into Scotland about an hour ago, and at least half of their journey remained ahead of them. It had been Warren's idea to transport her in a supply wagon. Apparently, Scottish raiders had been increasing their activity along several major roads that crossed the border.

She shivered at that. Although she was none too happy to be married off to some man she had never even met, at least he was English. She clung to the idea that he would adhere to knightly codes of honor, and even if he wouldn't let her help run the manor or make decisions beyond her wardrobe, at least he wasn't likely to physically hurt her. That much couldn't be said for Scots, or so she was told. She had never met one, but she had overheard tales from some of the men-at-arms involved in skirmishes. They were truly savages, according to these men. They were ruthless and lethal on the battlefield, dressed in strange clothes, and had no honor to speak of.

Warren confirmed such stories when he insisted that she not travel to him by carriage, but instead, conceal herself in a wagon surrounded by his guardsmen. He was sure that if any Scottish rebels saw a carriage fit to transport Lord Raef Warren's future bride to him, they would instantly attack and either kidnap her for ransom or kill her on the spot. She shivered again, tucking her knees up and pulling her cloak down over her slippered feet. She hoped the disguise worked. Although the soldiers surrounding the cart were Lord Warren's trained men-at-arms, there were only a dozen of them—enough to provide the illusion that they were protecting a load of supplies, not a noble lady.

To further carry on the ruse, Alwin had been forced to leave behind all of her trunks and even sweet old Betsy. The parting with her had been bitter; Betsy was Alwin's only true ally in her father's manor. Many a night, Betsy sat with Alwin as she cried herself to sleep, sometimes out of grief for her mother's passing, others out of frustration and anger at her father's treatment, and lately, out of worry for the future she was heading toward. Betsy was the only one whom

Alwin let see her true fears and hurts. Lord Warren had apparently assured Alwin's father that upon her arrival, she would have new clothes made to fit her new station as his wife, and that after the wedding, a few of her personal affects would be sent along with the dowry. She would also be granted another maidservant, but none could replace her dear friend.

She supposed some would consider her fortunate for such a marriage, but it did little to alleviate her sense that she was being shipped like cargo rather than a bride. She again tried to push these thoughts aside and remind herself to be strong; this represented a new beginning for the new year and her life ahead. But somewhere in the pit of her stomach she knew she was terrified, not just of this day-long journey, but of what awaited her at the end.

Once again, she chided herself for giving into her fears for a moment, and reminded herself that she could find ways to resist her future husband should he try to control her as her father had. She refused to be broken.

As she rearranged herself yet again, the wagon rolled to a stop. They had stopped a few hours back, but she had been told by one of the guardsmen that they wouldn't stop again for several more hours. Her skin tingled as she strained to hear what was happening beyond the canvas-covered cart. The silence stretched, and then just when she thought she would go mad from the quiet, all hell broke loose.

Chapter Three

Robert glanced off to his right, making sure he and his men were still moving parallel to the road, but far enough back to be swallowed from sight by the forest. They moved nearly silently, quite the feat for ten men on horseback to accomplish while navigating through the underbrush. The cold rain that had just begun to fall helped to baffle their noise. It hadn't soaked through his thick wool plaid yet, but judging by the deep gray of the sky visible through the trees, the rain wasn't going to let up any time soon.

The men didn't notice or mind, of course. He had been leading covert patrols, raids, and intelligence gathering missions just like this one for nearly four years in the Lowlands. Ever since the battle at Roslin, he and the allied clans knew the English wouldn't lick their wounds for long before they began plotting another assault. Despite having plenty to do back home as Laird, he had volunteered to lead several of these covert missions, feeling personally responsible for his clan's well-being, and longing to be a thorn in the side of the English war effort.

These days, he spent more time on these secret Lowland patrols than he did back in the Highlands. And it had been worth it. Over the years, he had intercepted countless supply trains, weapons transports, soldiers being relocated, and missives regarding the English's plans. The loot he had secured in the process was only a bonus; the real reward had been knowing that he thwarted their efforts to further subject and oppress his people.

Aye, he thought with an inward smile, he had been a thorn all right. He even knew that some of the interceptions he had made had been headed toward Raef Warren's holding. His mirth slipped at that. It still made his blood boil that the man had gotten away unscathed so many years ago, and to add further insult, the snake held land in Scotland. The borderline between the two countries hadn't been clear for years, but the castle Warren held was one of the farthest north into the Lowlands that the English had managed to secure. Robert knew a direct attack on Warren now would be foolish, of course. He could wait, though, and bide his time.

Instead, he would have to settle with a slower form of Warren's undoing, where it really hurt him the most—his ledgers. Robert couldn't guess at how much his attacks along these roads had cost Warren and the English, but trying to calculate it was one of his favorite activities to pass the time during the quiet moments. He suppressed another vicious grin at the thought.

Suddenly, the mirth left his mind, and before even realizing what he was doing, he threw up his fist, the signal to halt his men. They responded immediately to him, the only sound the pattering of rain through the winter-bare trees. After several tense seconds, he registered a faint sound along the road south of where they were concealed in the crisscrossing branches. His instincts had served him yet again. He motioned for several of his men to go farther north and cross the road out of sight of whoever traveled toward them, so as to be able to attack from both sides. He positioned himself and the remaining men on their side of the road.

"What do you think?" Burke's whisper was only audible to Robert.

"Small group—sounds like ten, fifteen armored men at the most, and only a few horses. Supplies?"

Burke gave a quick nod, and though he remained tense and ready to spring into action, a small smile quirked the corner of his mouth. Robert knew what he was thinking. This would be easy pickings.

As the sounds of the travelers grew louder, Robert caught several glimpses of the procession through the trees. Twelve soldiers on foot, and one on horseback in the front, surrounded a canvas-covered cart drawn by two draft horses. Their clunky armor gave them away as English. Robert squinted at their coat of arms and had to stifle a noise.

They bore Warren's coat.

He ran a hand down his bay stallion Dash's neck, reassuring the animal and himself. He was going to enjoy this, but he had to be patient. Each step the procession took seemed to stretch, and it felt like ages before they drew near enough. Robert deepened his breathing, trying to calm his body and clear his mind. He forced himself to focus only on this moment, his hands loosely holding Dash's reins, the soft patter of the misty rain on the bare branches overhead, and the anticipated weight of his sword resting in his palms.

Just as the party on the road came parallel to its awaiting trap, the rider at the front seemed to sense something and halted the wagon. Not giving them time to figure out what was afoot, Robert let out a piercing whistle, and he and his men came crashing through the forest onto the road to surround the procession.

The soldiers wasted no time in drawing their swords, but the Highlanders were already falling upon them. The clang of metal and screams filled the air, and time seemed to slow again as Robert swung, connecting his sword to the foot soldier in front of him. His strike found a weak spot in the soldier's armor where the helmet met the shoulder. The soldier barely had time to scream in agony before he was dead. Even through the haze of battle, Robert could tell within a matter of seconds that the Highlanders' element of surprise, their advantageous position atop horses, and their lack of cumbersome armor made the outcome inevitable. Robert let out a guttural growl as he dispatched another soldier toward front of the train, and somewhere in his mind, he registered the sure swing of Burke's sword to his right.

The man that Burke had just run through fell backward and toppled lifelessly onto the two horses pulling the supply wagon. The horses spooked, reared, and tried to bolt, but got tangled in their harnesses. As they lurched forward in confusion, the cart began to tip precariously onto two wheels. The horses continued to struggle and rear in the mayhem of blood and noise, and with a groan, the whole cart rolled over to rest on its canvas top, the wheels spinning slowly.

Robert pulled his attention away from the sight and back to the battle, which appeared to be over already. His men had made handiwork of the soldiers, but at a shout from one them, Robert turned to see the lone mounted soldier disappear in the distance farther up the road. The coward must have bolted the second the skirmish began, Robert thought with disdain. Although he could tell his men wanted to give chase, Robert help up a hand to stay them.

"Let the deserter deliver a message," he said in a clipped tone. "And let us hope he goes straight to Warren to tell the tale of how yet another one of his supply routes has been intercepted!"

At that, his men gave a hearty "Aye!" and began dismounting and cleaning their blades. Robert had his eye on the upturned wagon, though. The draft horses had managed to get their feet under them, but were twisted in their harnesses and spooked from the battle. Robert motioned to Burke to see to the horses, never taking his eyes off the wagon. What prize would he find inside this time, he wondered as he approached the rear of the cart and threw back the canvas cover.

Chapter Four

A sharp whistle cut through the muffling canvas. Then Alwin's ears were met with a cacophony of war sounds—the clang of metal on metal, the battle cries of the victorious, and the screams of the dying. Panic seized her as she got on all fours and began crawling toward the back of the cart. She didn't know what she planned to do, but she was sure as hell not going to remain trapped in here. As she reached the back flap of the cart's canvas covering, she stopped herself, however. Which was better: stay hidden inside the wagon, or walk right into a battle? If her guardsmen won the encounter, then the wagon was best. If they lost, it didn't matter, and she could count herself dead already. She attempted to scoot back toward the front of the cart, when the whole world seemed to tip on its side.

She felt her body hurtling into first the side wall of the wagon, and then its hooped canvas top. Pain shot through her, but it seemed distant as her panic increased. She tried to right herself, but more pain seemed to radiate from her body, and her legs got tangled in her dress and cloak. Somewhere in the back of her mind, she registered the fact that the noise outside was dying down. Fueled by sheer terror, she again tried to crawl toward the rear of the wagon. The battle must have been decided, and she had to face her fate.

Just then, gray light flooded the dim interior of the cart as the canvas flap was pulled back. She heard a sharp intake of breath, and then saw a large shadowy figure reach inside the cart toward her. Unable to see who it was, she tried to struggle backward, but two enormous, strong hands closed around her arms and dragged her forward. As she was pulled through the canvas door and into the weak gray afternoon light, she felt a scream rising in her throat, but it never came out.

On the ground in front of her feet, the bodies of the soldiers guarding her were strewn, their metal armor bloodied and dull under the misty sky. Her eyes traveled from the bodies to the men who stood over them. A band of fierce-looking Scotsmen stood wiping their blades and speaking quietly to each other in what she assumed was Gaelic. Unlike the English soldiers, they wore no armor, but instead had belted kilts of red wool around their waists, with a length of the same material draped over their shirted shoulders.

Her worst fears had come true. Her head spun, and bile rose in the back of her throat at the sight of the dead bodies and the Scotsmen standing over them. With the realization that she would now probably be murdered by these savages, she felt her knees give out beneath her. The hands on her arms jerked her upright, though, preventing her from collapsing, but also bringing her attention to the man in front of her.

She felt the color drain from her face and her eyes widen as she gazed up at the man holding her. He towered over her by at least a head. Like the others, he wore a bright colored plaid around his waist and over one shoulder, the fabric splattered with mud and blood. She could see his frame beneath his shirt was heavily muscled and battle-honed, the build of a true warrior. Hair as black as night settled around his wide shoulders, and the iciest blue eyes she had ever seen bore into her with a look of menace.

This time she did scream, or at least started to. As the sound left her throat, he clamped one of those huge hands over her mouth, stifling the sound. By now, all eyes had turned to her, and she quickly registered the range of expressions on the other Scottish warriors' faces. Surprise flitted across most, to be quickly covered in unreadable masks. They waited for what their apparent leader would do.

"What have we here?" the giant in front of her said in English with a heavy Scottish bur.

One of the other warriors approached the man holding her and leaned in, murmuring something that sounded like a question in Gaelic.

The giant's eyes flickered, and then a slight smile touched his lips, but not his eyes. She tried to draw back from the dangerous look on this savage's face, but he held her fast with one hand circling her upper arm and the other still clamped over her mouth.

The giant responded in Gaelic to the man who had spoken to him. Somewhere in the back of her mind, she realized she would have to come up with another word for him besides "giant," because as her eyes again flitted over the other men present, she registered that they were all tall, hulking warriors.

With a nod of his head, he sent the rest of the men back to their business. Despite their apparent interest in this turn of events, they went back to cleaning their blades, securing their horses, and dragging bodies out of the road, except for the man who had spoken softly to the one holding her. He remained at the apparent leader's side.

The two men made eye contact and seemed to be communicating something to each other. Alwin stood trembling, her blood still rushing through her veins. What would they do with her next? She would probably die, but by God, she would not go down without a fight. Without waiting to consider her actions, she sank her teeth hard into the hand that was still clapped over her mouth. Just as she felt his grip release slightly from her face, she brought her knee up swiftly between his legs. She heard a groan, but had already turned to flee from the road and into the cover of the trees. She sprinted as hard as she could through the forest, even though she could already hear her pursuers giving chase. It would be futile, she knew. Even as she ran, she waited for the blade she was sure was behind her to sink into her back. *Let them earn my death*, she thought as she heard them closing in.

Chapter Five

Robert had been shocked speechless for a moment at the sight of the inside of the cart. It had been empty except for a shadowy figure crumpled up and trying to scramble away. When he had dragged the figure into the dim light, he received another blow. Looking up at him had been a beautiful lass. Her creamy white skin had been flushed with fear, her light brown tresses tumbled and askew, and her eyes—those wide gray eyes—had gazed at him with such awe and terror. She was slight in frame, but he could see that she was a young woman, not a girl; her gentle curves were noticeable even through the cloak that lay slightly off kilter on her shoulders. He had been so startled by not only her presence, but also her beauty, that he couldn't piece the situation together until Burke had pointedly asked about the rumors they had been hearing. A few weeks back, he and his spies had begun to hear murmurs of a union being planned for Warren and some English lass. Robert knew if the whispers were true, it could mean trouble. If Warren had managed to ally himself through marriage, it could be another sign that war was imminent.

This lass's presence fit the puzzle pieces together—Warren's men providing a guard, the whispers about a marriage arrangement, even the underhanded way she was being transported. Warren was up to something. That thought had made Robert glare fiercely at the maiden, and he watched as the color drained from her face. He had felt her tremble and nearly faint, too. Good. Her fear would hopefully make her easy to handle. A plan had started to form in his mind, and he had looked to Burke for consultation.

Just then, though, the little hellion had sunk her teeth into his hand! At the same moment, he took a swift kick to the bollocks, and had toppled over backward into Burke. The two stumbled, but righted themselves quickly. Robert caught a flash of brown cloak disappearing into the woods off the road, and he growled his frustration. His men, noticing what had happened, looked to him for direction. He waved them off, trying to hide his ire.

"If I can't hold on to one little lass, I'm hardly fit to lead you all," he said gruffly. That brought a few chuckles from his men, but Burke refused to stand down.

"I'll go with you. She might pull that trick on you again, and we can't have our Laird unable to produce an heir," he said with the faintest hint of teasing in his voice.

Robert scowled at that, but let Burke follow as he

took off in the direction the lass had taken. They went on foot; the horses wouldn't be able to maneuver as easily in the thick underbrush. And with any luck, neither would the lass.

Alwin stumbled as her dress caught on a shrub. She could feel the energy which had given her the strength to escape just moments before begin to seep from her body. She simply couldn't keep running at this speed for very much longer. There was still some distance between her and her pursuers, but she could hear that they continued to give chase. She wondered fleetingly if they were toying with her, keeping just enough distance between themselves and her to give her hope and hurry her flight. Was she wasting her energy? She forced herself to keep her legs moving, despite the fatigue and pain settling over her. What was the alternative? Sit down and wait for them to kill her? That thought gave her another little burst of energy, and she kept running deeper and deeper into the forest. She didn't know where she was going, and she didn't care.

Just then, her slippered foot snagged on a root, and she went tumbling to the ground. By the time she sat upright, she could see two bright red splashes of cloth through the dense foliage moving toward her. She tried to scramble to her feet, but faster than she though possible, the two men had closed the distance.

Suddenly the one she had bitten and kicked dove forward and tackled her to the ground, knocking the wind from her lungs. He pinned her with his body weight and managed to wrap up both of her wrists in one hand. He yanked her hands upward and held them to the ground above her head. His warm breath fanned her face as she struggled to inhale underneath his weight.

"Stop," he commanded curtly.

"I'll never give in," she panted between gasps for breath.

She seemed to confirm something for him when she spoke, and a cold, menacing look settled over his face. After a moment, he turned his head toward the other man with him, who stood to the side.

"Prepare rope and cloth."

The man's bur was even more noticeable now. Alwin didn't understand at first why he had spoken to the other man in English, but then it dawned on her that he had wanted her to understand what he was saying. He wanted her to know he would kill her now. She struggled even harder beneath the giant warrior.

The other man nodded, and headed back through the forest toward where Alwin guessed the skirmish had taken place. The man on top of her stood up abruptly, dragging her upright with him by her wrists. She tried to twist out of his grasp, but that only seemed to annoy him. Without a word, he hoisted her up and over his shoulder like a sack of wheat. She shrieked in protest and slammed his back with her fists, but it seemed to have no effect. His arms held her in place like iron vises, and her blows appeared to bother him no more that the tickle of a feather. He began to trudge back the way she had run, and sensing the hopelessness of her struggles after several minutes, she grew still. Her body began to tremble as she acknowledged to herself that she would not escape, and her life was probably over.

The injuries inflicted from the flipped wagon and her dash through the forest began to throb. She had scratches on her cheeks, hands, and neck, and she felt deep bruises forming on her left hip and knee. Her feet began to feel numb, blessedly, for she was sure she had done some damage, her thin slippers providing little protection against the forest floor. She silently cursed her father and Lord Warren for agreeing that since she would remain in the cart for the trip, she didn't need winter boots. Tears formed in her eyes as she felt herself swirling helplessly. She was at the mercy of these savages, and from what she had heard, they didn't grant mercy.

Her captor was silent, although she was sure he could feel her trembling, and despite her best efforts, a few moans of pain, frustration, and hopelessness escaped her as she jostled on his shoulder. After what seemed like an eternity, she saw the forest floor give way to the road beneath his boots. Just then, he tipped her down onto her feet, and her head swam as the blood rushed behind her eyes. He held her steady, though, preventing her from crumpling to the ground.

Unfortunately, it meant she was face to face with him. She wanted to cast her eyes down so that he wouldn't see her tears, but his cold blue eyes pinned her in place. She thought for a moment she saw something flicker there, but it was replaced with ice so quickly that she doubted herself.

He broke their gaze and nodded to someone behind her, who handed him a length of rope and a strip of cloth. Her eyes widened on the rope, and she realized they were going to hang her right there and then. Although she longed to try to break free again, she knew it would never work a second time. This man before her could overpower her and snap her neck with one hand in the blink of an eye.

Fearing the answer, she asked in the strongest voice she could muster, "What are you going to do with me?"

He glanced at her but didn't answer. Instead, he asked brusquely, "What is your name?"

She hesitated, but decided it wouldn't make a difference. What did this savage care that she was a lady and from a respectable family as well? He probably hadn't even heard of her family name. On a shaky breath, she managed, "Alwin. Lady Alwin Hewett."

He frowned, drawing his dark brows together and down, but then nodded. Taking the length of rope in his hand, he grabbed both of her wrists and began tying them tightly together. She watched him, suddenly uncertain he meant to hang her. He looked up from her hands and met her eyes again, pausing briefly. Slowly, he wrapped the cloth over her mouth, reaching around her to tie it behind her head. Finally, he spoke.

"We are taking you with us, lass. If you behave, no harm will come to you. If not, well…I make no promises."

With that, he turned away from her wide and teary eyes and motioned for his giant warhorse to be brought over to him.

He turned to the rest of the men and barked something in Gaelic that sounded like an order. They mounted and waited for him. He smoothly slid into the saddle, then, with his giant hands under her arms, pulled her up in front of him so that she too straddled his horse. He reached around her waist and took hold of the reins, making a cage out of his muscular arms. She could feel his legs give the animal a little nudge, and then they were off.

Chapter Six

Robert couldn't believe his luck. Warren's betrothed! And Hewett's daughter, no less! He had hoped the supply wagon had held household goods or perhaps weapons at best, but this? He had no idea what he had done to deserve such a blessing, but he thanked his lucky stars all the same. She would be a powerful bargaining chip.

Hewett, the old fool, and been filling the air with his boasts of late about the dowry he had pulled together for his only child, a beautiful daughter, or so he bragged. It was no surprise that Warren had taken the bait. He doubted Warren cared for the girl at all, but if the price was right, the snake would likely marry a mule.

The lass pressed against him was certainly no mule, though. Her exceptional beauty must have sweetened the deal for Warren. Again, the man's pride controlled him; he would want to be talked about at court for having a pretty lass on his arm. Warren fancied himself an up-and-coming nobleman, and he went to a good deal of trouble to advance himself—even at the cost of others' lives, he thought with disgust.

Warren would take the dowry money gladly, and the beauty he could have on his arm at court was likely just an added bonus. Aye, that would explain Warren's willingness to align himself with the equally greedy and manipulative, if slightly more foolish, Lord Henry Hewett. Robert was familiar with the Hewett holding further south on the English side of the border. Hewett was of aristocratic blood, and though his holding was small and had almost no influence at court, he had amassed a fair bit of wealth in recent years, mostly by overtaxing his tenants and being ruthlessly tight-fisted.

With his bride kidnapped, Robert was sure Warren would go to great lengths to secure her back into his possession in order to save face—and collect the dowry. The man's pride and greed would prove useful to Robert for once.

Word would likely be reaching Warren soon of their attack, and Robert doubted the man would take it well. He and his men would have to travel hard back to Sinclair land. They were still within reach of Warren's holding, and would be for several hours of hard riding. Hopefully, the relatively mild weather would hold and they would only have to deal with rain and mud, not snow. The going would probably be tougher with the lass along, though. Despite the fact that she had put up a hell of a fight, she was a lady, and wouldn't be used to such conditions.

She appeared rather fragile as well—or, perhaps

that was the wrong word. Robert shifted his eyes to one of the legs that was plastered against his, down to her small slippered foot bobbing in front of his booted one in the stirrup. She was lithe, slim. Her bones were delicate, but she had shown real grit in her attempted flight from him. He frowned at her foot again. She was dresses all wrong for the travel they would be doing. Those house slippers were already torn and soggy. He could only imagine how frozen her toes must be. He glanced at the brown material of her dress, which poked out from her cloak. It was finely made but too thin for the outdoors in winter. It was also not particularly showy. It looked like Hewett's daughter was also subject to his tight-fistedness, despite the alliance her existence allowed him to make with Warren.

Perhaps the man didn't think much of her now that the arrangements had been made. Her cloak, at least, was stout wool with fur lining but probably wouldn't be enough at night, especially if she were sleeping on the ground. He couldn't allow himself to think she was too foolish, though, for she had surely had no idea when she departed—probably this morning, if his memory of the location of the Hewett holding served—that she would be kidnapped and spirited off to the Highlands to serve as a bargaining chip in a war she likely knew nothing about. Shock probably still enveloped her for now, but Robert would have to keep an eye on her when it started to wear off to make sure she didn't freeze to death.

He sensed the tension in her as she tried to keep herself rigid and separate from his body. That was difficult, given their position. He could feel the curvature of her body from her slim shoulders to the slight scoop in her lower back, and farther down, the softness of her bottom against his inner thighs—and groin. He had also noticed the way her waist curved inward pleasingly. The insides of his forearms brushed her sides so that he could reach the reins. A vision of her face came to him, her high cheekbones giving her a regal look, while her large gray eyes revealed both fear and strength. Before he had clapped a hand over her mouth, he had also caught a glimpse of full, rosy lips. And now, her long, soft brown hair, tumbled and loose, was only inches in front of him at nose-level. Giving himself an inward shake, he tried to analyze her looks from a distance. Aye, she was a beauty, but that would only help him wield her against Warren and Hewett.

He refocused himself on the task at hand. He and his men would have to travel hard to reach the Highlands and avoid being trailed. He could only hope this lass, this *Alwin*, wouldn't cause too much trouble.

Alwin fought against exhaustion, trying to stay upright. Although she had been too frightened at first to pay much attention to her surroundings or how much time had passed as they rode, she had slowly begun to come down from her panicked state. As she did, she began to chew on what was to become of her in these men's hands. It seemed unlikely they would kill her now; if they had wanted her dead, at least initially, they would have killed her back at the road. Likely, they wanted to ransom her, but she wasn't sure if it was to her father or Lord Warren.

She also didn't trust that they wouldn't still harm her. As her captor had said, he made no promises regarding her safety if she resisted. She also struggled to push away the thought that they might harm her in…other ways. She had heard the stories. She knew what these savages would do to innocent ladies they kidnapped. No one had yet made any such move, but she was uncomfortably aware of her captor's masculine strength behind her. Although she tried to keep their bodies from touching, she could feel the hard planes of his torso behind her and the corded muscles of his arms and thighs brushing her waist and legs.

She guessed they had been riding at a steady and swift clip for at least four hours. The already dim light of the day had slipped into an eerie bluish glow, which was now turning black. She had shivered for a while after her initial fear had ebbed, but now she seemed beyond shivers, beyond cold. The horse's stride beneath her had grown monotonous, and she feared she would go into a trance of shock, frigidness, and exhaustion soon. The man behind her gave no indication of his own fatigue, nor did those riding around them. She wished she didn't have to be so embarrassingly close to him—she was a lady, after all—but then again, his body radiated heat, which she was grateful for. Although she refused to succumb to the desire to lean into him, she no longer fought to create space between them. She would do what was necessary to survive, she told herself.

It seemed as though these men weren't going to harm her, at least not right away. That thought buoyed her, and also gave her time to plan an escape. Her mind was too jumbled with the events of the day to think of details at the moment, but she was sure of one thing: she wouldn't go willingly with these savages. Although she was not so proud as to try to deny her own fear, she wouldn't let it rule her. She was stronger than that—or at least she hoped she was. She had never had to face something like this before. She could only pray her spirit wouldn't fail her now.

Her thoughts were interrupted when the man behind her let out a soft whistle and halted his stallion. He dismounted smoothly then reached up to pull her off his horse. When her feet hit solid ground, she gasped and then groaned through the cloth covering her mouth. She hadn't realized just how numb her feet were or how sore the rest of her was. She felt like she was propped up on two wooden pegs, and she wobbled. Luckily, the man's hands stayed around her waist, steadying her. She looked up at him through the darkness but was met with a menacing frown and cold eyes. She tried to give him her fiercest glare back, unwilling to be cowed by the threat in his expression. Unexpectedly, he spoke.

"We stop only for a moment. You probably want to see to your needs."

She nodded, and he began to unwind the rope around her hands. When they were free, she yanked off the gag over her mouth.

"Who are you? Where are you taking me? What do you mean to do with me?" she demanded in a rush with more fire than she thought she could have mustered.

His scowl deepened, and she wished for a moment that she hadn't spoken so rashly. Nevertheless, she refused to cower despite her fear of the giant warrior before her.

"See to your needs," he repeated curtly. "I won't be far off, so don't try anything."

She hesitated for a moment, but sensing that if she didn't hurry she would miss this opportunity to relieve herself, she turned and hobbled awkwardly toward a copse of bushes. She registered that her hands were free and that she would be out of sight of the men for a moment, but quickly decided against an attempt at escape just yet. She would need more strength than she had right now. With each passing hour on horseback, her chances of escaping and finding a friend to aid her grew slimmer, yet to try to run now would likely only involve her hobbling a few yards on her frozen feet before being tackled and bound again.

With a sigh, she concluded her business and stumbled back around the bush, only to find her captor looming in front of her. She gasped in surprise but quickly tried to mold her face into an unreadable mask to match his.

"We will ride through the night," he stated.

She thought that was all he would say, but after a second, he spoke again.

"I am Robert Sinclair, Laird of the Sinclairs of Roslin."

Despite the darkness, Robert saw realization flit through her eyes. She had likely heard of the Battle of Roslin, though he imagined her countrymen had a different version of events than he did. She didn't speak on the matter, though, so he wasn't sure what she made of his name and title. It was just as well. He wanted this to go as smoothly as possible, and he hoped she wasn't the sort to ask too many questions.

He took her by the elbow and drew her back to where Burke and the others were. He hadn't yet spoken his plan to his second in command, but he didn't need to—not yet anyway. Burke followed his thinking about taking the lass for ransom. They would need to discuss the matter further, though, but not now. He still itched to put more distance between them and Warren's lands. The closer they got to the Highlands, the safer they would all be.

He halted in front of Dash, his hand still wrapped

around Alwin's elbow. She looked up into his face with a question in her eyes. Hesitating for a heartbeat, he pulled an extra length of thick wool plaid from his saddlebags and draped it around her shoulders. He had known she was suffering from the cold, and for some reason he felt a twinge of guilt. That didn't mean anything, he told himself. After all, he was to blame for her being here. Of course, Warren, the bastard, was also to blame for putting her in such a dangerous situation, but Robert pushed his anger aside. Aye, he would be the one dragging her along through the freezing night, and he could at least try to ease her discomfort.

Without acknowledging the surprised look on her face, he lifted her onto Dash's back then mounted behind her. He gave a signal to his men, and they pushed forward once again into the darkness. The lass seemed to try to stay alert for a little while, but soon exhaustion must have overtaken her, for she slumped against his chest and slept.

Chapter Seven

As the warmth at her back vanished, Alwin stirred. She felt a pair of warm, strong hands pulling her downward, and she opened her eyes slowly. She was standing in front of her captor—Robert Sinclair, she reminded herself. Weak winter sunlight tried to break through the clouds overhead, casting the gray light of mid-morning. The events of the last twenty-four hours began seeping back to her. They seemed surreal and dreamlike in her half-awake state. The man in front of her was very much real, though. She had been enveloped in his warmth and scent all night, a constant reminder of his awe-inspiring visage. She had dreamed of those blue eyes boring into her, looking at her with icy anger and something else—something...She couldn't put her finger on it but it was...intense.

"We will rest here for a few hours," he said, turning from her to tend to his horse.

His curtness frustrated her. Now that it seemed she would be with him and his men for a while, she longed to know what they had planned for her.

He seemed to sense her eyes on him and turned

back to her, pinning her with a look before she could get her questions out. "Hold your tongue, or I will gag you again."

"I will not," she said heatedly. "You can gag me if you choose, but I want answers." She noticed then that he had dark rings under those light blue eyes. She had slept, but he had not. She felt some of the fire drain from her, feeling a fluttering of guilt that she had taken his plaid and nodded off for hours while he rode. But why should she feel bad? He had brought her along with him, apparently to use her for his own gain. She would take whatever kindness he offered and use it against him without remorse. Besides, despite his lack of cloak, neither he nor his men seemed overly affected by the cold, damp conditions. She steeled herself with that thought, and charged ahead.

"Tell me where you are taking me, and what you intend to do." She refused to include his name or title, as it might indicate to him that she respected him, which she didn't.

He looked at her for a moment, considering, then turned away as if she hadn't spoken. Frustration and anger consumed her. He sauntered over to one of his men, the one who had been at his side earlier, and the two brought their heads together, speaking quietly in Gaelic. Alwin's blood boiled. Why did the man have to be so damned stony toward her? He refused to answer even her most basic questions and glared at her like it was somehow her fault that he had kidnapped her.

She was near screaming with frustration for several moments, but then a seed of an idea began to grow. All ten of the men surrounding her looked as weary as Robert did. They had all fought in a battle the day before then ridden hard through the night on high alert. Several of them had already pulled out bedrolls from their saddles and had settled themselves on the ground to sleep. She still stood in front of Robert's horse. He and his man had their backs to her now.

Feeling her rage turn into energy, she made a split-second decision. She threw herself onto the huge warhorse's back, wheeled it around, and dug in her heels. In a split second, she was crashing through the forest in the direction she thought the road was in, hearing a commotion behind her.

Before she had gone twenty yards, however, a whistle pierced the air, and the horse beneath her lurched to a stop. She nearly flew over the damned beast's head but managed to hold on by flinging her arms around his neck. Scrambling down, she bolted on foot, but knew instantly that she would never make it. Hard hands plucked her from her feet in mere seconds. She writhed and screamed, but was once again thrown over Robert's shoulder as he marched back to their makeshift camp.

He dumped her unceremoniously on the ground, to the chuckles of the group of men. Their laughter at her helplessness brought hot tears of shame to her eyes. Before she realized it, Robert was back in front of her with the rope and gag again. Without meeting her eyes, he retied her aching wrists. She raised her chin, despite the tears streaming down her face.

As he fastened the cloth over her mouth, he said "You've got spirit, lass, I'll give you that." The faintest hint of respect touched his voice, but it abruptly changed to cold steeliness. "But know this: you will not succeed in escaping me." Nodding toward the horse that stood patiently awaiting his master's instructions, he continued. "Dash follows my command, and you would do well to do the same."

He stepped behind her, pulled the saddle from his horse's back, and carried it toward her. He dropped it next to her, then to her horror, began tying her already-bound wrists to the saddle's pommel. The enormous leather saddle, sized for the giant warrior and his steed, would be far too heavy for her to drag behind her if she attempted to escape again.

Seeing the dread in her eyes, he said, "I think you get the idea, lass."

After fastening her to the saddle, he seemed to all but dismiss her from his mind and went about arranging a bedroll on the forest floor. By now, all his men had bedded down, and some were already snoring. Alwin gave a few half-hearted tugs on the saddle but knew it was useless. She had kept herself going so far, she realized, by telling herself she would escape. She acknowledged somewhere deep inside that such a plan would never work. She was stuck with these savage kidnappers for as long as they found her useful. The thought frightened her, but her fear could not ward off the hopelessness that crashed around her now. Wrapping the length of plaid tightly around her and setting her head down on the saddle, she did her best to stifle the sobs that shook her.

From his bedroll several feet away, Robert could hear Alwin's muffled crying through the cloth over her mouth. He hated women's tears. He never knew what to do to make them stop. And many women he had encountered over the years used their tears to terrify and manipulate men. Such a thought about Alwin was misplaced, though, given her current circumstances. She was not trying to put on a show and wasn't asking for anything. Her grief seemed real, and why wouldn't it be? She had been tumbled inside a wagon, then seen what were likely her first dead bodies, and had then been kidnapped by a band of Highlanders.

He quickly shuttered himself from any sympathy for her. She would be trouble, aye, but he had to admit he admired her courage. Even now, she attempted to put on a brave show in trying to muffle her crying. That spirit would be put to the test in the next several days, he thought grimly.

He resisted the rising urge inside himself to protect her from the coming challenges of their travels north. There was nothing special about her, he told himself; it was just that he never wished to inflict pain or discomfort on any woman. She didn't belong out here. She would likely only slow them down and distract him with her delicacy and that damned feminine scent, like roses and warm skin, which emanated from her soft brown hair. Once he was safe inside the walls of Roslin, he would think further on the matter of what to do with her, but for now, he would continue with the plan to sell her back to Warren. The bastard didn't deserve such a spirited beauty, he thought as he drifted off to sleep.

Chapter Eight

"A soldier rides in, Milord! One of ours!"

Raef Warren looked up from the papers strewn across the ornate wood desk he sat behind, a frown on his face from the loud intrusion. He sighed then waved to the page at his study door to bring the rider to him immediately.

A few moments later, a mud-covered, sweating foot soldier rushed in. With a quick bow to Raef, he said, "Milord, we were attacked on the road from England."

Raef, who normally didn't trouble himself overmuch with the lowly soldiers guarding his keep, wrinkled his brow, trying to remember who the man in front of him was and what he was doing on the road.

Seeing his blank stare, the soldier went on. "We were transporting the…Hewett delivery, Milord, when a band of Scottish rebels attacked."

Realization slammed into Raef, and he stood so quickly that the heavy oak chair he sat in went tumbling behind him. "What? How could you have allowed yourself to be attacked? What happened?

Speak, man!"

"They surrounded us about twenty miles south of here, Milord. They appeared out of nowhere, and it looked like..." Here the soldier faltered, because he realized that he couldn't tell his lord what had happened without revealing the fact that he had turned and bolted just moments after the attack.

Raef's hazel eyes narrowed on the man before him. "Were the rebels victorious in overpowering a dozen of my trained and battle-ready soldiers?" he asked with deadly calm.

The soldier swallowed then slowly nodded. "Aye, Milord. From what I saw, our men went down, and the...contents of the cart should be considered lost."

Forcing his anger down, Raef turned his back on the muddy soldier. At least he had brought the message here. Now he could try to stay ahead of the news of this embarrassing loss before it traveled too far. This was going to make him look bad. The Hewett girl was meant to be a symbolic gesture, a sign to the English that his alliances were strong and his holding in Scotland was secure. With a slow but steady trickle of money going missing from England's war cause against rebellious Scotland, there was only so much he could blame on Scottish raiders before eyes would begin turning to him. The thought of losing the girl's dowry made him compress his lips in frustration.

The soldier interrupted his thoughts. "Milord, I thought I might have seen...Sinclair colors."

Raef's heart missed a beat as he spun back around to face the soldier. Sinclairs! He ran a hand through his sandy-colored hair. Ever since he had been embarrassed on the battle field four years ago by the Sinclairs and the rest of those Scottish scum, he had held an especially black corner of his mind for thoughts of their torture and destruction. The Sinclair leader in particular had made him and his troops look foolish in front of Edward I and the other noblemen he was trying to ingratiate himself to. He would not stand for another affront to his reputation at the hands of those savages.

Perhaps, though, he could use this disaster as an opportunity. With a flick of his hand, he dismissed the soldier. He would have to devise some punishment later for the coward.

He righted his chair and resumed his seat, smoothing his hands over his fine silk breaches. The Sinclair attack could be just the spark needed to ignite the fires of war he had so carefully been priming for the last few years. Whether the girl lived or not didn't matter; she was just one woman, and the stakes were far greater. Either way, he could spin it into reason enough to retaliate with a full-fledged attack on Scotland. Even setting aside his personal vendetta against the Sinclairs, the Scots had to be brought to heel. It was dangerous for all Englishmen, not just those on the borders, to have barbarians roaming nearby, raiding and looting, or worse, making alliances with the French against English interests. The world needed order, by any means necessary. And though war often meant chaos, ultimately he knew bringing Scotland under England's control would be safer.

He pushed the missives and ledgers on his desk aside and began crafting an outraged message to every English holding with a reasonably sized force of soldiers he could think of. He would demand action for this attack on his beloved bride and call for the raising of an army to finish what the British started and failed to complete at Roslin.

He would also need to attempt a rescue effort, he calculated with annoyance. It wouldn't appear as though he really cared about the girl unless he put together his own men and acted like they were looking for her and her captors. Wars often centered around symbolic injustice. The loss of a beautiful English maiden to a savage Highland barbarian would certainly raise the ire of his countrymen.

His mind raced as he planned his next moves, sensing an opening for glory, riches, and perhaps even a Barony. He would be remembered as the man who led England to victory over those Scottish beasts. Then the entire island of Britain could be run smoothly, sanely. The padding to his coffers only sweetened the prospect, he thought with a smile as he set aside the message he had written and called to his page on the other side of the door of his study. "Tell the captain to gather thirty of his best men. We ride north in an hour."

Chapter Nine

Alwin woke to the smell of smoke. She slowly opened her eyes, which she could feel were puffy from crying, to the overcast sky. The clouds obscured the sun so much she couldn't tell what time of day it was; she could have been sleeping for an hour or five, and she wouldn't have known the difference. Luckily, she was still wrapped in Robert's plaid, which had kept her warm.

Sitting up, she found the source of the smoke. Several feet away from her was a dug-out fire pit with a small blaze working its way through a few sodden logs. Robert's men sat around it, talking quietly to each other and chewing on dried meat and biscuits. Robert was a little way off from the fire, in discussion with his man again. From across the fire, his eyes locked with hers, and his gaze was intense, though she couldn't tell if he was angry with her.

With a few more words to his man, Robert strode over toward her. Still tied to the saddle, she didn't make a move, but sat and waited for him. When he reached her, he crouched down without a word and untied her hands. Not wanting to risk losing the opportunity, Alwin said nothing but yanked the gag from her mouth and rubbed her freed wrists, which were sore from the rope and the awkward position they had been forced into.

Finally, he spoke. "You'll be wanting to see to yourself. There is a copse of bushes over that way, and a stream over here where you can wash your face." His tone was emotionless and businesslike, but at least he wasn't glaring at her.

She nodded and began to push herself to her feet. Pain stabbed through her left knee and hip where she knew bruises had formed from her crash in the cart. The bruises were made even more stiff from all the horseback riding and contorted sleeping. She inhaled sharply and stumbled, nearly falling, but Robert's hands scooped her upright.

He frowned at her as he held her steady for a moment, then said, "Tend to yourself. Then we will see about your injuries."

Alwin walked stiffly toward the bushes he had pointed out, sensing that although he gave her privacy, he wasn't far off. When she was done, she went to the stream he had indicated on the other side of their little camp. She first scrubbed her hands in the frigid water then cupped them to splash water onto her face and swollen eyes. She even made time to quickly re-braid her disheveled hair. By the time she was done, she felt surprisingly refreshed.

Turning back toward camp, she nearly ran into Robert, whom she hadn't noticed looming behind her. Avoiding contact with him, she skirted around him and walked back to their makeshift camp with as much dignity as she could manage. Not knowing where else to go or what else to do, she sat down on the saddle she had been strapped to a few feet away from the other men. Robert trailed her and crouched down in front of her when she was settled on the saddle. Before he could speak, however, his man approached.

"I have not introduced myself yet, my lady. I am Burke Sinclair," he said with an inclination of his brown-haired head to her.

She eyed his politeness with a touch of suspicion. So far, all she had been met with was hostility or curtness at best. This Burke seemed a bit more relaxed than his leader, though, and certainly more kind. Although he was a battle-hewn warrior just like the rest, a hint of softness touched his dark blue eyes.

"Are you a relative of his?" she asked, inclining her head toward Robert.

He quirked his lips, seeming to find her brusqueness and refusal to use Robert's title amusing. "Aye, I am a distant cousin of the Laird's."

"I am glad to know your name, Burke," she said grudgingly, granting him a sliver of politeness in return.

Just then, Robert reached for the hem of her skirt and started to lift it. Shocked, Alwin let out a screech and yanked her hem down, tucking her legs under her.

"Calm down, lass," he said, his voice full of irritation. "I mean you no harm. I just want to see what is causing you to limp so badly and see if I can do anything about it."

Staring wide-eyed at him, it took her a moment to register what he was saying. She glanced at Burke.

He gave her a little smile of encouragement and said in a soft voice, "Laird Sinclair has tended to many a wound on the battlefield, my lady. You can trust him to look after any injuries you might have."

Alwin locked eyes with Robert again. His cool blue gaze seemed to penetrate her, but she couldn't quite read it. She slowly nodded, not breaking their look, and untucked her legs. This time, he paused after taking her hem in his large hands, seeming to wait to see if she would protest again. When she didn't, he raised it slowly up her left leg, exposing first her stockinged ankle, then her calf to the wintery air. When her hem brushed her left knee, he stopped, letting go of the material. He glanced down at her exposed leg, scrutinizing it. She didn't realize it, but she had been holding her breath, and she let out a shaky sigh as he inspected her. She looked down too but didn't see anything amiss with her leg.

"Remove your stocking...please," Robert bit out through clenched teeth.

Alwin hesitated, afraid of this powerful and, she admitted inwardly, handsome warrior's gaze on her naked leg.

"Turn away," she said, her voice sounding a bit strained to her ears. Glancing over Robert's shoulder, she noticed all of his men had suddenly become absorbed in looking at the trees, the sky, anything in the opposite direction of where she sat. Burke, too, without hesitation, turned on his heels and gave her his back. Robert alone kept looking at her, his eyes like blue fire. She thought he was angry with her for her girlish modesty, but perhaps she read something else in him?

Ever so slowly, he stood to his full height. From her seat only a few inches off the ground on the saddle, his height and battle-honed breadth seemed even more intimidating. He crossed his large forearms in front of his chest, and she could see his muscles straining against the cloth of his shirt. Finally, he broke their stare and turned around.

Quickly, Alwin reached up under her skirt and undid the ties on her left stocking, then rolled it down past her knee. "All right," she said quietly when she was ready.

But only Robert turned back around, the other men still pretending to be preoccupied. He crouched in front of her again, his eyes locking on her exposed skin. Just as she had expected, her left knee was a purple and blue mess. He reached out a hand toward her knee with deliberate slowness, seemingly trying not to spook her, then gently prodded the swollen knee. She could feel heat rising to her face at his touch. She clamped her eyes shut, attempting to block out the image of his large, callused hand on her bare leg and instead focus on the discomfort his poking and prodding caused. When his touch disappeared, she opened her eyes and realized yet again she had been holding her breath.

"Just a bad bruise. Doesn't look like any permanent damage," he said gruffly. Then he coughed and it almost sounded like he was uncomfortable. "I noticed you are favoring your left hip as well. I assume it's more of the same?"

"Yes, just a bruise, probably," Alwin blurted out. There was no way she was going to let him give her hip the same inspection he had just given her knee.

Not waiting for him to turn away again, she swung around on the saddle so her back was to him and quickly reached under her skirt once more to pull up and retie her stocking. When she turned back around, Robert had stood, and his gaze flickered from her face to her neck.

"The rest looks to be scrapes and scratches," he said of the marks the tree branches had left in her first attempted flight.

She nodded, lowering her eyes and feeling even more warmth in her cheeks than before. Why did she feel so uncomfortable under his scrutiny? Although he emanated coldness and calculating distance, it seemed to Alwin that his raw, animalistic strength and masculinity lingered just under the surface whenever his pale eyes bore into her.

"Very well."

Turning from her, he spoke to his men in Gaelic, and they all started to rise and prepare to leave. One kicked dirt over the fire, while others went to their horses and began saddling up. Turning toward her once again, Robert extended a biscuit and a piece of dried meat in one hand. Alwin realized all of a sudden that she was starving. She took the proffered food and set into it quickly while he watched her. In only a few minutes, she had devoured everything he had handed her. He offered his waterskin, from which she pulled several long swigs.

She handed it back to him, but before he could turn away, she said, "How long have we been here?"

Robert considered her for a moment before answering. "A few hours. You slept deeply." He said this with the lightest touch of teasing in his voice, which she found disconcerting for some reason.

"Why must we leave so soon?"

"You ask too many questions," he said flatly, all trace of lightness gone.

He began to turn away, but she reached up and touched his arm. "Please—I—I'm not going to cause trouble, I just—" She trailed off. The begging in her voice frustrated her, but she was desperate to know anything about what was going to happen to her.

He froze and stiffened under the light pressure of

her fingertips on his forearm. Turning back to her, he considered the pleading look in her eyes, and after a second, said, "We are still on your betrothed's lands. We have already overstayed, and it will be safer for us all if we keep moving."

She gasped, her hand dropping from his arm. "How do you know about Lord Warren?"

Her response appeared to confirm something for him. "Most Highlanders know of Warren. His cowardice and deception claimed the lives of many, and he profits from making war between our two countries."

She had thought she had seen his anger already, but the intense hatred in his voice eclipsed the coldness and annoyance he had shown thus far, shocking her.

And then there was what he was saying about Lord Warren. Granted, she knew next to nothing about her intended husband, but certainly Robert's accusations couldn't be true. Lord Warren was an Englishman, after all, and bound by honor and nobility. She couldn't blame the man for wanting her dowry; her father had made sure that everyone in Northern England knew of the money that would accompany her, but that didn't make Warren greedy—no more than every other man who had sought her hand in marriage. The thought of all those people Robert claimed Warren had killed, however, made her picture the scene of the slaughtered guardsmen on the road the previous day. For some reason, she very much doubted that death was something Robert talked about lightly; would he lie about something so serious?

Registering the disbelief on her face, he gave her a look of scorn. "So, you haven't met the man, have you? If you had, you would be begging me to take you away from him. As it is now, you'll just have to trust me." He put heavy sarcasm on the word "trust"; the ridiculousness of her trusting him, her kidnapper, apparently wasn't lost on him.

With those words spoken, he lifted her by her elbow off the saddle and onto the ground, then picked up the saddle and walked it over to his stallion and began fastening it to the animal. She was left standing there, stunned by his accusations about Warren and suddenly unsure what to believe.

Chapter Ten

They rode at a brisk pace as the hours stretched on. Alwin was at first so lost in her swirling thoughts that she hadn't noticed the fact that Robert had not bound her wrists or gagged her this time, for which she was grateful. She became very aware of his presence behind her, though. She could feel every small squeeze he gave to the horse beneath them with his rock-hard thighs. His torso was like a wall behind her, yet heat radiated from his body and into her back. She could not see his face, but she could picture the strong line of his jaw, likely clenched in concentration as they traversed the tangled forest. Since she had first laid eyes on him more than a day ago, his jaw had become increasingly covered in the dark shadow of the beginnings of a beard. She wondered absently what it would feel like if she were to brush her palm against it, and then was horrified at the wanderings of her own mind.

She could feel him glancing up every few minutes now. About an hour into their ride, the temperature had noticeably dropped, and a light snow had begun to fall. In the last half hour or so, as the light had started to fade, the snow had begun to cling to the trees, and some of it even managed to settle onto the forest floor where their horses' hooves churned it in with the mud.

After checking the sky yet again, Robert made a sound of annoyance then whistled to his men. They halted reluctantly, glancing at each other with concern.

"Why do we stop?" Alwin asked softly.

"The snow won't be letting up any time soon, and if it keeps sticking, we might as well roll out a carpet for anyone trying to follow us," he responded, frustration tightening his voice.

"Oh," was all she said back.

In theory, she should want someone to be following them, and for their movements to be easily trackable by the slushy, muddy path they left in the snow. But she did not relish the thought of another battle, especially if she were going to be in the middle of it. She had seen enough bloodshed—or at least its aftermath—when Robert and his men attacked her procession to last a lifetime. Though she had lived near the border her whole life, she had always been sheltered from seeing the worst results of warfare. She inwardly acknowledged that being the daughter of a nobleman had granted her the privilege of such naiveté. The more time she spent with Robert and his men, the more she realized perhaps she didn't know the world as well as she thought she did—and perhaps she wasn't as brave, either.

The smallest sliver of her also didn't like the idea of Robert, Burke, or his other men dying out here in the forest, to be covered up quietly with falling snow and forgotten like they had never existed. She shivered at the image in her head. No, surely it was simply that she did not wish for *anyone* to die; these particular men were nothing to her.

Robert dismounted behind her, pulling her out of her morbid thoughts. Reaching up, he took hold of her around the waist and drew her from Dash's back and onto the ground.

"We will wait here."

Alwin wanted to ask what they were waiting for but figured he wouldn't answer and might even gag her again for asking questions. She noticed, though, that neither he nor his men removed the saddles from their horses and seemed to stay on alert. Some took out their weapons to clean or sharpen them.

Robert pinned her with a look and said, "Stay next to Dash," then stepped over to Burke's side so the two could talk in low voices. Shortly, he returned to her side.

"Will we have a fire?" she asked, rubbing her arms. She was still wearing Robert's plaid, but the cold penetrated deep, and the frigid air kept slipping up around her ankles.

"Nay."

She gritted her teeth in frustration at his brevity. Instead of pushing him with more questions, however, she walked around him and approached Burke. Perhaps the apparent second in command could set an example for his lord in how to be more polite, she thought with a twinge of smugness.

"How much farther is it to your land, Burke?"

A faint smile touched his mouth, "Oh, a ways off still, my lady. We ride to the farthest northeast corner of the Highlands. If we encounter no problems and the weather cooperates, it is perhaps another week's ride away."

"Oh." She felt her face fall.

"My lady, Roslin is beautiful. It is worth the effort to travel there. At least, I have always found it so," he said.

To her surprise, he winked at her. She couldn't help the little smile that formed on her lips.

"And when the Laird isn't spending all of his time scowling, he is a beloved leader of our clan," Burke went on, merriment shining in his deep blue eyes.

Alwin gasped at his boldness then covered her widening smile with her hand. Suddenly, she felt as if she hadn't smiled in years and was grateful to Burke for his touch of humor and kindness. Finally able to straighten her face, she lowered her hand and asked, "And why does your Laird scowl so much at present, Burke?"

Burke's smile slowly faded. "These are dangerous times, my lady, and we are in dangerous territory. But rest assured, while it may seem hard to believe just yet, Robert will not harm you, nor would he let someone under his care come to harm. He is honorable."

She frowned at that. "But he kidnapped me, and he has yet to tell me what he plans to do with me. How do I know I will be safe?" she asked in a low voice.

Even as she said the words, she felt a part of her resist the idea that she wasn't safe with Robert. Burke's firm declaration in Robert's defense surprised her. All men spoke of their commander's strength and courage, but Burke seemed to know more of Robert's character. After all, he was his closest companion, from what Alwin had seen. And, she admitted somewhere inside herself, she had sensed as much about Robert even in the short time she had known him. He was rough, yes, but for some reason she *did* feel safe with him. At least her head was still attached to her shoulders and her virginity was still intact. Of course, she was still a captive. But he wasn't acting like the savage she imagined all Scotsmen to be.

"Aye, he is planning something," Burke said hesitantly, "but he is a leader and a good man at heart."

"He is your Laird, and I do not doubt that he cares for you and all his people," she said, surprising herself by meaning it, "but what if what is best for your clan is not what is best for me?"

Before Burke could answer, Robert strode over to them. "See to your horse," he snapped at Burke.

Startled, Burke gave him a questioning look, but obeyed, leaving them. For some reason Robert seemed to be furious, though all Alwin and Burke had been doing was smiling and talking in low voices with their heads together. He turned the full force of his dark frown on Alwin as she watched Burke leave. Suddenly, all those whispers inside her about the quality of Robert's character didn't seem to matter. Instead of being frightened by his scowl, though, she felt her ire rising.

"You don't have to be rude. Burke was only trying to reassure me of your honor, though if your behavior thus far is any indication, I doubt very much that I should believe him," she said tartly.

"I care not what you think of my honor, *my lady*," he said stormily, "just that you remain quiet so as not to broadcast our location to anyone with a pair of ears within a twenty mile radius."

She snapped her mouth closed on another retort and settled for glaring at him. He seemed unaffected, though, and went back to fiddling with his saddle and the sword strapped to his hip.

There was nowhere to sit—the snow kept falling harder, blanketing the forest floor in damp whiteness. So Alwin tried to busy herself by walking around the small group of horses and men. Most didn't look at her, but a few gave her little nods with their eyes down. They were all enormous like Robert and appeared to be capable warriors. Their ruggedness stood in stark contrast to the orderly English soldiers whom she had seen back at her father's estate and who had been escorting her to Lord Warren. She pushed thoughts of those men and Warren aside, still not sure what to make of all that had happened and all Robert had said. By her fifth lap around the group, however, she needed something else to do while they waited, or else her mind would begin to go in circles just like her body.

Straightening her spine and resolving to brave facing Robert, she started walking toward him. She was willing to risk the gag again if she could only get some more information out of the man about what he intended to do with her. Before she got halfway there, though, he threw a fist in the air, instantly stilling his men. She stopped in her tracks, unsure of what he was straining to hear. A long moment stretched with Robert poised and motionless, then he gave a signal with his hands, and his men swiftly and silently mounted and drew their weapons. Panic began to edge into her.

In three strides, Robert was in front of her. He placed a finger over his lips, indicating that she should remain silent, and she nodded her understanding. He took her hand and pulled her toward his horse. He mounted first, then lifted her up to sit behind him this time. His sword made the faintest rasp as he drew it from its sheath. With another signal from Robert, his men began to form a circle around his horse—around her, she realized with a start.

Alwin still hadn't heard anything out of the ordinary. The falling snow baffled the normal sounds of the forest. Then ever so faintly, she heard the crunch of a hoof on snow. Before she could gasp, sound erupted all around them, and armored men on horses poured from the dim forest in every direction.

Chapter Eleven

Robert's well-trained men waited for the attackers to get closer. An eternity stretched as Alwin watched the riders barreling toward them from all sides, weapons drawn. Finally, when the attackers were nearly on them, Robert let out a battle cry, which his men immediately took up too. They swung their swords just as the attackers got within range. Instantly, the air was filled with the sounds of ringing metal, screams, and horses' cries.

"Hold on, lass!" Robert shouted over his shoulder. She wrapped her arms tightly around his waist and pressed her cheek to his back. They were still inside the protective circle of his men, but the nearness of the battle made her nearly mindless with fear. Robert's men were severely outnumbered, yet all of them seemed to still be upright in their saddles and swinging their swords mightily.

But they couldn't stem the tide of attackers forever. Glancing over her left shoulder, Alwin saw one of Robert's men go down, and several of the assailants wedged their way inside the circle. Robert wheeled his horse around to face them, letting them come to him. The first man to reach him got a slice to the stomach that quickly ended his charge. Then two more were upon them, and Robert maneuvered to block their blows. As he worked his blade fluidly back and forth between the two attackers, a third entered the circle but didn't attack. Instead, the rider wheeled his horse behind Robert's stallion.

The hairs on the back of her neck standing on end, Alwin sensed the rider before she turned. Her eyes widened with fear as she took in the helmeted man behind them, but he didn't raise his sword to them. Instead, he reached out with his free hand and grabbed Alwin's long brown braid. She screamed in pain as he yanked her from the back of Robert's horse by her hair. The rider scooped her up onto his horse and threw her across his lap, face down, then wheeled his horse back toward the opening in the circle.

Just as he was about to reach the outside of the circle, Alwin felt a lurch beneath her and went tumbling forward along with the rider across whose lap she lay. The horse they were riding on seemed to crumple, and the two of them landed in a heap on the ground. Her attacker quickly scrambled to his feet and wrapped her braid around his hand, yanking her up with him. He dragged her backward through the melee until they stood on the outside of the circle, the attackers' backs to them as they continued hacking away at Robert's men. But Alwin noticed through the frenzy that there were fewer of the attackers now, and almost all of the Highlanders still fought ferociously.

The man holding her hair breathed heavily beside her through his helmet and watched the battle continue to unfold. He, too, could probably see that his men were losing. He yanked off his helmet, and she was surprised to see a sandy-haired, hazel-eyed man underneath in the gray light of the evening. He would be considered remarkably handsome, except for the fact that he twisted her hair cruelly in his hand.

"Thomas!" he shouted over the din of the battle. One of his remaining fighters turned, and seeing his apparent leader, wheeled his horse around, leaving one of his compatriots to fight alone.

"Give me your horse," the man holding her demanded, and Thomas began to dismount.

"Who are you? Where are you taking me?" Alwin shouted, the terror in her voice piercing.

Without warning, the man lifted the hand not holding her hair and dealt her a heavy blow to the face. "Shut up, you stupid girl!" he screamed at her.

Just then, as if from a nightmare, Robert exploded out of the circle of fighting, blood dripping from his sword and death in his ice-cold eyes, which seemed eerily illuminated in the bluish light of dusk. He was coming straight for her attacker.

Instinctively, she knew she wanted to help Robert and not the man who had struck her and still gripped her braid in his fist. She began to fight with all her might. She kicked at his shins and clawed at the hand in her hair, despite his tightening grip.

His attention divided between Alwin's struggles and the terrifying warrior barreling down on him, her attacker shouted to Thomas again, who dutifully stepped in front of them to face off with Robert. Cursing, the man released her all of a sudden, apparently deciding he wouldn't get away with her struggling like a wild animal. Instead, he flung himself on Thomas's horse and kicked it into a gallop away from the dwindling battle, not even looking back to see if any of his men had survived the skirmish. A few of the remaining attackers, noticing their apparent leader's flight, disengaged with the Highland warriors and rode hard after him through the forest.

It was too late for Thomas, though. Alwin watched as Robert quickly dispatched the man with a blow that cut him downward from neck to chest. Thomas crumpled in a sickeningly lifeless heap at Dash's feet. She felt her stomach clench and flip.

Looking after the fleeing attackers, Robert seemed to consider giving chase, then decided against it after scanning the rest of his men. Her eyes followed his, and she thought she would lose the meager contents of her stomach right then. The fight was over, and Robert's men were victorious again, yet the sight of all the carnage assured Alwin that "victory" was subjective. None of the attackers left nearby remained standing, and the once-pristine snow was now a brownish red slush underneath the mangled bodies of men and horses.

Just as Robert's eyes swung back to her, Alwin felt her legs give out beneath her, and she slumped to the ground.

Chapter Twelve

Instantly, Robert was at her side.

"Are you all right, lass?" His voice sounded pinched and far away, even to his own ears.

Alwin gazed up at him in a daze, her gray eyes clouded. He ran his hands all over her, checking for injuries. When he was satisfied she hadn't been seriously wounded, his eyes went to her cheek, where a red mark in the shape of a hand stood out clearly, and the shadow of a bruise looked to be forming on her cheekbone.

"I will kill that bastard. I swear it," he said to himself with quiet heat. Then he scooped her up in his arms, cradling her, and carried her past his men.

Burke rushed to his side, fear in his deep blue eyes. "Is she—?"

"She'll be all right. But she shouldn't see this," Robert replied, indicating the bloodied snow and lifeless bodies strewn on the ground with his head.

"And you, Robert?"

"Just a few cuts and scrapes," he said, the sting of the few minor injuries he had sustained registering at last as the heat of battle drained from him. Burke quickly nodded, turning back to see about the injuries the rest of the men had received.

Robert carried Alwin to a nearby stream. He cleared the snow from a rock on its bank with his boot then sat her down as gently as he could. She was still dazed, based on the far-off look in her eye. He had seen such a gaze in boys after their first battle. He had once felt that way as a lad, but years of warfare had crushed such innocence from him.

He quickly dunked his hands in the icy stream, rubbing away the blood as best as he could. Then drawing his freezing hands from the water, he placed one against the red mark on her cheek, cradling her face. He longed to rub his callused thumb over her quivering lower lip but resisted the urge. Instead, he lowered his eyes to her hands, which rested in her lap. He noticed that there was blood under her fingernails. The lass had managed to get in a few good scratches to Warren's face, he thought, and a flutter of pride in her strength brushed somewhere in his chest.

She blinked a few times at the cooling sensation of his hand on her flaming cheek. Robert could see her eyes clearing as she shook away the battle's haze and her cheek cooled under his icy hand. Before she could start to piece things together, though, he wanted to distract her, to be the one to ease her pain and confusion for a few minutes. He resorted to his best attempt at small talk. "Alwin. Isn't that a man's name in your country?"

She gave him a startled stare for a moment then a shy smile crept to the corners of her mouth. "Yes. My father was convinced that he would have a boy." Then the sadness returned to her face and voice. "I was always a disappointment to him."

Robert sensed the deepness of that wound and redoubled his efforts to keep things light for her. "The man sounds like a stubborn old mule. I can see where you get it from."

A shocked look crossed her face, then she gave him a wobbling smile, and he felt his heart pinch a little.

"He is that. I always thought I got more of my character from my mother, but perhaps you are right about the source of my obstinacy."

Before Robert could rummage another conversation topic from his brain—which was rusty at making small talk with anyone—Alwin took a deep breath and asked, "Who were those men?"

Robert's hand, which was still cradling her cheek, slipped down to his side. He surmised that she knew they were her own countrymen based on their armor. He had initially thought to hurt her by rubbing in the proof of what a monster her betrothed was, but now he found that he didn't want to inflict more pain on her. He hesitated a long minute, looking into her weary and confused eyes, trying to gage how much she could handle. Finally, he said, "The man who held you, who—struck you—" he nearly choked on the words with his rage "—he was Raef Warren."

Her face transformed from tired openness to horror. "No!" she cried. "He wouldn't—"

Robert felt himself turning cold at her disbelief. Why did she trust the man when she clearly hadn't met him and didn't even know anything of his character? "Aye, he would. And he's done much worse than you saw here today."

He didn't mean to cause the frightened look that took hold of her features, but he also would not stand by and let the lass think something other than the truth about Warren. A part of him longed to reach for her again, to comfort her and tell her soon Warren wouldn't be able to harm her or anyone else again. But another part of him wanted to shock her, to make her see the truth.

Just then, Robert heard Burke cough a few feet away. His eyes snapped to his second in command, silently demanding an explanation for the intrusion.

"Laird, I have made an account of the men," Burke started.

Robert glared at him, for he spoke English.

Burke cleared his throat again and finished in Gaelic. "Minor injuries for the most part. But Robert," he said, then hesitated. "Liam has fallen."

"Is he—?" Robert's irritation fell away instantly, and fear for his man replaced it.

"He lives yet, Laird, but not for long."

Alwin looked between the two men, trying to parse what was happening. She heard Burke emphasize the name "Liam," and her eyes sought Robert for a reaction. His face hardened, but she noticed his eyes went hollow with a deep grief. He gave Burke a nod and stood, then looked down at her.

"What has happened?" she asked, dread lacing her voice as she gazed in his eyes with concern.

"Your betrothed's men have slaughtered a husband and father."

Robert's voice was so filled with icy rage that Alwin actually recoiled slightly from her position on the stream-bank rock. Before she could move further away or speak her disavowal of Warren and his actions, though, Robert grabbed her elbow and hauled her to her feet then pulled her back toward the site of the battle.

As they approached, Alwin had to throw a hand over her mouth to keep from crying out at the sight. The clouds had broken up somewhat, allowing the large moon overhead to illuminate the horrible scene. Yet again, her eyes were filled with the bodies of English soldiers. She tried to tug out of Robert's hold, but he only tightened his grip and dragged her along toward his men. They had dismounted and seemed to be forming a circle around something on the ground. Robert and Burke, with Alwin trailing in Robert's grasp, pushed their way toward the center. Alwin caught a glimpse of a Scot on the ground. The dark blood soaking his shirt matched his tartan in the moonlight. She vaguely recognized the man's face. He was young, perhaps only a few years older than she. His labored breathing seemed to fill the otherwise silent air.

Robert released her elbow, now completely focused on his man. He went down on his knees and clasped Liam's hand in his.

"Mara..." Liam began, but was soon coughing, and blood came out of the corners of his mouth.

Robert leaned in, speaking in soft and soothing Gaelic close to the man's ear. A faint smile touched Liam's lips, and then Alwin watched as the light behind the man's eyes seemed to dim and go out. Without realizing it, she had fallen to her knees and reached out a shaky hand to rest lightly on his blood-soaked shirt. She watched him leave, felt it. She willed his spirit to heaven, and though she didn't know the man, she knew he was good, and that he should have a place of peace to rest.

Everything seemed frozen for several minutes. Robert held Liam's hand fast in his own. Alwin lowered her head, feeling the tears streaming freely. The men creating a circle around them bowed their heads, some whispering a prayer.

Robert broke the spell when he gently laid Liam's hand down on his still chest and stood. He cleared his throat, then in a gravelly voice, instructed his men to find a proper place to bury their fallen comrade. Alwin slowly withdrew her shaking fingertips, gazing at the faint red tint left on them from Liam's shirt. As she looked up, her eyes locked with Robert's. She feared his cold gaze; she was sure that she would crumble to pieces if he gave her one of his icy glares.

Instead, she found sadness in his eyes, and solace. He extended his large, callused hand toward her, and she took it, allowing him to draw her up and to him. His gaze moved from her eyes to her cheeks, where her tears glistened in the moonlight. He raised his hand to her face, and with his thumb, he wiped away a tear as it slid past the bruise on her cheekbone. She let out a breath at the contact, and her eyes closed at the warmth and gentleness in his touch.

His hand left her face all too quickly, though, and when she opened her eyes, he had already turned his back on her. She watched as he strode over to Burke a few feet away and talked quietly with him as his men began digging a grave as night settled in.

Chapter Thirteen

Robert sensed Alwin's eyes trailing him as he strode away from her. A part of him longed to return to her side, take her into his arms, and wipe away each tear that fell from those large gray eyes. For some reason, her tears did something to him. Perhaps it was because he sensed she was actually quite a strong person and that her emotion was genuine.

Her deep grief for Liam had surprised and moved him. He had sensed it earlier, but now he was sure she was not like Warren. Nor could she be like her father if what he knew of the man was true. She didn't seem to fully grasp the connection between Warren and the death he brought with him, though, which angered him. She had clearly led a very sheltered life, judging by her naïve reactions to the realities of battle and of Warren's malevolent nature. He shouldn't think so harshly of her, he thought with an inward sigh, for she was surely getting an education in the ways of the world since his path had crossed hers.

It was also beginning to trouble him that he found his thoughts focused on her more often than not, and that his eyes followed her when she wasn't near him. It was just her beauty, he told himself. It had been a long while since he had shared the company of a beautiful lass, opting instead to go on these secret missions. He was simply longing for female contact. That explained the fact that his eyes followed her, that he couldn't get the smell of her hair out of his mind, that his thoughts kept drifting back to the feel of her softly curved bottom pressed against his—

Pushing her from his mind, he reached Burke's side. His friend's eyes were pinched with grief. Despite the danger he and his men were regularly in, they had suffered very few losses. Robert's skill in striking quickly and quietly, as well as their much-honed fighting abilities, had made them the victors of nearly every encounter. The blow was made all the worse by the knowledge that Liam left behind a young wife and son. Robert would be the one to deliver the news. It was his responsibility as Laird.

"The others are seeing to their wounds. It looks like only a few stitches will be needed. How do you fair, Robert?" Burke asked.

"I'm fine," Robert said, waving away his friend's concern. "You?"

"The same. It seems that Lady Alwin will be all right?"

Robert's eyes narrowed at the anger Burke held in check but which nevertheless seeped into his question about Alwin.

"Speak what is on your mind, Burke," he responded with irritation.

"I can tell you are plotting something, Robert. When will you inform me of your plans?"

"Is that why you are angry? Because you think I have slighted you by not including you in my thoughts yet?"

"Nay, it is not that, or not just that," Burke replied, running a hand through his hair. "I am…concerned for the lady's wellbeing."

Robert saw red at that. For some reason it made his blood boil to think that Burke was being protective of her. He had no right, he thought angrily. Robert didn't stop to question why he felt that *he* should be the one to protect her.

Before he could respond to Burke's comment, though, Burke answered his thoughts. "I am making no claim to her, Robert, so you can stand down. But you must recognize the fact that every moment she is with us, she is in danger. She already has more scrapes and bruises than she has likely accrued in her entire life."

"Aye, of course I know that, but what would you have me do? Hand her back over to Warren?"

Burke's fierce scowl matched his own. "You know that is not what I mean. You plan to ransom her, but to whom? I want Warren to suffer just as much as you do, but collecting his money is not enough justification to give Alwin to that monster. And returning her to Hewett would result in the same thing, since her father would likely continue with the betrothal."

Robert exhaled, trying to calm his nerves. He had been thinking along the same lines as Burke, circling back over his plan to ransom her and trying to solve the knotted problems it caused. It bothered him that he might pass up an opportunity to thwart Warren, but letting him have Alwin was clearly out of the picture, so he couldn't trade her back to him for ransom money. He wasn't sure when he had become so possessive of her, but he didn't have time to think on the matter now. He had been chewing on an alternative plan for a few hours but wasn't sure he was ready to reveal it to Burke. He knew his friend wouldn't be happy about it.

"Out with it, Robert. I know you too well. What do you plot now?"

Robert smiled inwardly. Of course he couldn't keep his thoughts from Burke. Taking a deep breath to steel himself against his friend's anger, he said, "What if I were to marry her?"

Burke opened his mouth to speak, but words seemed to fail him.

"Hear me out," Robert proceeded. "As you say, we cannot just ransom her and return her to Warren. The bastard will never lay hands on her again," he said heatedly, picturing the red mark and bruise on Alwin's cheek. "We also cannot ransom her to her father, who will just turn around and hand her over to Warren. But think on it. That Hewett fool has laid a path for us. He has made it clear to practically everyone in England that he has gathered a dowry for his daughter that will only be paid out after a marriage. That is probably why Alwin was traveling in that empty cart. The greedy bastard likely wouldn't even shell out a chest with a few dresses in it for the lass until the deed with Warren was done."

Burke nodded, though his brow was knitted.

Robert continued. "If I wed her, he will have to pay out, and thus we will snatch that money from Warren's grasp, who has likely already counted it among his coffers."

"And what of Warren? Clearly, he knows we have the lass and has at least made a show of coming after her," Burke pointed out.

"Aye, but he needn't know I will have wed her. Before I collect from Hewett, I will open negotiations with Warren for his beloved bride to be returned—for a price. Once he has paid out for her—and I'm sure he will, as long at it saves him face—I will break the news to him that in the eyes of the church, she is mine. She will be out of his grasp forever, and we will have dealt Warren a double blow to his coffers, not to mention to his pride and reputation."

Burke gazed hard at him. "It's clever, Robert, but I don't think you have thought this all the way through. In the first place, everyone in the clan knows you do not wish to marry. You may best Warren with this maneuver, but don't forget you will also pick up a wife for the rest of your life in the process."

"Aye, I've considered that. I'm sure once the transaction is complete, we can undo the arrangement," Robert said coolly. He hated being so harsh, but he had to keep his sights on what was most important—his clan.

"Would you truly use her so callously?" Burke said, anger rising in his voice.

"If it means dealing a blow to Warren that could put a stop to his warmongering, then yes, I would," Robert responded, heat entering his voice as well. "She is one lass, Burke. I don't like the thought of hurting her, but think of the lives it would save. And no, I don't relish the thought of being married, but as you have pointed out more than once, the clan needs me to. Isn't this the best thing for the clan? Our fortune will be secured, and perhaps an heir will even come of it."

"Oh, so you *do* intend to keep her around! Wed her, bed her, get an heir on her, and *then* discard her when you no longer wish to have a wife—is that it, *Laird*?"

Burke's fists were clenched at his sides, and Robert sensed that he was close to taking a swing at him.

"Careful, Burke," Robert said, hoping the ice in his voice would cool his friend's mind. "You are not the lass's champion. You are my second in command."

"Someone needs to look out for her, since you seem to have discounted her interests in all your plotting. That's another problem—how do you plan to get her to even agree to this ruse?"

"She'll not know until afterward," Robert said, setting his mouth in a grim line.

At this, Burke's eyes widened. "So, you would trick her into marrying you?"

"You know the place I have in mind. Father Paul only speaks Gaelic."

"This is wrong, Robert, and you know it. It isn't fair to the lass to keep her in the dark about this. And I may be your second in command, but if you harm her—"

"I do not wish to, my friend, but if deceiving one lass could save the lives of hundreds, perhaps thousands, of others, I know I can still count on you to trust in my honorable intentions," he said softly.

He watched as a war waged across Burke's features. Just as he had expected, his good-hearted friend was angry with him, but he also knew that Burke was loyal to him still. Burke hated Warren and the war he brought with him just as much as Robert did. Burke knew Robert's character. He knew that his Laird didn't make decisions based on greed or revenge but on what was best for his clan and country. As much as they were both willing to fight to the death to protect their home, they longed for peace.

Robert saw the resignation on his second's features, but Burke nevertheless said, "I'll not be a part of your lies to her, Robert. It's your plan, and you can be the one to explain what you've done to her." Burke seemed to be finished, but then spoke again. "And I'll not let you forget that you are a man of honor."

With that, he turned away angrily and returned to the other men. They had finished digging a grave for Liam, and Robert joined them as they lifted their clansman's body and settled it gently into the earth. After covering him, they bowed their heads once again and whispered a prayer.

Raising his head, Robert caught Alwin's eyes on him again. She had watched his conversation with Burke from a distance, but since they spoke in Gaelic, she couldn't know what had transpired. Still, she searched his face for answers, confusion and grief clouding her gray eyes, which shone in the moonlight. He hardened himself to her vulnerable look, refusing to give in to his desire to explain everything, to wrap her in his arms until she felt safe and warm again.

He forced a cold distance once again into his eyes as he approached her and spoke. "Ready yourself. We ride north. Hard."

Chapter Fourteen

They kept a grueling pace for the next several hours. No one spoke, but Alwin could feel the tension in Robert's men. They were exhausted, with only a few hours of sleep in the last two days, and had engaged in two battles that left one of their own dead. Burke seemed particularly stiff on his horse, keeping his back rigid and riding a few paces farther away from Robert than he had earlier. The snow had stopped falling and no longer clung to the ground. Instead, the forest floor was a soggy mush underneath the horses' hooves. It appeared as though they were going to ride through the night without stopping.

Finally, longing to break the tension, Alwin turned slightly in the saddle in front of Robert to look up into his face. His jaw was set in a hard line, and his eyes looked forward.

"Robert?" she said softly.

He jerked slightly, presumably at her use of his given name. She realized that it was the first time she had spoken it. He let his eyes fall to hers, waiting.

"What did you say to Liam as he…when he…" She

had been forming the question in her mind for hours as they rode, but now she couldn't seem to get the words out. She stopped trying and simply held his eyes, holding her breath and hoping he wouldn't be angry with her for the bold question.

After a while, he spoke, and his voice was soft and low. "I told him that Mara and little Danny, his wife and son, would be well cared for. I told him not to worry, and that he could be at rest and find peace at last."

Alwin exhaled and nodded. She felt the tears springing to her eyes but forced herself to swallow them back. She had to be strong. She couldn't let herself get lost in her own grief and burden Robert and the other men with the need to coddle her.

He seemed to read the struggle on her face, and a light of admiration came into his eyes. He said no more, and she turned around to face forward again. Unexpectedly, though, he suddenly let go of the reins with his left hand and wrapped his arm around her middle, pulling her back into his chest. She gasped at the contact and his firm hold around her waist, but then sank into the warm hardness of his chest, letting herself draw strength from him. After a while, she felt her eyelids grow heavy, and she succumbed to the weariness clinging to her. The last thing she remembered before slipping off to sleep was the feel of him letting his nose brush the top of her head and inhaling deeply in her hair.

The rocking of the horse's motion suddenly stopped, and Alwin felt herself coming awake. She blinked a few times in the bright morning sun. There were still a few white and gray clouds lingering, but much of the sky was blue, and judging by the sun, it was about an hour after dawn. The countryside had changed while she slept. Earlier, they had been riding through dense forest, but the terrain had turned more mountainous and rugged, and while trees still abounded, she saw more rock outcroppings and clumps of heather.

She felt Robert dismounting behind her then he reached up to pull her down. He looked haggard. There were dark smudges under his blue eyes, which were hazy with fatigue. It looked like he had been dragging his hand through his black hair because it was disheveled. The stubble on his face darkened his jawline. He clasped her around the waist and brought her off his horse, and she noticed that the other men were dismounting also. It was then that she caught sight of the cottage in front of them. A look of uncertainty crossed her face, and she looked to him for explanation.

"We will rest here for a few hours," he said, exhaustion straining his voice.

"Do you know these people?" she asked hesitantly.

"We are safe here. We have put enough distance between ourselves and Warren for the time being, and my men and the horses need rest." He didn't mention himself, but obviously, he could use some sleep and a meal as well, she thought. "Stay here," he said as he turned away and walked toward the cottage.

Robert rubbed a hand over his face, trying to clear his mind. It was just fatigue that was making him feel so scrambled and out of sorts, he told himself. It wasn't the smell of roses in her hair and skin, nor was it her eyes, which he had thought were gray. Then when he had stood on the ground looking up at her perched on Dash's back, she had opened her eyes with the morning sky behind her, and he had realized they were actually blue-gray, the same color the Highland sky over Roslin so often was. The lass seemed to be coming to trust him. She no longer struggled against him or sought to escape, and had allowed him to embrace her last night as they rode, sleeping undisturbed against his body. He grimaced internally as he imagined what she would think of him in a few hours' time when his plan was complete.

Upon reaching the door to the cottage, he knocked lightly. A moment later, a wrinkled and slightly stooped man opened the door. Recognition filled the old man's eyes, and he extended his arm to Robert.

"Laird Sinclair! What can I do for you, my son?" he asked, his voice only slightly weakened with age.

"You are kind to offer your assistance, as usual, Father Paul," Robert said with a weary smile. Many a time on his travels between the Highlands and Lowlands, he had stopped by this cottage with his men for a hot meal or a place to sleep. "We could use a place to rest, and I have another request as well."

"I will provide you with whatever I can," Paul responded without hesitation. As a man of God, he did not involve himself in the battles between the English and Scottish, but several of the Highland chieftains—Robert included—had always made sure that Paul was protected and looked after. He belonged to a long generation of Highland priests, whose ancestors had worked with generations of Lairds to care for the Highlands and its people.

"I would like you to perform a wedding ceremony," Robert said levelly. "For me," he added with a bit more difficulty.

Paul went into a coughing fit at that, but quickly regained control of himself. "And who is the lucky bride?" he asked, managing to sound relatively calm.

"That lass over there," Robert said, pointing toward Alwin, who stood next to Dash, looking a little unsure.

"Ah. I can see what has changed your mind about marriage, then," Paul said with a chuckle, bobbing his head approvingly at Alwin's beauty. A band of sunlight was resting on her hair, highlighting the dark gold streaks in the soft brown tresses. Even from several paces away, he could see both the blue and the gray in her inquisitive eyes, which stood out against her pale skin. She still had his plaid wrapped around her slim shoulders, and for some reason, the sight of her in his clan colors tugged at him. For a moment, Robert let himself drink in the sight of her.

He gave himself a little internal shake, trying to refocus. Not wanting to explain everything to Father Paul, Robert gave a curt, "Aye. But she is English, so she won't understand the Gaelic ceremony. Burke will speak in her stead, though."

"English, eh?" Paul frowned and scratched his balding head.

"It is probably best if you do not ask, Father. Before the ceremony, I would like to catch a few winks and freshen up. We won't be staying long."

"Yes, yes, of course Laird. Make yourselves at home."

Robert nodded then turned to his men, who eagerly awaited word that they could unroll their blankets and sleep. With the go-ahead from Robert, the men tethered their horses around the back of the cottage, then tromped inside to the fire-warmed interior. There was enough room on the floor for all ten of the men to lie down, and within minutes the sounds of soft snores and deep breathing filled the cottage. Alwin stood waiting outside as Robert tied Dash. Then he beckoned her to enter the building.

It appeared that the inhabitant of the cottage lived alone, but the inside was spacious, warm, and tidy. Robert guided her to the side of an old man who was moving about the small kitchen, pulling ingredients and utensils together in preparation for a meal.

"This is Paul," Robert said simply to her in English. She nodded and started to introduce herself, but Robert stopped her with a raised hand. "He only speaks Gaelic, so he won't understand, but he knows that you are a guest of ours," he said.

"Very well. Please thank him for his hospitality," she said to him.

He said something in Gaelic to the older man, who bowed his head and smiled at her. Robert guided her away and through the piles of sleeping warriors on the floor. Toward the back of the room, a ladder led up to a loft. She climbed up, with him following behind her. At the top of the ladder, she saw that this was where their host slept. The ceiling was too low for her to be able to stand upright, so she remained on her hands and knees. A mattress rested on the ground in one corner, and a few personal items, including several books, covered a low table next to it. Alwin hesitated, feeling like she was invading the kind old man's space.

"It's all right, lass. Paul always lends us his home when we pass through this area," Robert said from behind her. "You can take the mattress, and I'll sleep here on the floor."

A look of horror must have transfixed her face, for he said with a wicked gleam in his eye, "Unless you want to share the bed?"

She shook her head furiously and felt her cheeks coloring with embarrassment. "No thank you."

He snorted but seemed too tired to tease her further, and instead, wrapped his plaid around his shoulders and lay down on the wooden floor in front of the ladder. Within minutes, she could hear his even breathing and knew he was already asleep. She crawled over to the bed and lay down on it. It was wonderful to stretch out on a mattress, a luxury she didn't think she'd ever take for granted after a day in a bumpy cart and more than two riding on horseback, sleeping on the ground or upright in the saddle when she could. She too drifted off to the hushed sounds of sleep that filled the cottage.

Chapter Fifteen

An hour later, judging by the slant of the sun through a small rectangular window in the loft's wall, Alwin woke, feeling surprisingly refreshed. She had slept more than the other men by virtue of getting to lean against Robert, she reminded herself, stretching.

She sat upright and noticed that Robert still slept deeply. Not wanting to disturb him, she crawled across the floor as quietly as she could, but stopped when she reached him. He had positioned himself lengthwise across the loft so as to completely block the ladder. She cursed silently. Did he think she would try to run away again?

She surprised herself by acknowledging that she hadn't considered it once since Raef Warren's attack. She felt safe with Robert, Burke, and the rest of the men. She wouldn't let herself trust Robert all the way, since he still hadn't told her his plan for her, but she no longer feared for her life. Though she was still a captive, she was coming to see that she would be treated decently.

That was something she would have to think more on later, she told herself firmly. Right now, she just wanted to see to her needs and perhaps have a bite to eat.

Slowly, she eased one leg over the sleeping giant blocking her path. Next she placed her hands on the opposite side of him. Just as she began drawing her other leg over his body, he stirred and mumbled something. She froze, unsure if he was waking or not. His eyes remained closed, so after a second, she continued to bring her body to the ladder's side of the loft. Once there, she climbed down wrung by wrung, and at the bottom, she carefully tiptoed between the warriors covering the floor.

She noticed that Paul, their host, was still working in the kitchen on what looked to be taking the shape of a stew. She nodded to him then eased out the front door and into a copse of bushes next to the cottage. Coming back through the cottage door a few minutes later, she considered returning to the loft, but decided against it. Crawling back over Robert's large and muscular frame would be challenging, and, she admitted to herself, she was beginning to find it difficult to be in such close physical proximity to him. She was a lady, and it wasn't proper that contact with his ruggedly handsome form brought about a fluttering inside her stomach.

Instead, she made her way to the kitchen where Paul was chopping carrots and tossing them into a large caldron on the table next to him. Knowing he wouldn't understand her if she spoke, she remained silent but picked up a second knife and joined him in preparing the stew. She thought it odd that this man didn't speak any English. Their two countries had been at war for so long that she assumed most Scots had at least been exposed to English.

Then again, he was older and perhaps wanted to live undisturbed by political struggles. And although she didn't know exactly where they were, she knew they were far from any road. This remote area may have remained blessedly untouched by invasion and war. Either way, she found it easy to remain working next to him in an amicable silence.

Once their chopping was done and the caldron was nearly full, the two of them managed to maneuver it to the hearth a few feet away and hang it over the fire. Alwin sat watching as the old man stirred the stew, occasionally adding this or that herb. As the smells of the food, the warmth of the fire, and the sounds of sleep soon blended together, she felt herself slip into a lazy haze of relaxation.

She didn't know how long she had been sitting like that, but finally, she glanced at one of the windows and was surprised to see the sun sloping toward the mountainous horizon with the light of late afternoon. She shook herself from her daze and stood, smoothing her now wrinkled and dirty dress. Thankfully, it was brown, so the mud and dirt she had accumulated over the last few days didn't show as clearly.

After crossing out of the cottage door once again, she walked over to a small stream on the far side of the building and went about freshening herself up. Who knew when the next chance to do so would come, she thought to herself as she went about re-plaiting her long hair. When that was done, she scrubbed first her hands and then her face in the icy stream. She couldn't do anything about her dress but smoothed her hands over it again in an attempt to press out a few of the wrinkles.

As she finished, she heard the cottage door bang against the wall, causing her to jump. Turning, she saw Robert barreling down on her, fury in his eyes. Surprise quickly turned to fright, and she tried to back away as he kept plowing toward her, but realized her back was to the stream, and there was nowhere else to go.

"What are you doing?" he barked at her.

Why was he so angry? "I—I was just—" She gestured toward the stream. She took a deep breath, attempting to calm her nerves in the face of this fierce warrior's temper. "You can lower your voice. I was only washing up before Paul and I served the stew," she said, proud that her voice no longer shook.

He leveled her with those frigid blue eyes. "When did you leave the loft?" he said in a slightly more calm tone.

"Oh, hours ago. I didn't want to disturb you, so I crawled over you and went downstairs," she said.

"Crawled?" He raised an eyebrow at her.

"Yes," she said quickly, feeling heat rush to her face. "It seemed like you needed the sleep, so I just…"

He grunted, then said tersely, "Don't go wandering off again. Although we are in the Highlands now, it is not necessarily safe." With that, he took her by the elbow and steered her back toward the cottage.

She wrenched her arm free. "I am perfectly capable of walking, Laird Sinclair," she said acerbically.

He gave her a cool smile that didn't touch his eyes then sarcastically swept his arm toward the door. "After you, then, *my lady.*"

Keeping her chin level, she glided past him without a glance in his direction. Why was he so annoyed with her? She had done nothing wrong. He likely was frustrated about something else and was taking it out on her. What that something might be, though, she had no idea. He had seemed distracted when they arrived at the cottage. Alwin had chalked it up to exhaustion, but perhaps there was more to it than that.

Back inside the cottage, the men on the floor had begun to stir and sit up. Looking for something to do to distract herself from Robert's gaze—which she could feel boring into her back—she joined Paul again, and the two of them began ladling out steaming stew to the awakening men. Once they were all served, including a scowling Robert, she dished Paul and herself a bowl each, and finding no place else to sit, plopped down on the ground next to Burke.

At first, the group was silent as they all dug into their first hot meal in days, but soon, the air was filled with hearty thanks and compliments on the stew. She let a faint smile creep onto her lips, surprising herself by how pleased she was at these men's gratitude.

As the meal wound down, she caught Robert gazing at her intently again. She couldn't interpret his look, though, and apprehension filled her. Just then he stood and ordered his men to leave them alone in the cottage. Soon, only she, Burke, Paul, and Robert remained, and the space felt strangely empty. Her apprehension continued to grow as Robert spoke to Paul and Burke in Gaelic. Burke began to frown, and even looked angry at his Laird. Paul nodded then went up the ladder to the loft, returning with a book.

Alwin glanced between the three men, trying to figure out what was going on. Something was afoot, but the three seemed determined to keep her in the dark about it. Paul began to read aloud from his book in Gaelic, and no one would make eye contact with her. Then Robert said something to Paul, who turned to Burke. Through clenched teeth, Burke responded, still in Gaelic, all the while shooting daggers with his eyes at Robert.

"Robert? What is going on?" she demanded, fear edging her voice. It seemed strange for them to carry on a conversation in Gaelic in front of her; normally either Robert or Burke would switch to English for her benefit.

Robert didn't answer, and instead, kept his eyes locked on Paul as the old man continued to read aloud from his book. Paul concluded his reading and made the sign of the cross in front of her and Robert.

What happened next upended her world.

Robert leaned in and kissed her on the mouth.

At first it was just the lightest brush of his lips against hers, but he lingered there, and she felt his hand snake around the back of her head, holding her in place while he deepened the kiss. Her eyes fluttered closed, and everything seemed to spin. She felt electricity course through her body from their point of contact. His lips were soft yet firm on hers, and his days-old growth of beard gently scratched her cheek and chin.

He finally released her lips from his and let his hand drop from where he had held her head. She wobbled on her feet and could only stare up at him open-mouthed and wide eyed.

"You've done it now, Robert. We'll leave you to explain yourself," Burke said bitterly from behind her. He took Paul's elbow and guided him outside. He closed the door behind him, leaving Robert to face Alwin's look of shock alone.

Chapter Sixteen

He watched as Alwin brushed her fingertips over her lips, her eyes still wide.

"What—why did you do that?" she managed.

He couldn't blame her—he was rather surprised by their kiss as well. He could have guessed that her lips would be soft, but he had no idea that there would be so much heat in the encounter. Her rose scent had enveloped him, and her lips had responded to his with innocent interest.

He ran a hand through his hair, warring with himself. Once he told her of what had just happened, she would likely never let him do what he wanted to do again more than anything else right now. He tried to regain control of his desire to taste her lips more fully, and almost had a rein on his craving when she lowered her fingertips and unconsciously licked her lips. It was not an intentionally seductive motion, for he was sure she was innocent, but that thought ended up being his undoing.

In one stride, he closed the small space between them. He placed one of his hands on her lower back and the other around the nape of her neck, then without considering the consequences, he drew her fully against him. Before she could let out a sound of surprise, he planted his lips on hers once again. He started where he had left off a moment before, with a firm pressure on her soft and yielding lips. As the kiss stretched, she went to pull away, but he tilted her head farther, and at her gasp, he invaded her mouth with his tongue. Her warmth overwhelmed his senses as he slowly claimed her mouth, his tongue stroking hers. Soon she was leaning into his body, and he felt her arms come up to loop around his neck. She was tentative at first, but then she met his tongue with her own, and her caress sent the blood rushing to his manhood. He molded her body to his, feeling every delicate curve crushed against him. If he didn't stop this soon, he realized, he didn't know when or if he could.

He finally managed to will himself to pull his mouth off hers and stepped back so their bodies no longer pressed together. She exhaled sharply at the loss of contact, and her cloudy gray eyes shone with confusion and something else—passion. He saw in an instant that his touch had awakened something inside her that no other had.

That thought had him cursing himself silently. Why had he kissed her again? Was it simply a matter of his male need? Was it just that he was curious about the sparks of desire he felt after their first kiss? And if so, was his need or curiosity any more sated than it had been a moment ago?

The answer, he realized, berating himself, was no. Now all he wanted was more. But he had to tell her what he had done, the decision he had made for her future. He had been selfish and controlled by passion, which would likely make his task now all the more difficult. He raked a hand through his hair again and cursed, this time aloud.

His expletive caused Alwin to jump and seemed to break the spell of what had just happened. And what *had* just happened, she wondered. Their first kiss had been so startling that she had hardly registered what had occurred when suddenly he was kissing her again.

The second kiss was like nothing she had experienced. She had only shared a stolen peck on the lips a few times before, and in honesty, those had stopped once she had started to become a young lady. Those kisses were sweet, tame, but this kiss—it was heated, intense, and, she thought with a blush, very intimate. When he had entered her mouth, she had felt her head swim and her body tingle all over, but especially in a few private places. His raw strength had made her feel both possessed and protected, and his scent, clean and masculine, had surrounded her, clouding her senses. And just as she felt herself grow heavy with longing for something she didn't fully understand, he had released her.

"Robert, please," she whispered, "what is happening?"

He cleared his throat and appeared to be genuinely struggling to respond to her plea. Then, he let a detached mask fall down over his face, turning his eyes flat, cold. The change frightened her, but nothing could prepare her for his words.

"We are now married."

She stood there for several seconds staring blankly at him. Then she blinked as if finally comprehending what he had said. "What do you mean?" she said in a low voice.

"Paul is actually Father Paul. He just conducted a marriage ceremony in Gaelic. We are wed." His voice was even, though he watched her closely.

"Wed?" Her confusion was beginning to turn to anger. "How can we be wed? I did not say I do!"

"Burke spoke for you."

"Burke?" She registered somewhere in the back of her mind that she had just yelled but didn't care.

"He did not wish to put you in this position, but he his loyal to me. I asked him to speak for you."

"And why in the bloody hell would you do that?" she shouted.

"Calm down, and I will explain," he ordered.

She wasn't sure if it was his words or his tone that caused her to snap, but either way, in a flash, she launched herself at him, ready to claw his eyes out. He caught her wrists before her nails could reach him, but a look of surprise at the force of her attack flitted across his face. He stumbled backward and tripped on one of his men's bedrolls that still lay on the floor. He went tumbling to the floor with her on top of him. Luckily, his body broke her fall, for she hardly knew what was happening, only that fury surged through her.

In an instant, he flipped them both over so that he pinned her to the floor. He pressed her wrists into the wooden floorboards despite her continued thrashing and attempts to scratch him. She jerked up her knee toward his crotch, but he blocked it with one of his legs.

"Get off me!" she shrieked angrily. Then a shadow crossed over her mind, and she redoubled her efforts to escape his grasp, this time with fear as her motivation. She let out a wordless scream that was edged with terror. He was going to consummate the marriage right here on the floor. He was going to rape her.

Robert struggled to understand the change in her for a second, then realization dawned on him, and he instantly released her hands and stood. He had deceived her, forced her into a marriage, and now she thought he would force himself on her to complete the union. The thought disgusted him, but she didn't know that. She scrambled to her feet and away from him, putting her back into one of the corners of the cottage. She panted, eyes still wide with fear, but also with a glint of determination and fight in them.

He held up his hands in front of him, gesturing that

he would not advance on her. "Let me explain," he said again, this time with caution.

She stood there panting for another moment, occasionally brushing a stray strand of light brown hair from her eyes. Finally, she nodded.

"You have now met your betrothed, and I hope you recognize him for the vile excuse for a man he is." He waited for a response from her, but she just continued to stare at him with a guarded look. "As I told you before, he makes a living by leeching away the lives of others. He profits on warmongering. You have heard of the Battle of Roslin?"

She nodded again, still remaining silent.

"I was there. Roslin is my home, and as Laird, the land and people are my responsibility. I was also there for the negotiations attempting to prevent war. That was when I first met Warren. He lied to the king and the English gathered there that several Scottish chieftains plotted a secret attack. That lie, along with the falsified documents he made to accompany it, set Longshanks—your King Edward—on a warpath. Only a few months after negotiations broke down, I was fighting for my life and the lives of my people on my own land. We were victorious, but many of my men died, and the land took years to recover."

He paused, letting her process his words.

"Warren was there on the battlefield at Roslin. Just as you saw him do yesterday, he turned and ran when it became clear that his side would not be successful. I vowed on that day to do everything I could to make him answer for the lives he cost with his deceit."

"And you will dole out your punishment for Warren on me?" she asked, her voice filled with bitterness.

"Nay, Alwin," he said softly, taking a slow step toward her so as not to frighten her. "Believe me when I say I do not desire to hurt you, and I wish there had been another way besides this."

"Did you know that I would be in that wagon? Did you attack us intentionally?"

"Nay, though I have been working in that area on and off for several years," he said honestly. "I have been conducting intelligence-gathering missions around the Borderlands, trying to learn all I can about an impending war and doing everything in my power to thwart it."

"Why? Do you truly hate the English so much?"

He paused, considering the hurt underlying her question. "The English have done much wrong to Scotland, but nay, that is not the reason for my actions."

"Then why?"

He held her eyes with his. "Peace. We have all lost far too much to the feuding between our countries. My clan, and most others as well, long only to rebuild, start families, and grow prosperous for the next generation. We fight because we must, but our goal has always been peace. And freedom from the threat of invasion and usurpation."

Alwin sank down to the floor, all the fight seeming to go out of her. "But why did you have us married? How does that bring peace?"

Her sudden exhaustion and deep grief tugged at him, but he maintained his distance, both physically and emotionally. "Warren will want you back, if for no other reason than to save face. I plan on negotiating a ransom with him for you."

A look of horror transfixed her features. "You would hand me over to him for *money*?"

He could see the fury building in her again, but this time it ran deeper. Before he could speak, she went on.

"And that must be why you've arranged this little wedding ceremony as well. You wanted my dowry, and somehow you knew my father would only pay it out after a marriage."

"Alwin, let me explain—"

"No! Your actions already have! You're just like *them*!" she shouted. She pulled her knees into her chest and huddled in a ball in the corner. Tears of rage and betrayal began flowing down her cheeks. "All you want is money, and all you see in me is a pawn for you to control! Don't touch me!" The last was screamed as he took several steps toward her, reaching out to soothe her.

Robert felt desperation claw at him in response to her words and tears. He had to get through to her. She could hate him if she wanted, but she had to know his real motives and intentions. He knelt in front of her and took her arms in his hands, giving her a little shake.

"Listen to me, Alwin. You must listen. I won't ever let Raef Warren touch you again. I said I would negotiate a ransom payment from him, not that I would give you over to him. If he has to shell out a huge ransom, then that money can no longer be used to fund his warmongering. And as for your dowry, that money too would just be going to Warren. Think of the lives that will be saved if all that money cannot be used to wage a war on Scotland."

He knew she had heard him, but she burned him with a gaze filled with betrayal and hate.

"Even if I believed all that you have said," she said bitterly, "I will never forgive you for the wrong you have done. You have taken away my choice and my freedom. You have made me a pawn, a bargaining chip for your own schemes. And in that way, you are just like my father and Raef Warren."

He let his hands fall from her arms. His chest squeezed in fear at the thought of her hatred of him. He tried to push the feeling away, though. One lass's loathing was worth the lives of hundreds, perhaps thousands. He had to live with his betrayal of her and her justified abhorrence of him. That was his burden as Laird and leader of his people.

"I cannot change your mind, then," he said curtly, standing. "We continue north in an hour's time. Be ready."

Chapter Seventeen

Burke could hear Alwin's angry shouting from where he stood several paces from the cottage. The men, who had been slowly readying their horses to resume their travel, turned to him with a spectrum of curiosity and concern on their faces. He returned them to their tasks with a wave of his hand, but Paul, who stood at his side, gripped his forearm and stared at the door.

"Is everything all right, Burke?" he asked.

"Aye, it's fine, Father. Just a newlywed's quarrel, I'm sure," he said through clenched teeth.

Robert had done it this time. He understood his friend's motivations, and knew he sought the greatest good for his people, but damn the man for hurting an innocent lass in the process. To make matters more complicated, Burke had noticed the way the two of them had been drawn to each other like magnets from the start. Their eyes followed each other when their bodies weren't plastered together atop Dash. Robert had even seemed to soften somewhat, showing her kindness and being considerate of her comforts, what little they were, along this harrowing journey. When Alwin had been struck by the bastard Warren, Burke had seen a protective side to Robert that he had never revealed before. And though he did not know Alwin well, he guessed she didn't let just any man wrap her in his arms and allow herself to fall asleep against his chest.

The shouting had died down somewhat, but Burke could still hear their voices coming from inside. He secretly hoped Alwin wouldn't bend under Robert's force of will, that she wouldn't let her spirit be crushed by Robert's disregard and callousness toward her. From what he had seen of the lass so far, he imagined the struggle between them was only just beginning.

The bang of the cottage door as it slammed against the wall with a good deal of force startled Burke out of his thoughts. He turned to see Robert storming through the doorframe, looking like an angry bull.

He stomped right by Burke, but as he passed, he said in a low and dangerous voice, "Not a word." He kept walking until he was amongst his men, where he silently saw to saddling up Dash.

All the preparations for departure had been made, and half of the men were already mounted when Alwin finally emerged from the cottage. Her cheeks were dry, but Burke could see the tear tracks down her face, and her eyes were red-rimmed and tight. She held her chin steady, though, and glided over to Burke's side.

"Although we have a thing or two to discuss,

Burke," she said tautly, "I would like to ride with you the rest of the way to Roslin if that would be all right."

Just then, Robert wheeled Dash over and glared down at them. "No, that will not be all right. You ride with me, lass." The deadly calm in his voice belied the fire and ice warring in his light blue eyes.

Alwin stared up at him, first with disbelief in her clouded eyes, then with a combination of hate and sadness. Burke caught the slightest quiver in her lower lip, but then she pressed her lips together to steel herself.

She turned to him and said, "Please thank Father Paul for all he has done to…help us." She seemed to nearly lose control again in getting out those words, but before she could, Robert scooped her up from the ground and placed her in front of him on the saddle.

Burke rushed to thank Father Paul for his hospitality then mounted up with the others, and after a whistle from Robert, nudged his horse into a trot toward the mountains in the north.

Raef Warren slammed the door of his study in the curious face of his page. Thankfully, none of his staff had voiced their questions, but they didn't need to. They had all witnessed him ride back through his keep's gates with less than a third of the men he had ridden out with earlier. Those who had returned had been in a sorry state—some were injured, and most had scrapes and dents in their armor. And Raef was no exception. Deep red scratches ran down his face and neck from where that little bitch had clawed him.

He flopped down in the finely upholstered chair behind his desk and drew a small circular mirror from one of the drawers. He cursed loudly at the sight of his face. She would pay for each scratch, never mind the fact that they would heal in a matter of days. It wouldn't happen soon enough for Raef, though. Undoubtedly, there would be whispers within his walls of his being bested by the tiny little twit of an English girl, the one whom he was supposed to be rescuing. Word of her resistance would also be a problem.

A soft knock on the door interrupted his thoughts. "Who is it?" he shouted crossly.

"It is Jossalyn, brother," came the timid reply through the door's thick wood.

"Come," he said with irritation.

His sister eased the door open and stepped into his study hesitantly. She was carrying a few jars in one hand. "I thought you might want me to see to those scratches," she said quietly, keeping her blond head lowered and her green eyes on the floor. "I already saw to the men who returned with you. They will all be fine, I think."

"I don't need any of your little ointments, sister," he said coldly. "Is there anything else?"

She shook her head and backed toward the door but hesitated and seemed to search for resolve. Finally, she spoke again, trying to hold her voice steady and clear this time. "Perhaps your people would respond better to you if you let them see me for healing. While you were gone, I went to the village and treated a boy who—" Her voice was cut off as his fingers wrapped around her throat. He had flown from his seat in a flash and now squeezed her neck with one hand. She tried to swallow her fear—he had done the like before to her—but couldn't get her throat to work properly.

"Keep your thoughts inside your pretty little head, Jossalyn, unless you want me to dash them from you with my fists," he hissed in front of her face. "You are not to go into the village, and you will assist only those I tell you to."

She nodded as best she could, but he gave her neck an extra squeeze before releasing her. She scurried out the door and shut it quickly behind her, leaving him alone with his thoughts once more.

If only his intended bride had been as easy to control as his sister, he thought with frustration. The little hellion had fought back, which Jossalyn had given up doing long ago. He forced himself to cool his thoughts, though. He needed a plan, something that would cover this most recent misstep and reposition him to lead the English to victory in Scotland—slowly enough so that he could skim some of the plunder off the top for himself.

Perhaps he would have to consider Alwin Hewett a loss, he thought with a sigh. The idea of giving over a ransom to a Scot—a Sinclair in particular—grated. He simply couldn't do it. He might as well announce to all in England and Scotland that he was weak, couldn't keep his woman under control, couldn't even outsmart or outmaneuver a Highland barbarian. But perhaps he could still turn this situation in his favor yet.

He sat down in his chair once more, and smoothing his hair and silk breeches, he pondered the possibility of arranging for her death.

Chapter Eighteen

Alwin sat rigidly in the saddle, trying to keep space between herself and Robert. She had scooted as far forward as she could without sitting directly on the pommel and kept her back rod-straight so as to avoid contact with the apparently indifferent Scot behind her. A knot had long since settled in her lower back, and she had to distract herself yet again by raising her ire. The uncaring, controlling, manipulative…man!

She had begun to trust him in the short time that she had been with him—been kidnapped by him, she reminded herself. She had been a fool to think that a barbarian who had slaughtered dozens, if not hundreds, of men, and who had likely been thieving from the English for years, would treat her as anything more than a pawn in his scheming. Why had she believed that he could be trusted?

It was a sign that she was a naïve and silly girl. She had thought herself strong because she had stood up to her father a few times. She cursed herself, grief replacing her anger for the hundredth time this evening. Now she could see the truth. She was easily duped by the tiniest gestures of kindness he granted her. She had longed to believe that underneath his gruff and cold exterior, he was honorable, brave, strong, and kind. He had likely sensed her growing trust, perhaps even the pull he seemed to have over her, and had used it against her. This thought brought heat to her face and the sting of tears to her eyes yet again. Aye, he had even used his kiss against her, making her think for a moment that there was a spark of genuine desire between them.

She inhaled a lungful of cold evening air to clear her thoughts. The sun was just setting behind one of the many mountains that had replaced the forests and rolling hills of the Borderlands and Lowlands. They traveled in the open now, since there were only low shrubs, thickets of heather, and jagged rock outcroppings to move between. She guessed they had crossed over into the Highlands; not only had the landscape become more rugged, but also the men seemed a bit more at ease with their surroundings. Nevertheless, they maintained a quick pace, and Alwin wondered if they were going to ride through the night again.

She had her answer a few hours later. Robert wheeled his horse off the line they were making northward, and their group moved west for several minutes. Alwin noticed a lighter colored blob emerging in front of them through the early night darkness, and as they drew nearer, she realized it was a large outcropping of pale rock. Robert halted them in front of the rock, which Alwin guessed stood over twenty feet high. He dismounted and pulled her down after him, then took her by the elbow and guided her even closer. He moved with assuredness despite the darkness. For her part, she stumbled several times, only staying upright because of his firm grip on her elbow.

Just when she thought they could get no closer to the rocks in front of them, Robert seemed to almost walk through them. She realized they were headed into a shallow cave. It was only about ten feet deep but provided shelter and cut the slight breeze that had picked up after the sun had gone down.

Robert released her elbow, and without a word, went back outside the cave to his horse. He returned a few moments later with his saddle and bags. Tossing them on the ground, he removed his bedroll, water skin, and a few more biscuits and dried meat wrapped in parchment. Setting those things aside, he went about starting a fire toward the mouth of the cave. All the while, his men were doing as he had. Some spread out their bedrolls several paces away from the cave, out in the fresh crisp air. When the fire was started, Alwin saw that a dark smear of soot covered the cave's roof. These men, or others like them, must have used this spot before.

As the fire blazed cheerfully, the men chewed on hard biscuits and talked quietly, seeming to pick up on the tension between their leader, his second in command, and their captive. Not wanting to sulk in the shadows, though, Alwin adjusted the plaid she still wore around her shoulders, and sat on the ground in front of the fire. She let herself gaze into the flames, mesmerized by their dance and content to not look at, talk to, or touch Robert.

All too soon, though, he interrupted her thoughts. Coming up beside her, he silently offered her food and water, an unreadable look on his face. She hesitated, not wanting to take anything from him, but then decided she wasn't going to let herself starve. She could use him for her benefit just as he was using her. She took the proffered food and chewed slowly, forcing herself to dismiss him again from her mind and return her eyes to the fire.

After they were done eating, the men around the fire stood one by one and walked to their bedrolls, which were scattered out in the open. Within a few minutes, she could hear light snores coming from outside the cave. Two men were assigned watch, and they too disappeared into the night. Soon, only Burke, Robert, and Alwin remained by the fire.

"Burke, may I have a word with you?" Alwin said flatly, her voice cutting through the tension.

"Aye, my lady," Burke said reluctantly. He stood and offered his hand to assist her in rising. Robert stood too, but without a word, turned and strode out of the cave, leaving the two of them alone.

Alwin trained her eyes on Burke, trying to sort through all her thoughts and questions, not to mention her frustration and fear.

"When did he come up with this plan?" she finally said, arms crossed in front of her.

"He first told me of it after Warren's attack, my lady. I do not know how long he had been thinking on it, but I can tell you with certainty that we were all genuinely surprised to have found you in that supply wagon."

"What did he say to you to convince you to go along with him in this madness?"

Burke sighed and ran a hand through his brown hair. "He is my Laird," he said simply after a moment.

"Is that it? You do what he tells you because you are forced to give him your loyalty?"

"I am not forced," he snapped in response, heat edging his voice. "I follow him because he leads our clan toward prosperity and peace."

"Prosperity?" she spat out. "You mean stealing from Warren and conning away my dowry?"

"Nay, my lady, I mean rebuilding, protecting our people so they can farm and raise livestock again and save enough to build a better future for their children. I know Robert's heart. He is looking to do right by the clan."

"And what of me? My life doesn't matter?" She took a breath to try to calm herself. "I don't think either one of you can understand what it is like to struggle your whole life for the freedom to make your own choices then have the hope of such freedom taken away in a single moment." Her voice grew tight as she continued. "I knew I would have to become a wife one day, and that I likely wouldn't have any say in the matter, but this? I might as well have been a load of supplies in that wagon in the Borderlands, for that is how everyone treats me!"

Burke's eyes softened as he watched her struggle to maintain control of herself. "You may be surprised by how well the Scots understand your desire for freedom, my lady," he said quietly. Shaking himself a little, he continued more firmly, "I do not know what the future holds, but I am positive it will prove better to be wed to Robert than Raef Warren. He is not perfect—he can be harsh, but he is also not cruel."

"I refuse to accept that we actually *are* wed, Burke. What happened back there at the cottage?"

Burke lowered his eyes, not wanting her to see both his anger and his shame. "Father Paul is indeed a priest. He conducted the ceremony in Gaelic so you wouldn't understand. Robert spoke the words, and I spoke them for you."

"And what were those words?" she asked, fear creeping in. She realized that although she hated Robert for what he had done, a part of her didn't truly believe that it had actually happened, that they were wed in the eyes of God.

"That you are his wife, and that you will obey and honor him, for better or worse, until death."

Alwin sputtered and nearly choked. *Obey? Honor?*

Her kidnapper? She hadn't spoken those words! Though they may be bound for the time being, she most certainly wasn't going to behave according to something she hadn't even agreed to. She straightened her spine and said levelly, "The moment that it is possible, I *will* have this deceitful union undone."

"Aye, you may try, my lady," Burke said cautiously. "Though truthfully, once we are back at Roslin, I doubt anyone would want to go against both their Laird's wishes and Father Paul's actions. Both are well respected and loved throughout the Highlands."

"Thank you for your honesty, Burke, though I am not sure I am ready to forgive you for your part in this lie."

"I understand, my lady. I am not sure I am ready to forgive myself either," he said with a little sideways smile touching his lips.

Just then, Robert stomped back into the cave's mouth, a frown darkening his features. "You'd better get some rest while you can, Burke," he said coolly.

Burke nodded, and with another glance at Alwin, he moved out of the dying light of the now-low fire.

"You don't have to be rude," she said crossly.

"Forgive me, but I do not like other men smiling at my *wife*," he responded harshly.

She couldn't stop the gasp of shock that escaped her lips. Why would he say such a thing? Was he just trying to get under her skin, to remind her of the powerless position she was in thanks to his plotting? Or was there also a genuine note of jealousy in his tone?

She pushed aside the thought, not wanting to fret over his actions. All she could do now, all she had ever been able to do, was control her own reactions and responses. She had already learned the hard lesson from her father that she couldn't change men's control over her life. Robert was just another one in a line of men who were trying to use her. She had to take control of her own destiny. That meant getting out of this farce of a marriage, but for tonight, she would have to settle with ignoring Robert's mysterious comments and actions. She had decided somewhere along the way that she would no longer attempt to escape from him and his men. From what she had seen of Raef Warren, she grudgingly admitted, Burke was right: she was better off with Robert. She would allow him to take her to his home, but once there, she would find a way out—she would claim her freedom.

She smoothed her face and walked farther back into the cave, settling herself on the ground, which was surprisingly soft. Centuries' worth of dried leaves had settled inside the cave, making a carpet of sorts over the rocks beneath. She rearranged the plaid so it both covered her and cushioned her head then gave Robert her back and attempted to fall asleep. She could feel his eyes on her for several moments then heard him arranging his bedroll only a few feet from her. She nearly turned over and demanded to know what he was doing sleeping so close to her but then reminded herself that she was strong enough to ignore him. He was likely just trying to assert his power over her again, to cloud her thoughts with his masculine scent and intimidate her with his honed and muscular body.

She silently thanked the stars he had not claimed his husbandly right yet. That thought had her reeling again. Even though she considered their marriage a sham, technically he could consummate the union, which would thwart any attempt she might make for an annulment, as well as any chance she had to return home to be wed to another. She shuddered inwardly, frightened to think of how her life now balanced on a knife's edge. With the slightest nudge one way or the other, she could fall to ruin.

As sleep took her, she thought again of Robert's kiss, but instead of being frightened, she felt that strange heat suffuse her and a longing for something from Robert she feared she shouldn't want.

Chapter Nineteen

Sometime well before dawn, Alwin awoke to the sound of mumbling. She recognized Robert's voice but couldn't make sense of what he was saying. She realized that he was talking in his sleep, so she sat up and reached out in the dark with her hand to try to wake him. On instinct alone, she ducked just in time to miss one of his massive arms go whirring through the air right where her head had been. He was fighting someone in his sleep.

"Robert!" she hissed. "Wake up! You are dreaming!" Cautious of his powerful limbs, she placed a hand on his shoulder and shook him.

All of a sudden, though, his arms came up and wrapped around her, dragging her down onto his chest. She squirmed and struggled to get out of his embrace, but his arms were too heavy for her to lift, and besides, he was clutching her tightly.

On a pause for breath, she realized that his mumbling had stopped, and that his hold on her seemed to be calming him. Instead of fighting against his grip, she eased her arms from between them to a more comfortable position then adjusted her neck so her head rested on his chest. He inhaled slowly, deeper sleep returning, and she heard his heartbeat resume a steady beat.

She lay there tense for a long time, unsure of what to do. The last thing she wanted right now was to be snuggling her body against his as he slept—wasn't it? His warmth enveloped her, and she soon found her eyelids drooping. His slow breaths soothed her frayed nerves, and she felt herself slipping back into slumber. This was not exactly taking control of her destiny and distancing herself from him, she thought just before sleep claimed her once more.

Robert slowly drew out of a wonderful dream. He had been lying on a bed of roses with a warm lass in his arms—and not just any lass. In the dream, he had felt every one of Alwin's delicate curves pressed against him, the scent of her hair filling his nose. He cracked his eyelids open to see the first hint of dawn beyond the cave's mouth.

Suddenly, something tickled his neck. He thought to brush at it, but realized that his arms were wrapped tightly around—Alwin! She was warm and limp in his embrace, still deeply asleep. One of her legs was thrown over his thigh, dangerously close to his very awake and needy cock. Her hand rested on his chest, and her head was nestled on his shoulder. As she exhaled, her warm breath fanned over his neck.

He nearly jerked upright but managed to control

his body so as not to disturb her. She made a little noise in her sleep and nuzzled closer to him. He cursed silently to himself. He doubted she had simply crawled into his arms during the night. More likely, he had been having one of his dreams again, where he battled and endless sea of English soldiers but could never quite stay ahead of their attacks. He had long known he had such nightmares and that they caused him to flail and talk in his sleep. He hoped he hadn't frightened her, or worse, accidentally swiped her with his thrashing.

He hated to think that she might wake and assume he had pushed his body onto hers during the night, but he had to admit that the thought of sleeping like this again appealed to him. His dream had made the blood rush to his cock, and the reality he found upon waking only increased his desire. As slowly as he could manage, he tried to peel her from his body as he sat up. Based on her attempts to keep her distance from him since they were wed, he guessed she would be none too happy at their current position. His movement disturbed her, though, and she blinked her eyes open. Cloudy gray, with just a hint of deep blue, enveloped him for a moment, and he felt like he was gazing deep into the Highland sky.

She jerked out of his embrace. "You were talking and thrashing in your sleep" she said quickly.

"Aye, I guessed as much. Did I hurt you?"

"Nay, you just sort of...held me and wouldn't let

go," she said, averting her eyes. A beautiful flush was rising up her neck and settling in her cheeks.

"I apologize," he said simply.

"I'm fine. You knew not what you were doing."

He chewed on that. She made it sound like if he *had* known what he was doing, he wouldn't want to embrace her and have her sleep in his arms all night, which, he realized, wasn't exactly accurate.

Pushing that line of thinking aside, along with his bedroll, which had scooted out from under him so that it covered both of them, he stood. She did the same, brushing stray leaves from her dress and cloak.

"We'll ride shortly. You'd best ready yourself."

He stomped out of the cave, pretending to be preoccupied. In truth, he had to turn away from her and readjust his kilt to try to obscure his hard manhood standing at attention. It was just his body's natural reaction to the prospect of taking a tumble with a beautiful lass, he told himself. But the thought did nothing to ease his discomfort, for he didn't want just any lass. Her scent seemed to cling to him, teasing and haunting him. He wanted Alwin.

So, it was back to that, was it, she thought with irritation. He seemed all too ready to return to his cold and distant demeanor with her. But why should it bother her so much? His indifference, even his harsh coolness, made it easier for her to hate him. Some part of her whispered that he was a good man and that she couldn't deny her draw to him. She ignored this inner voice, though, reminding herself she was his captive, and now his wife.

He stepped out of the cave and began to rouse his men, some of whom had already begun to stir and rise. She glanced at the sky. Dawn was breaking in a blue sky to the east, but a heavy mist was encroaching from the west, and from the looks of it, would settle over them in an hour or so. She hoped her dress, cloak, and Robert's plaid would keep the damp chill out. If not, she thought with a sinking feeling, a combination of dread and longing, she could always share Robert's warmth again.

When the camp had been cleared and preparations completed, Robert boosted her onto Dash's back then took to his saddle behind her, a position that was becoming all too familiar to her. His rock-solid arms wound around her waist so he could grip the reins with his large, strong hands. His chest behind her somehow managed to radiate warmth and be hard as stone at the same time. Her soft, slim legs pressed into his muscular thighs. Their hips were plastered together and would soon be rocking in a slow unison when he gave his horse the signal.

This last thought shocked her but also brought a new warmth to her skin. Though she couldn't see his face, she had stared at his handsome visage long enough to be able to picture with perfect clarity the hard line of his jaw, now covered in dark stubble, his straight, strong nose, his black hair disheveled from the hand he frequently ran through it when thinking. And his eyes—they bore into her with a combination of heat and ice that set her stomach fluttering. He nudged his horse forward, and they were off yet again.

Chapter Twenty

The next several days passed in a similar fashion. They rode at a brisk pace during the day, stopping only for the horses and their most basic needs. A heavy mist sat atop the countryside, which grew increasingly barren and rugged as they rode on. Alwin found it breathtakingly beautiful, though. She was used to the green fields and soft rolling hills of England and had never seen such jagged mountains or desolate expanses. She wondered how this awe-inspiring landscape would change its personality in each of the seasons then chided herself for such thoughts. Why should she care what this place might look like at different times of the year when she would be back in England as soon as possible?

As the sun began to set each evening, Robert would guide their party to some shelter he and his men seemed to be familiar with. She was struck at how well they all knew their country. She had never been more than a few hours' ride from her father's keep—that is, until the day she was sent to wed Raef Warren. Instead, she had met and been wed to Robert Sinclair, a

Scottish Laird and warrior, and was now being whisked away to the Highlands. How things had changed in the last week, she thought ruefully.

After the night in the cave, Robert slept farther away from her with his men, gruffly explaining to her that he didn't want to risk accidentally bumping into her with his flailing. She didn't protest, of course, but found the nights colder without him nearby.

Nearly a week after they had all slept at the cave, the men awoke in a particularly good mood. They joked and laughed with each other as they slowly prepared for another long day of travel and even ribbed Robert good-naturedly.

"Perhaps once we return to Roslin, we will no longer be subjected to the sorry sight of that scraggly beard, Laird," the one named George said.

Seamlessly, all of Robert's men had switched over to speaking English in her presence rather than Gaelic. Alwin had realized this a few days ago and found herself surprisingly touched. Ever since the ceremony at Father Paul's cottage, they seemed to treat her with greater respect and deference, and she felt included by their language switch.

This ribbing comment brought a raised eyebrow from Robert. His stubble had turned into a week's worth of scruff, which he rubbed thoughtfully with his hand. "Aye, mayhap, George," he replied. "And in exchange, I'll kindly ask you to bathe. Your stench is chasing away any game we might catch and eat."

The men laughed heartily around their makeshift camp. To Alwin's shock, even Robert quirked a smile, which transformed the hard lines of his face into a mischievous handsomeness.

Unsure of what brought about the change, Alwin approached Burke, who stood smiling a few feet away. "Why are the men so happy, Burke?" she asked softly.

"We are on Sinclair land now, my lady," he said, his eyes twinkling. "We are perhaps only a day or a day and a half's ride from the keep at Roslin."

"Oh," she replied. Her heart seemed to accelerate a few notches. She wasn't sure how she felt about their imminent arrival at Robert's keep. On the one hand, she longed for a hot bath, a meal, and a change of clothes. Robert might as well have directed his rib about stinking toward her. She was tired of only being able to freshen up her face and hands in the icy waters of the streams they passed. Her dress was wrinkled, torn, and stained, and she could feel her skin itching underneath the dirty cloth.

On the other hand, though, she was worried about what would happen once they reached Roslin. Would she be able to get her farce of a marriage annulled? Would Robert release her once her father and Raef Warren paid him out, or would he keep her for any other uses he could devise for her? She wasn't sure what to make of the swirl of emotions she felt at the thought of Robert putting her aside or sending her away. It would mean she could be free of his control, but she would no longer get to see those pale blue eyes or have his scent and warm arms wrap around her.

She also didn't know what the other members of the Sinclair clan would think of Robert bringing home a brand new English bride. Would they hate her? Would they treat her like a pawn or bargaining chip, just like Robert? What if—she swallowed hard—what if there was another woman who would loath her for her new position as Robert's wife?

She told herself she was being silly and childish, getting herself all worked up over something she had no control over and couldn't know until they arrived. But based on what Burke just said, that would be sooner rather than later.

Robert's voice interrupted her thoughts. "We have a stop to make, lads," he said, the smile fading from his face and his voice turning serious.

The men's smiles slipped too, and they nodded and prepared to break camp. Alwin looked questioningly at Burke, but he had already begun to turn away to ready his horse for the day's ride.

Alwin wouldn't get her answer until that evening, when their party veered off their course and began to approach a small farmstead in the distance. She was about to ask Robert what was going on when she realized that all the men had fallen into a stony silence that she sensed should not be broken. They rode on for an hour this way, drawing ever closer to the farm.

When they were perhaps one hundred yards away, the door to the farmhouse opened a crack, and a little blond mop of hair poked out. The door closed, then was opened again, but this time a woman stood in the doorway with the blond head peaking out from behind her skirts. When they were only a few paces away, Robert dismounted silently, along with all the other men. He seemed to completely forget about Alwin, his eyes trained on the woman and boy in the doorway. Alwin slid down from Robert's massive warhorse and crept up behind the group, peering around their shoulders.

The woman called out to them cheerfully, saying something in Gaelic, but her eyes quickly scanned the group of men before her. Alwin watched as the woman's eyes widened and fear seemed to rise in her when she could not find what she was looking for.

"Liam? Liam?" she said, her voice hitching higher with panic.

"Mara…" Robert began softly.

He began to speak in Gaelic, but before he had gotten far, the woman screamed in agony. She collapsed to her knees in the dirt in front of the door, clutching Robert's shirt. He lowered to his knees as well and wrapped her in his arms as she screamed and sobbed and thrashed against him. The men stood around them with their heads bowed and eyes lowered, some unabashedly wiping at the tears that flowed freely down their cheeks.

The little boy next to Mara didn't seem to understand what was happening. He was perhaps four years old at most. He began to tug on his mother's sleeve, confused and frightened. Mara, lost in her grief, did not see or feel him.

Without realizing what she was doing, Alwin pushed her way through the giant Highland warriors to come to a halt in front of Robert, Mara, and the boy. She too went to her knees, scooping the little child into her embrace. He let her hold him but began speaking in Gaelic in a high and frightened voice. Not knowing how to soothe him in his own language, Alwin began to sing softly in English. She sang a lullaby her mother had taught her as a child about a little girl chasing a cow in a meadow. It had always helped her nod peacefully off to sleep as a girl. As she reached the end, she started over, all the while slowly rocking the boy. Gradually, he went limp in her arms, gazing up at her face with bright green eyes.

She didn't know how long she had been crouching there with the boy in her arms, for the song had created a kind of hypnosis in both her and the child. She thought of her mother, of the pain of losing her, of all she still wished she could have taught her before she died. This boy would have to go through the same thing, but with his father, who was buried in an unmarked grave somewhere in the wilderness.

Glancing up, she realized that darkness had fallen. Mara still cried and Robert still held her, but her screams had turned into low moans that were becoming less and less frequent. Finally, she released her clenched hands in his shirt and laid a hand on her face, as if feeling herself to make sure she was still real. Slowly, Robert helped her to her feet.

"Who will watch over Mara and little Danny for the night?" Robert said, his voice like sandpaper.

Instantly, George and another man stepped forward. While the other man walked Mara into her little farmhouse, George came over to where Alwin was crouched with the boy in her embrace. Gently, George lifted Danny from her arms and carried the near-sleeping child inside. Alwin saw the soft light of a candle being lit through the window but knew the cheery light would do little to ward away the pain of the family's loss tonight.

She tried to stand, but her legs had grown cold and stiff from hours of crouching, and she nearly toppled over. Suddenly, Robert was at her side, holding her up with his strong, warm hands around her waist. He turned to glance over his shoulder and gave orders to his men to make camp a half mile away from the farmhouse, far enough to give the family privacy but close enough to be of help if they needed it. As the men moved off to the west of the house, Robert and Alwin were left alone.

Exhaustion slammed into her body, and she felt like she would come to pieces at any second. She tried to suppress the tears that seemed to bubble up out of nowhere, but she knew it was a losing battle. She had always been quick to tears—it was simply her way of expressing any intense emotion, whether it was anger, frustration, or, as was the case now, pain and sadness. She was not embarrassed about her response—she knew her tears didn't make her weak—but she had to admit she had shed more tears since meeting Robert than she thought possible. Why did this man seem to tap straight into her core, either raising her ire and frustration, or uncovering her deepest sorrow? Would she ever shed tears of joy in his presence?

Tears started streaming unchecked down her cheeks, and her legs wobbled again. Not caring about the consequences of her actions, she threw her arms around Robert's neck and pulled their bodies together. She felt guilty for demanding more of him after he had given so much to Mara but longed to feel his warmth, his aliveness, against her.

He responded, circling his arms tightly around her and squeezing her so hard that she couldn't breathe for a moment. She felt a drop of moisture on her forehead, where his chin was pressed to her hair, and drew back slightly. In the light of the half-moon, she saw that a tear had rolled down his cheek as well.

Mesmerized by the intensity in his eyes as they bore into her, she leaned forward and raised up onto her toes, letting her lips brush the track the tear had left on his cheek. He shuddered at the delicate contact. As she drew away, she saw that his eyes were now filled with a rawness and hunger that made her gasp. Before she could exhale, though, his lips came crashing down on hers.

Their first kiss had been light, soft. Their second had been exploratory. This one was pure desire. His tongue plunged into her mouth, demanding, hot, and urgent. She met him with an intensity she didn't know she possessed. Her fingers dug into his shoulders, pulling him even closer as her tongue moved with his. His invasion of her mouth sent waves of heat radiating through her, and the warmth seemed to pool especially between her legs.

One of his hands pressed against her lower back, plastering her body against his, while the other went from her waist to the underside of her breast. He lingered there for a moment, seeming to make sure even through the fog of passion that she would allow the touch. When she made a noise of longing in the back of her throat, his large hand slowly moved upward to settle over her breast. The touch made her tingle even through her clothes, and she instinctively arched her back so that the contact was fuller. At that, he groaned, and she could feel the hard length of his manhood pressing against her belly.

He began moving his thumb over the peak of her breast, which shot fiery sensation through her, and she gasped against his mouth. He switched his hands so he could cup her other breast and give it the same caress. She could feel dampness between her legs, and an ache was building there, but she didn't know how to relieve it. She pressed her hips into his, longing for something she didn't fully understand. Her body was responding all on its own, suffused with heat, climbing toward something, hungry for more.

Suddenly he tore his mouth away from hers and held her at arm's length. She was so shocked at the loss of their contact that she stood there, mouth open and eyes wide, for a long second.

"We shouldn't do this. Not here. Not now." His voice came out gravelly with passion. He wiped a hand over his face then through his hair, trying to clear his thoughts. Damn, but he had nearly thrown her on the ground and tossed her skirts up right on the spot. His desire for her startled him. Aye, it had been a while since he had been with a lass, but he couldn't remember a time when anyone had ever moved him so much, had ever made him so hot and hungry before. He wanted her—badly, he admitted to himself.

What was it about her that was driving him half mad? At the moment, it was her swollen lower lip, still damp from his kiss, which she was now working gently with her teeth. Aye, she was one of the most beautiful women he had ever seen—*the* most beautiful, he corrected himself, but not just because of the perfect feel of the weight of her breasts in his hands, her trim waist, the womanly yet delicate curve of her hips and bottom, those blue-gray eyes a man could drown in, or the tumble of rose-scented tresses that always seemed to be coming loose from her braid.

He realized with a jolt that despite his desire to taste, to touch, to explore every inch of this goddess in front of him, it went deeper than lust. He wanted to know more about her, wanted to learn about the thoughts that raced behind those eyes. How could she be so naïve to the world, and yet so brave to stand up to him, to fight back against Warren, to comfort the child who had lost his father?

She was innocent when it came to men, though, he reminded himself. He couldn't lose control of himself like that again. Otherwise, the consequences would be irreversible. He had to stop this. He had to remember his mission. She wasn't his to take, or to keep.

Shame, embarrassment, and a sense of rejection washed over Alwin as he silently raked her with his eyes, an unreadable mask on his face. He was right to have stopped. What were they doing? How could she have acted like such a wanton, and after everything that had happened this evening? And moreover, she had told herself over and over that she hated him for using her like a pawn.

Why couldn't she quite believe it, though? Why did her body seem to know what it wanted, to know the truth about him—that he was worthy of her desire? She didn't know what to make of what had just passed between them; it was like nothing she had ever experienced before. She had lost herself in his embrace, in his heated touch. She had felt his raw passion, and she had matched it with her own. She wasn't thinking about what it would lead to; all she knew in the moment was that she had needed to feel his aliveness, to remind herself of the warmth in her own blood, which had never stirred except in anger. Suddenly, she felt like she had uncovered an entirely new and foreign part of herself. Just as her fiery spirit had kept her from bending to others' will, it seemed to also suffuse her with a passion she had never experienced before—never before Robert.

But now he stood at a distance, and she felt ashamed at her own desire. She tried to salvage what little shred of dignity she had left, not wanting him to see the longing he had created in her, especially if he did not feel it equally. She smoothed her hair, strands of which had come loose from her braid, and straightened her dress where it had become disheveled.

"We should join the others," she said on a shaky breath.

"Aye," he responded, his voice resuming some of its normal flatness.

She lowered her eyes, shamed again by his levelness. She felt like her whole world had been tumbled upside down at their embrace, while he remained cool, unaffected. She knew he had wanted her as they kissed, but perhaps for him it was merely a...bodily longing? She didn't know enough about men and women to understand but was hurt by his ability to control himself when she felt completely jumbled.

They both turned and walked over to Dash, then without speaking, they mounted and rode the short distance to where the other men had set up camp for the night. The crisp night air cooled her cheeks somewhat, but Alwin was unable to find rest once she was stretched out on the ground with Robert's plaid wrapped around her. She tossed and turned the whole night, tumbling over and over in her mind what had passed between them.

Chapter Twenty-One

The next morning, the party prepared to set out early. All the men were eager to return to Roslin and their families, bathe, and have a hot meal. Burke informed Alwin that they were only a few hours' ride from Roslin. As she spoke to him shortly before they left Mara's farm, she noticed that Robert headed back to the farmhouse on horseback. He returned alone soon after, telling Burke that George and Collum, the other man, would be staying with Mara and little Danny for a few more days to help her around the house. Neither man was returning to a wife or child, and both were more than willing to help out the widow of their fallen friend. Just moments after Robert returned, they were riding at an urgent pace once again, but this time they rode eagerly toward home.

Their home, Alwin thought as she grew more and more anxious. What would their arrival at Roslin mean for her? What would her role be there? Would she be greeted as the new mistress of the castle? Unlikely, she thought fretfully, nor was that a role she wanted to inhabit. As the lady of the Hewett manor, she had been trained to run a keep, but she was unsure of how they did things here in the Highlands. Moreover, she was still in disbelief that she and Robert had actually been married. Since she planned to seek an annulment immediately, she hardly even thought of the union as real.

Nevertheless, she was in fact the mistress of Roslin now. Would the Sinclair clan hate her for that? She had not asked for such a role. She would let Robert take the lead on how to tell his people of their marriage and watch him closely for how he treated her in front of others. Perhaps he thought of the union as just as much of a farce as she did. Perhaps he wouldn't expect her to run the keep as mistress but serve her function as a pawn in ransom negotiations until the money came in from Warren and her father.

One thing she knew for sure, though: he may not see her as the true mistress of the Sinclair holding and clan, but she would not be treated poorly. She refused to be controlled or disrespected by him or any of the other clanspeople. Even if they hated her, even if he saw her only as a pawn, she would demand basic human decency. She had not chosen this, and she would keep fighting for her freedom. She wasn't exactly sure what that would entail in this new and unknown environment, but she trusted that her spirit would never break, that she would always instinctually defend her freedom. And that meant not being controlled by her feelings for Robert or crushed by his distance this morning—and getting an annulment as soon as possible.

While she chewed on these thoughts, she lost track of time. As the sun reached its midday height through patchy clouds, they began climbing a slope. Soon they reached the top of the rise, and a whiff of salty sea air had her jerking her eyes up. She gasped at the sight before her.

The rise they had climbed sloped down to a flat, open expanse, which was slightly browned now in the winter, but she guessed it was normally coated in a carpet of bright green grass. The expanse narrowed to a point over several miles, and at the tip of that point stood an imposing castle. From their vantage, she could see at least four towers within an enormous stone curtain wall. The castle was perched on what seemed to be the edge of the world; it could be approached by land on its front side but was surrounded on its other three sides by cliffs and ocean. A breeze was whipping up the whitecaps on the sea and occasionally Alwin saw a blast of mist shoot up behind the castle where the waves crashed against the cliffs atop which it sat.

Burke reined his horse alongside Robert and Alwin. "Didn't I tell you, my lady? Roslin's beauty makes the journey home well worth it."

She could only nod, her eyes still locked on the sight before her.

Although Robert couldn't see the look of awe and

wonder on her face, she felt his chest swell behind her and heard a deep rumble of pride in his throat. He nudged Dash forward to cross the last expanse standing between them and home.

The watchmen along the curtain wall must have spotted their colors but waited until their faces became visible to raise the portcullis. Alwin could hear a cheer go up from within the walls, and the open square in the middle of the castle started to fill with people. As their party made their way under the portcullis, another cheer went up, and the men began jumping off their horses and embracing what Alwin guessed were wives, family members, and friends. Her chest pinched in fear. Despite the fact that she still wore the clan colors around her shoulders, she was an outsider. No one knew her here, and she was not likely to get any kind of warm welcome.

Robert slid off his horse then reached up and drew her down as well. A few eyes were beginning to find her, and despite her efforts to keep her back straight and chin high, she flinched under their scrutiny. Robert surprised her, though. Taking her hand, he laced it through his arm so that her palm rested on his muscular forearm. He cleared his throat, and suddenly, the square was quiet.

"It is good to be home!" he said.

The crowd gathered around cheered loudly again. But they returned to an expectant hush, waiting for his next words.

His face was set in an easy confidence and command. Only Alwin was close enough to see the slight tension in his jaw. "This is my wife, Lady Alwin," he said in a deep, clear voice.

Alwin realized that he had spoken in English, and probably not just for her benefit. With a sense of horror, she guessed he was also indicating her country of origin to those gathered in the square. A gasp went up all around them, and a murmur of what Alwin interpreted as displeasure began to rise. Instinctively, she moved closer to Robert's side, trying to shield herself from the crowd's seeming discontent behind his powerful body.

After what felt like an eternal silence, the crowd cheered again, even louder than before. Amazingly, they seemed genuinely happy. Alwin let out a breath she didn't realize she was holding.

Suddenly, she was surrounded by people offering their congratulations. Men came up and clapped Robert on the back, and several women approached her and curtsied. Beneath lowered lashes, Alwin caught a glimpse of an older woman elbowing her way through the crowd. She was thin and wiry and wore a plaid in the Sinclair colors over the shoulder of her dress, as the other women did. Her graying hair was pulled back into a simple bun.

Once she broke through to stand in front of Alwin and Robert, she gave them both a hard, critical look. She inspected Alwin in particular from head to toe, no doubt taking in her dirty and disheveled appearance and Robert's plaid around her shoulders. Seeming to decide something, the older woman nodded and curtsied then pinned Robert with a scathing look.

"And how do you like this? Leaving your house and kitchen staff with only a few hours to prepare a wedding feast fit for their Laird and new Lady?" she said critically, glaring at Robert.

Surprisingly, Robert laughed. The sound was deep and hearty, startling Alwin and causing her to stare up at him. She had never heard him laugh before. She had to admit, it was quite a pleasant sound. She quickly averted her eyes and tried to school her mouth from matching the smile that now lingered on his lips.

"Stella, I have the utmost confidence in your ability to recover from my idiotic blunder," he said, his mouth still quirking at the corners.

Stella, the apparent head of servants, grumbled at his teasing, but a hint of a smile crept onto her face. Turning abruptly to Alwin, she said, "And I'm guessing you'd like to freshen up. Follow me, my lady."

Alwin was whisked away from Robert by Stella's firm hand on her wrist. Stella plowed through the crowd and into the keep, winding this way and that. It was all Alwin could do to keep up, and she was completely lost in a matter of moments. She followed Stella through several large rooms, wide hallways, and up one of the tower's twisting staircases. Suddenly Stella halted in front of a wide wooden door and, leaning her weight into it, pushed it inward.

Alwin's eyes were filled with what she could only assume was Robert's chamber. It was large and spacious and had a distinctly masculine feel to it. An enormous bed rested against the far wall, and to the right were an armoire and a desk and chair. To the left, there was a window covered with both wooden shutters and a heavy fur, and in front of the window stood a brazier. The room was cool, and the air inside was still, but Robert's scent lingered. A flood of doubt suddenly filled her.

"I shouldn't stay here, mistress Stella. This is Robert's...I mean, we aren't—we haven't—" She stumbled awkwardly over the words, unsure how to get out of sharing Robert's chamber.

"Just Stella, my lady. You are the mistress now. And the way I see it, you two are married, so this chamber is just as much yours now as it is his."

The words stunned Alwin, but she managed a mute nod. She didn't know how to explain to the older woman the...unique situation she was in.

Tactfully ignoring Alwin's struggle, which she was sure was playing across her face plainly, Stella said, "I'll have a fire built up, my lady, and the lads will bring up the tub and some hot water for a bath."

Alwin felt such a strong rush of excitement and gratitude at the thought of a bath that tears sprung to her eyes. "Thank you, Stella, that sounds wonderful."

Stella turned and whisked out of the room, and

Alwin could hear the older woman delivering orders for a fire and bath as she marched back down the stairs.

Alwin found herself suddenly alone, and the tears that had threatened a moment before overwhelmed her. Stifling a sob in her hand, she went over to the bed and sank down to sit on its edge. Loneliness and uncertainty swept over her, and she unexpectedly found herself missing her old home at her father's keep and Betsy's kind and familiar friendship.

She quickly wiped her tears away when a soft rap on the door came. She ushered several servants in, one of whom set about making a fire in the brazier and creating a little gap in the furs covering the window to let the smoke out, while three others walked in carrying a large wooden tub. Even as they positioned the enormous tub, other servants began coming in with buckets of steaming water. They filled the tub bucket by bucket until the air seemed to be filled with warm dampness. Stella returned with several soft-looking towels and a bar of soap. She shooed the servants away, who had completed their tasks and were lingering to steal curious glances at their new mistress.

"Come, my lady, before the boys' hard work hauling all that hot water is wasted," Stella said matter-of-factly.

Alwin hesitated then turned her back on Stella to undress. She had only ever been naked in front of Betsy before. She unwrapped the plaid and set it on the bed then unfastened her cloak and began fumbling with the ties on her dress. When all her garments but her chemise were shed, she hesitated again, then felt a light tap on her shoulder. She turned to find Stella with an unusually soft look on her face.

"No need to be shy, mistress. I'm just an old lady who's seen it all by now," she said gently.

Alwin blushed and lowered her eyes, but nodded, grateful for Stella's tact and compassion. Loosening the strings on her chemise, she pulled the worn garment over her head and tossed it on the corner of the bed with the rest of her dirty clothes. She scampered over to the tub and quickly threw her feet over the edge, sighing at the warmth of the water. She sank all the way in on another sigh.

"I imagine you've been missing this, judging by your appearance," Stella said with a smile. "Now, now, I mean no offense by that, my lady. I'm just furious with the Laird for not taking better care of you on your journey."

Alwin picked up on the woman's gentle prodding for information about just how and where Robert had found her, how they came to be married, and why she was in such a tattered condition upon arrival at Roslin. She didn't wish to try to explain, though, so she didn't take Stella's bait, and instead, dunked her head underwater.

Letting the subject drop easily, Stella approached with the bar of soap and began working a lather into Alwin's dripping hair. Soon the smell of lavender filled the chamber, and Alwin could feel all the aches and tensions from the last week begin to ease away. She dunked her head again to rinse out the lather, then Stella handed her the bar of soap, and Alwin went about scrubbing away the dirt, and likely a fair bit of skin. The sensation of being clean was intoxicating, though.

Stella let her dally in the tub for a while longer as she went around the room straightening things that didn't need it. When she reached the pile of Alwin's filthy clothes on the bed, she scooped them up, saying, "We'll have these cleaned for you, mistress. For now, though, you'll have to wear some borrowed clothes. The Laird's late mother wasn't as tall or slim as you, but..." Stella trailed off, her brow furrowed as she mentally catalogued clothes. She dumped Alwin's garments in a pile in front of the door then went to the armoire and pulled out one of Robert's clean white shirts. She draped the shirt over the back of the chair then picked up one of the towels and returned to the tub.

Alwin stood reluctantly, but she knew if she lingered in the bath any longer she was in danger of falling asleep. The fire was burning cheerfully in the brazier now, filling the room with warmth. As she dried herself off with the towel, Stella retrieved the shirt and held it out to her. Although it felt too intimate to put on one of Robert's shirts, she didn't have anything else to wear, and it was better than nothing. As she slipped the shirt over her head, Robert's clean, masculine scent surrounded her. She was becoming very familiar with that scent, and she secretly admitted she drew a fair bit of enjoyment from it.

Stifling a yawn, she squeezed as much water from her long hair as she could while she walked over to the bed again. She longed to stretch out and let sleep take her, but before she did, a question popped into her mind. "Stella, does everyone here speak English?"

The older woman paused in her tidying of the soap and towels and turned to her. "Aye, my lady, just about. There have been so many invasions and wars fought over this land that we have all learned it."

Alwin lowered her eyes in embarrassment, but Stella went on.

"That's no burden for you to carry, my lady. You didn't bring the wars to us. Besides, these days we normally only speak in Gaelic for special occasions or traditions. If you hear people around the castle speaking English, trust that it is no comment on your presence. And if you hear people speaking Gaelic," she said, a twinkle coming into her eye, "then they're likely talking about you."

Despite her fatigue and worry, Alwin smiled at that. Well, she was the mysterious and foreign lady their Laird had shown up with unannounced. A little gossip was only natural. She would have to make sure they had nothing to use against her. She had become very good at acting the part of the lady even as she worked to undermine her father's control over her, she thought, the mirth leaving her. She could do it again.

"I'll let you rest now, mistress," Stella said briskly. She scooped up the pile of clothes in front of the door and eased out but left the bath. She would have to twist Robert's ear about the exhausted and filthy condition the girl was in, as well as pry some answers out of him about what he meant by resisting marriage for several years then returning home after a two-week journey with an English bride no one had ever seen or heard of before. She could tell by Alwin's modesty that she was still innocent, which was another puzzle. Something was afoot, she was sure.

She saw the strain in Alwin's face and took note of the way the girl stumbled over her words and appeared frightened to share Robert's chamber or use his shirt. The girl knew something, but Stella doubted that she had somehow manipulated or threatened Robert. More likely, the blockheaded Laird was planning some tactical scheme, but Stella knew not what. She had also not missed the looks that passed between Robert and Alwin. Aye, the lass was still a virgin, but something grew between the two of them.

Stella tried to suppress the joy bubbling up inside her. They had all hoped so desperately that the Laird would marry and settle down soon. Many in the clan knew about the covert missions he ran against the English in the Borderlands and were grateful for his counter-war efforts, but the clan needed him here to lead them, not off gathering information and stealing supplies and weapons. Not only was Robert wed now, but Stella suspected the union could be a happy one based on the heated looks they gave each other and the protective stance Robert took toward Alwin. She seriously doubted either comprehended it yet, though. Well, she thought, she was going to enjoy watching them come to realize it.

Chapter Twenty-Two

Robert passed Stella on the stairs on his way up to his chamber. A faint smile touched her lips, and he wondered absently what could have her looking so mischievous.

"I take it you saw to Alwin?"

"Aye, Laird, she has bathed and is now resting," she replied, her eyes twinkling.

He nodded and began trudging up the stairs again, but she said, "A bath awaits you in your chamber, Laird."

"Thank you, Stella. That sounds wonderful," he said, his exhaustion fully hitting him.

She curtsied and scurried past him, covering a chuckle behind her hand. He was too tired to guess at what had her so amused, so he simply kept walking until he reached his chamber door. He pushed it open unthinkingly but froze halfway through the doorway.

Stretched out on his bed was Alwin, asleep.

Asleep and half naked, he realized, swallowing hard.

She looked to have collapsed there, not even managing to pull a blanket over her bare legs. She wore one of his shirts, which was quite large on her, but still only covered her to just above her knees. Her legs were long and slim, and her skin glowed warmly in the light of the fire. He could see her form through the material of his shirt; she seemed so delicate and slight, and yet the gentle curve of her hip was incredibly sensual. He could see her full, firm breasts rising and falling with her steady breathing. The laces at the neck of the shirt were loose, and the slim column of her throat was exposed. Her hair, still damp and loose from her bath, splayed out around her head, soft golden brown in the firelight. Her red, full lips were slightly parted, and the dark fringe of her lashes lay still against her ivory cheekbones.

He stood there staring for several minutes, drinking in the sight of her spread out on his bed. Then he caught a glimpse of the tub, the water still steaming a little, and realized why Stella had been acting so mischievous. She had sent Alwin to his chamber to bathe and rest, and had conveniently neglected to mention it to him, all the while encouraging him to go to the room and find Alwin. He had returned perhaps an hour ago, and already his head servant was plotting something, he thought ruefully with a shake of his head.

Well, he wasn't going to pass up a hot bath, even with Alwin sleeping right in front of him. She was just as exhausted as he and was unlikely to wake anyway. He began unwinding his plaid from his shoulder then undid his belt buckle. He tossed his belt and sporran on the desk chair and caught his plaid and kilt in the other. He draped them over the chair as well. He loosened the strings at the neck of his shirt, all the while keeping his eyes on Alwin's form to assure himself that she was still asleep. As he pulled the shirt over his head, the thought crossed his mind that perhaps he would like it if she were to wake at this moment. He could just picture her rosy lips forming the shape of an O of surprise and her gray-blue eyes going wide as she drank in the sight of him naked before her. The thought made his cock harden even more that it had at seeing her lying on his bed wearing nothing but his shirt.

He quickly slipped into the tub before he started letting his eager cock make decisions for him. He could take her if he chose—it was his husbandly right. But the thought of forcing her turned his stomach. He had seen enough of that kind of behavior from wave after wave of English invaders over the course of his lifetime to know the damage, both physically and mentally, such actions caused. He would never force himself on her, but damn if he didn't find his thoughts continually returning to her. Her lithe and graceful form, not to mention those delicate curves, seemed to pull his eyes no matter how far away he was. Her regal face, full lips, and seemingly depthless eyes drew him in. And her scent, of warmth and roses, was nearly driving him mad. Thank God, they would no longer be sharing a horse all day, with her body plastered to his, their hips grinding together in rhythm, and her hair right at nose-level.

He picked up the bar of soap next to the tub and gave it a sniff. Lavender. Well, he'd smell like a woman after this bath, but that was better than how he smelled now. He washed absently, still chewing on the puzzle of his body's response—and one part of his body in particular—to Alwin. He was becoming familiar with her little gestures and thought patterns. He liked the way she carried herself with a delicate dignity, even under the worst circumstances. And his heart had nearly burst seeing her genuine emotion for Liam, Mara, and little Danny. She could clearly care deeply, but she was no weakling. She had leveled him with the harsh comparison of being like Warren and her father when he had secretly wed them.

He frowned at that thought. He didn't like the idea of her thinking so poorly of him. Without his permission, his mind jumped to thoughts of how to make things right by her, how to get her to forgive him and prove that he was a good man. He chastised himself for such a wandering mind. He didn't need to prove anything to her. He knew who he was and why he was doing this. Besides, once their marriage had secured its intended purpose—thwarting Warren—then she likely wouldn't be in his life anymore anyway—would she?

Robert hadn't let himself consider any other possibility than returning his life to the way it had been before he met her, but he also couldn't figure out what to do with the lass once his plan had been executed. If he got the marriage annulled, Alwin's father could potentially cause problems, claiming her dowry should be returned. He could let the marriage stand and send her to a nunnery, but he rejected that thought immediately, not liking the idea of forcing her into such a life, and all because of his decisions for her. She couldn't be allowed to leave and marry another, though. Robert couldn't exactly explain to himself why this was so clear to him, but the thought of her with another man made his blood boil for some reason.

He had grown protective of her, he could admit. But it was only because he took responsibility for putting her in such a dangerous and precarious position. In a way, he realized, their marriage actually afforded her a measure of protection. She could not fall under the control of her father any more. From what Alwin had alluded to earlier on their journey, he was not a kind or loving man. Nor could that bastard Warren get his hands on her again, he thought heatedly.

If they remained married, she would have a place here, protection, and a home. But then again, he couldn't make such a decision for her. He had already done enough of that. He would also have to work hard to not compromise her further. It was bad enough that he had succumbed to his desire and kissed her. If he went any further, then her choices would be gone.

He sighed and ran his fingers through his wet hair. If he could keep his distance, then once his plan was executed, he could go back to the life he had before: working for his clan toward peace, without the distraction of an intoxicatingly beautiful English lass complicating things.

He dunked his head one last time in the now-tepid bathwater. Reemerging, he scanned the room for a towel. He cursed softly when he noticed that a stack of fresh towels sat atop his desk several feet away from the tub. Just as he began to stand upright to fetch one, a flicker caught his eye, and he looked over at Alwin. Her eyes were open, and she was staring right at him.

Chapter Twenty-Three

The sound of splashing water and Robert's muttered curse had woken her. But what she saw before her was not entirely different than what had just been filling her dreams. She had dreamt of Robert's kiss and the feel of his strong, muscular body pressed against her. Now she had a full view of that body, from his dripping hair down to his hip bones, which were just visible above the tub's rim.

She gasped at the sight of him. Every contour of his body was hard and honed. His jet black hair was finger-combed back from his face and dripped around his wide shoulders. His muscular chest tapered into a trim waist, and water sluiced over each ripple and contour. His arms, which were now resting on the tub's edge, flexed as he clenched his hands. She dragged her eyes away from his magnificent form and met his eyes, which were shooting fire toward her, but not, she registered somewhere in the back of her mind, out of anger.

She tried to swallow but found her mouth had gone dry. "What are you doing?" she managed to choke out finally.

"What does it look like I'm doing, lass? I'm taking a bath in my own chamber," he said dryly, but heat still radiated from his eyes.

"Oh, well, Stella showed me up here and had this bath prepared and told me I should not be afraid to be in this chamber and that I could wear this shirt while she found something else for me to wear," she said in a rush, feeling a deep blush creeping from her neck to her face as she heard her own frantic voice in her ears.

"She's a crafty one," he said, letting one corner of his mouth rise in a half-smile. "She sent me in here to bathe as well but neglected to mention that you were here."

"I'll go!" she said, leaping from the bed in a rush to escape his heated gaze and his godlike body, which was doing funny things to her insides.

"If you don't mind, lass, I was just going to go fetch one of those towels over there…"

She scrambled over, not wanting him to reveal any more of his body, else she lose her wits completely. She felt his eyes on her predatorily as she moved across the room, picked up a towel, and began to approach him. Had the prey ever wanted to be caught before?

He waited until she was directly in front of him before raising his hand to take the towel from her slightly trembling hand. She had never seen this much of a man before, and part of her was frightened out of her senses, but she was also rapt at his perfect, muscular physique. She couldn't stop herself from flickering her gaze between his hungry eyes and the smooth, naked planes of his chiseled torso.

"Thank you," he said softly as he grasped the towel.

She was so intently staring at him that she didn't release her hold. Their gazes locked, and lightning almost crackled between them. Something seemed to snap inside him. He tugged hard on the towel so that she was jerked forward against his wet chest. His arms wrapped around her, and his mouth came down onto hers.

She could feel each one of the rippling muscles she had just been staring at through the thin linen of the shirt she wore. She looped her arms around his neck, letting her fingertips skim across his broad and powerful shoulders. His body radiated heat, and he smelled like clean masculinity with a hint of lavender. His kiss seared her lips, and she moaned into his mouth as he deepened their contact. His damp skin was soaking through her shirt, making the material plaster to her skin and leaving only a thin barrier between them. His hand slipped to her bottom, and he pulled her hips against his. She could feel his manhood pressed against her, hard and large.

The hand on her bottom moved up to cup one of her breasts. The contact, inhibited only by the wet shirt, caused her to shiver and moan again. He moved his thumb over her nipple as he gently grazed his teeth over her bottom lip. She arched into him, and at that, he too moaned, the sound a deep and masculine growl.

Suddenly, he scooped her up in his arms and stepped over the rim of the tub, not breaking their kiss. He strode over to the bed and laid her down on it, leaning over her with his weight on one elbow while his other hand brushed up her calf. His hand was strong and callused, but he managed a light caress as he moved to her knee, then her thigh. Her head spun with the sensations of his lips and hand, and she felt as though she were in a fog. A very distant part of her screamed that she shouldn't let him go any further, for they were wading into dangerous waters. That rational side, though, was muted by the animal passion he had awoken within her.

His hand slipped under the material of the shirt, moving still higher up her thigh. She shuddered under his touch, longing for more. The spot between her legs had grown damp and ached for something, but she wasn't sure what. All she could register was that Robert's touch seemed to both cause the ache and might be able to relieve it.

Just then a soft knock sounded at the door, and Alwin nearly jumped out of her skin.

Through the heavy wood, Stella's voice said, "I've found some clothes that might do for Lady Alwin."

At the mention of clothes, Alwin looked down at herself and gasped. The white linen shirt she was wearing had absorbed the water from Robert's body and was plastered to every one of her contours, rendered almost completely see-through.

Robert's gaze followed hers. "Christ," he breathed.

Reclined in his arms was the most beautiful sight he had ever seen—nay, the most beautiful he could ever imagine in his wildest fantasies. Alwin's gray eyes were bottomless pools in the firelight. Her lips were redder than normal from their passionate kiss, and a pink blush warmed her skin. He could see her breasts clearly outlined through the wet linen of the shirt she wore, each firm, full curve topped with a rosy nipple the same shade as her lips. Glancing farther down, he saw his hand underneath the shirt's hem. His fingers on her creamy, smooth thigh were just inches from the apex between her legs. He was half on top of her, completely naked. His eyes traveled back up to her face, and he saw the look of horror there. She was so damned enticing, but what was he doing? Hadn't he just told himself that he couldn't compromise her further, couldn't play with the fire that seemed to spark between them?

Cursing himself again for being so controlled by his baser side, he leapt from the bed and spun around so his back was to her, all in one fluid movement. He snatched up the towel she had used after her bath, which was on the foot of the bed, and deftly wrapped it around his waist to preserve her modesty and innocence.

He strode over to the door and opened it a crack. "Lady Alwin fell into a deep sleep after her bath, and she still sleeps now," he said crossly into Stella's grinning face. "Give me a moment, and I will be out of your hair."

With that, he closed the door on her and turned back to Alwin. She had sat upright and tugged one of the bed's coverlets over her to shield herself. A look of shock and confusion lingered on her face, but there was also gratitude in her eyes for his lie to Stella. He doubted his shrewd servant had believed him, but it was the least he could do to try to alleviate some of Alwin's embarrassment. He went to the armoire and retrieved a thick robe to throw around himself then went back to the door. Without a look behind him, he strode through, leaving it open for Stella to enter after him.

Chapter Twenty-Four

Alwin quickly laid herself out on the bed again, closing her eyes and feigning sleep as Robert passed out of the door. She heard Stella bustling about the room and decided to give up the ruse. She blinked open her eyes and sat up, only half-heartedly acting like she had been asleep. Stella graciously didn't say anything or look at her for a few moments, and instead, collected the towels and the bar of soap. Alwin noticed that she had also draped some clothes over the chair when she had come in.

"Ah, mistress, you're awake," Stella said. "I've brought you some garments until we can have yours cleaned and make you some new ones."

"That's very kind of you, Stella. I'll be much obliged to have my own clothes back, but please, do not trouble yourself with making new ones for me." She didn't say that she had no idea how long she would be here, or in what capacity, but Stella seemed to pick up on her omission.

"We can cross that bridge when we get to it, mistress. For now, I've rummaged these from the Laird's late mother's closet. She was about your size, though perhaps a bit shorter. Nevertheless, these should do the trick for such a last-minute occasion." Stella retrieved a clean white chemise and what looked to be a deep blue gown from the chair and brought it over to Alwin. Alwin quickly scooted out of Robert's shirt. If Stella saw it, she'd notice it was wet on the front from Robert's embrace.

She let Stella slip the new chemise over her head. The older woman was right—the chemise only barely brushed her ankles, but by adjusting the ties in the front, the fit was fairly good. Next the dress went on, and Alwin found the fit quite flattering. The dress hugged her body closely, showing her slim waist, gently curved hips, and full breasts while still being modest enough for a lady. The color was breathtaking. It reminded Alwin of the deep blue of the pre-dawn sky.

Stella gave a satisfied nod. "I'll send up the lads to remove the tub, along with a few of the girls to see to your preparations."

"Preparations for what?"

"The wedding feast, of course! We can't let our Laird run off and get married without a proper celebration!" Stella replied.

"Oh." Alwin's nervousness was returning again. What was she expected to do during this feast? Should she act like she and Robert were happily married? Was she truly a part of this clan now—the mistress of the clan? Would Robert tell them he had only married her to further his own power play against Warren, or would he lie to his people the way he had lied to her? And how could she face Robert after their latest encounter? She had acted like a wanton, driven only by desire.

Even as she thought this, though, a part of her rejected it. She wasn't some harlot; her response to Robert was different than anything she had experienced before. And besides, they were married! But at the same time, she hardly knew him. Her instincts told her he was a good man, but the precarious position she was in was also his doing. She didn't understand how she could hate Robert so much for the position he was putting her in and still long for his touch, his kiss—and more. He had awakened some part of her that she never knew existed, and she longed to learn more about that side of herself, and that side of him. But she couldn't allow herself to be blinded by lust, to ignore the fact that he had taken away her freedom by sneaking his way into a marriage bind with her.

All these thoughts tumbled through her head, and she felt like she was drowning in a sea of confusion. She was only slightly distracted as Stella called down orders to have the tub removed and to send up two servants to plait her hair and make other preparations for the feast. The servants moved about the room quietly, sensing their new mistress's consternation. She hardly noticed as they offered her a new pair of slippers to go with her gown, plaited her tresses in an elaborate pattern that left half of her hair flowing down her back, and placed a circlet of gold atop her head.

Much time must have passed, however, for she realized she was starving all of a sudden.

At a grumble from her stomach, Stella said, "Well, that sounds like our cue. The clan has already gathered below to welcome you and celebrate your marriage, mistress. Shall we join them?" Stella extended her hand toward the door, ushering her out of the chamber.

With her mind still in turmoil, Alwin stood and glided through the door and down the stairs to the waiting crowd.

Chapter Twenty-Five

Robert fidgeted at the head table. What was taking so long?

He lifted his mug of ale to his lips again and let his eyes skitter to the stairs at the other end of the great hall. After leaving his chamber in a rush, he had gone to a different tower to don clean clothes, shave, and comb his hair in preparation for the impromptu feast. He had also sent off a missive to Raef Warren informing him of an acquisition he had recently made that might interest him. Though part of him had niggled at the thought of treating Alwin like a bargaining chip—just as Warren undoubtedly did—he pushed his doubts aside and ordered a messenger to leave immediately after the feast with the missive. Perhaps it would be best to get this whole scheme over with as quickly as possible, he thought, taking another swig of ale. How the hell he was going to manage to get Alwin's dowry and her ransom while keeping her from Warren remained to be solved.

Setting aside that tangled problem, he had joined his people in the great hall to await the start of the celebration. Ale had already been passed through the crowd, and the cheery buzz of conversation now filled the hall. His people were genuinely happy. Not only had their Laird returned safe and victorious, but he had also managed to secure a wife. He was expecting a bit more reservation from them about the mysterious circumstances under which he had wed and the fact that his new bride was English, but no one seemed to mind, at least not yet.

Their overwhelmingly positive response made Robert realize just how hard these last few years must have been on his people, and not just because of their slow recovery from the warfare of the past. He knew they appreciated his missions, but perhaps all those treks to the Borderlands had taken a toll. He had been away so much in the last four years. A thought crept into his mind. Maybe his people would be better served by his presence with the clan at Roslin rather than off in the Borderlands.

And as for marriage, he had never allowed Stella or the others' pleas to take a wife to penetrate much because he was always putting his missions first. He had no time to arrange for such a union and no inclination to be tied to a woman purely for political reasons. Of course, part of the reason this marriage to Alwin happened at all was that it had required no planning, no negotiations, no awkward talks of alliances and dowries. Instead of getting in the way of his counter-war efforts against the English, it actually aided them.

And he didn't anticipate the need to be tied to her for the rest of his life—only until he could execute his plan, he told himself firmly. Once his goal was achieved, he would figure out what to do next with their situation.

But even as he reassured himself of this plan, a little voice in the back of his head shouted that he was being a blind fool. Despite their muddled circumstances, there was something between them. The thought of their kiss had scorched his memory, and he couldn't stop thinking about it—about her. Her scent clung to him, threatening to drive him insane. Her beautiful face and body swam before his eyes, and the feel of her smooth skin trembling with desire under his hand sent his cock hardening all over again. And it wasn't just her beauty. He admired her courage, her unashamed vulnerability, her gracefulness. She possessed a regal air that was not just a product of her birth; rather, it was an outward sign of the intoxicating mixture of her delicacy and fortitude that he had never encountered before.

He took another gulp of ale. Perhaps it was time to change his plan, he admitted reluctantly.

Just then, a hush fell over the crowd in the hall, and he jerked his eyes once more to the bottom of the stairs. It was as if his thoughts had just materialized. And magnified. There Alwin stood. She had stopped at the bottom of the stairs, seeming unsure for a moment at the sight of all those strangers staring at her with awe. But her back was straight and her chin level, and she took a gliding step forward. She wore a fitted deep blue gown that looked vaguely familiar to Robert, and her soft brown hair, pulled back around her temples, flowed in loose waves down her back. A circlet of gold sat atop her head, drawing out the golden strands in her tresses. She hadn't spotted him yet, so she must not know where she was going. He stood and cleared his throat, drawing her eyes.

When her eyes met his from halfway across the hall, he felt as if he had been punched in the chest. The gown drew out the blue from her eyes, and her gaze pierced him. He felt like he was swimming in their blue depths for a moment. Her eyes were only intensified by her dark lashes and pale skin, scrubbed clean and glowing faintly pink at the moment. As she recognized him, her full, rosy lips parted on a little gasp of surprise. He could only guess what he must look like to her, clean-shaven, scrubbed, and wearing clean clothes for the first time since they met. Though simply dressed and a bit tumbled when he had first laid eyes on her, he had always known she was a true-born beauty, a lady of refined grace. But he never could have imagined in his wildest dreams that she could be as perfect as she was now as she walked toward him.

She continued to approach, seeming to completely forget her foreign surroundings or the unknown Highlanders all around. Her wide eyes stayed locked on his, and she glided toward him as if in a trance. When she reached his side at the head table, he took her hand in his and bent over it, pressing a kiss to her knuckles. Turning to his clanspeople, he said in a loud voice, "My lady wife, Alwin Sinclair."

The crowd roared their approval and raised their mugs in a cheer to their Laird and Lady.

At Robert's words, Alwin felt like she was awakening from a dream. When she had spotted him from across the hall, she doubted for a second that it was actually him. He wore a simple white shirt and his red kilt, with a length of plaid over his shoulder, just as he had looked when she had first laid eyes on him. But his hair was combed back from his face, and he had shaved off more than a week's worth of scruff, which made him look more…handsome, she admitted. He looked a bit younger and definitely less frightening, though she had watched as the muscles in his jaw twitched at the sight of her. She thought at first he was angry with her for some reason, perhaps for causing everyone to wait on her arrival. But then she had seen his eyes, which had burned into her like a pale blue fire. She saw unmistakable desire in them, and she felt herself being drawn toward him, and the promise in his eyes, like a moth to a flame.

But then with his words, reality came crashing back. Alwin *Sinclair*, he had called her, and she supposed it was the truth. She sat down heavily at his side, sinking into her worrying once again. What could ever come of their union? After he had completed his plan to collect her dowry and ransom money, what then? And what of her plan for an annulment? If they continued on the way they had begun, first with their kisses at Father Paul's cottage and outside Mara's farmhouse, and then up in his chamber, she wouldn't be able to get an annulment.

She wouldn't *want* one, a voice whispered inside her head. But what could a life as Robert's wife look like? Would he be gone all the time on raids against her home country? Would she never know if he were alive or dead? Would he actually want a union with her, and not just a marriage in name, as she had secretly always longed for? Would he give her freedom and love?

These last thoughts she pushed away harshly. She had no business fantasizing about a marriage in which she was truly valued, given freedom, and loved. All her life she knew she would be wed off to whomever her father decided. She had let go of her girlish dreams of affection, kindness, and trust in a marriage—hadn't she? She realized now that she could never have such a union with Raef Warren. Only a few minutes in his company had made that clear. So why should she be fighting so hard to get away from Robert and back to either Warren or her father, who would hand her over to Warren anyway?

She cast a sideways glance at Robert, who sat next to her. He had his clean white shirt rolled up around his forearms. She was becoming increasingly fascinated with his body. It was so different than hers. Her hand rested on the table a few inches from his. His wrist was at least twice the size of hers. His frame was tall and broad naturally, but his muscles were battle-hewn. She had caught a glimpse of several scars on his torso when he had been standing in the bathtub. But he was also more imposing and commanding, with the presence of a true leader, than all other men she had ever seen.

She realized then that it wasn't just his body which had been formed over years of training and fighting—it was also his personality. He was hard, unyielding. He demanded respect and obedience from everyone—his men, his clanspeople, and now her. But he wasn't a tyrant. From what she had seen, he led his people both with commanding authority and subtle compassion. Even she had been swept up by the combination in him of strength and tenderness.

No, he probably would object to the word "tenderness" to describe him, but what else should she call it when he gave her his plaid, or when he warmed her with his body, or when he had held vigil with the widow Mara? In her fantasies, she had always envisioned her dream husband as a courtly English knight, well-versed in the arts of flowery words and romantic gestures she had read about as a girl back in her father's study. But here was this hulking Highland warrior who lit the fires of desire within her, despite his gruffness and even cold calculating side at times. She was drawn to him, and she respected him, she realized.

Sensing her eyes on him, Robert turned to her and

pinned her with one of those penetrating looks. Thankfully, a servant placed a trencher of steaming food in front of them, breaking their gaze. She busied herself by reaching for the mug of ale that was placed in front of her and taking a gulp. Setting the mug back down, she scanned the crowd of people before her. They were all happily talking and laughing, many seeming to be fairly deep into their cups already. Luckily the servers were making their way around the room offering food, and many people began finding a seat at one of the several long tables that filled the great hall.

Robert's fingers grazed her arm, and she jumped at the contact. He had cut some of the meat on their shared trencher and was holding a knifeful up for her to eat. She glanced between the knife and him, hesitant to partake in this intimate ritual. But they were married, after all, so finally she leaned forward and took the bite of meat into her mouth. Apparently several other clanspeople had noticed the gesture as well, for a pleased rumble of satisfaction rose in the air.

Alwin blushed and lowered her eyes, embarrassed at having to carry on with these marriage rituals so publicly. Seeing her embarrassment, Robert gave her some reprieve and turned to his left, where Burke sat. The two men chatted for a while about household matters. It sounded to Alwin's ears like they were having some trouble keeping the castle ledgers straight. Apparently, Stella and the head cook had different ways of recording and keeping track of things, and it was creating problems. With Robert gone so much, Alwin gathered, he hadn't had time to sort it out yet.

She took another sip of ale and let herself return to her own thoughts. She needed to talk with Robert about what his plan was. She had wanted to ask him so many questions in the last few days of the journey, but had been torn by her anger at his actions and her own nervousness over arriving at Roslin. Resolved, she turned back to him and laid her hand on his forearm. His skin was warm beneath her fingers, and his muscles twitched at the contact. He turned to her, questioning in his eyes, but also a hint of heat.

Leaning in, she spoke so that only he could hear. "Is your plan the same, Robert? Will you ransom me and then collect my dowry?"

He raised a dark eyebrow at her bold question. "I sent a missive to Warren this evening informing him that if he wishes to save his reputation, he will pay for you."

Her face fell at his words. It was too late, then, to call off that portion of his plan. She hated the way he was using her, and that he played into the fact that Warren apparently saw her as nothing but a matter of pride without missing a beat.

"When will you get his answer?"

"A few weeks, or perhaps sooner, seeing as how this is a fairly urgent and delicate matter for him," he responded coldly.

"And what then? What happens after he pays you?"

"Then I will contact your father informing him of our nuptials and demanding what is my due."

She felt herself growing angry with him once more. "That was not what I meant. What will happen to me—to us—after you have completed your scheme?"

She saw a shadow cross over his eyes for a moment, then the cold, calculating look returned. "That is not your concern just yet, lass."

She wanted to scream at him but pressed her lips together and tried to cool her nerves. She decided a different tack. "Do you plan to tell your clan how we came to be married?"

A faint smile touched his lips. "I'll tell them the truth, but perhaps not all of it."

As if on cue, a large, stout clansman stood, swaying a bit on his feet. He raised his mug to the high table where Alwin, Robert, and Burke sat, and bellowed, "Pray tell, my Laird, how you met and married this gem of an Englishwoman! Surely there was some trickery involved for you to secure such a beautiful lass!"

Several in the hall chuckled and responded with ribald calls of their own. Robert glanced over at Alwin and noticed that the color had drained from her face and she had lowered her head in shock and embarrassment.

Robert cleared his throat. "Well, Rufus, your whiskey seems to have made you see clearer for once. I first saw Lady Alwin in the Borderlands, and I knew then that I had to have her."

At his words, Alwin's eyes shot from her lap to his face. He was being careful with his words, but told the truth in a way, she supposed. Yes, he had to have her—for the money she would bring.

But he continued, shocking her even further. "And you're right, Rufus. She *is* beautiful, and I'm sure I don't deserve her."

All in the hall laughed and cheered at that, and several hands dragged Rufus back down to his bench. Alwin couldn't stand another minute of this humiliation. She had gone along with the celebration of their farcical marriage, not wanting to set the clan against her right from the start. Secretly, she admitted to herself now, she had also longed to see Robert again. She didn't know what he stirred in her, but she yearned to explore it further with him. She had endured the wedding rituals of sharing a trencher and eating what he cut for her in front of the whole clan. And then she had had to sit there while some drunken clansman prodded into the disastrous events that had brought her here. But to listen to Robert compliment her, to hear what she thought was sincerity in his voice even when just moments before he had coolly reiterated his plan to use her, was too much.

She stood, feeling her cheeks burning and her eyes brimming with tears, and rushed toward the stairs that lead back to the privacy of the chamber. *His* chamber, she reminded herself, only deepening her humiliation.

She ignored the quieting of those gathered in the hall, and the eyes following her. She dashed up the flight of stairs, but only made it halfway.

Chapter Twenty-Six

Robert's strong hands wrapped around her waist and spun her around. She gasped but kept her eyes down, not wanting him to see the tears shimmering in her eyes.

"Lass..." he began, but seemed to falter. Instead of speaking, he gripped her chin and raised it.

She was a few steps above him, so their eyes were level. She forced herself to meet his stare, not wanting to be the coward she was acting at present. She didn't guard herself, but let him see the hurt, confusion, and embarrassment she felt. She thought she saw him flinch, but couldn't be sure.

"You should rejoin your people," she said, her voice thick.

"Alwin, I know this is difficult for you. If it could be any other way..."

"Don't say things you don't mean and don't make promises you can't keep," she choked out.

"I didn't lie in the hall," he said heatedly.

She knew he wasn't just defending his honor and veracity. Based on the intensity in his eyes, he was referring to his declaration about her beauty and how he didn't deserve her.

"But what of my future, my life? What will come of this ruse?" she demanded.

She saw that he struggled, his brow knitted and his eyes stormy. One of his hands was still firmly around her waist, and the other held her chin. His gaze dropped to her mouth, and she could see which side of him had won his internal battle a moment before his mouth closed on hers.

He kissed her urgently, pulling her close so that no space existed between them. She met him, her arms gripping the front of his shirt and her body melding to his, trying to communicate her frustration and confusion with her kiss. When his tongue entered her mouth, he groaned at the sensation. Wanting more contact, he pivoted with her and pushed her against the stone wall of the spiral staircase. She realized her leg had risen up the outside of his thigh of its own volition, but she didn't care. She wrapped her arms around his waist. One hand snaked its way to his upper back while the other went lower to his buttocks. She felt his muscles tense and ripple beneath her grip. Suddenly, he scooped her up, not breaking their kiss, and practically sprinted up the remaining stairs to his chamber door. He pushed the door open with his back and carried her in, closing the door again with his boot.

There was a frantic passion between them, both clutching each other as they kissed. He strode over to the bed at the far side of his chamber, and they both tumbled onto it. He propped most of his weight on one elbow to prevent from crushing her, but his other hand was all over her. He held the nape of her neck to secure his lips to hers then let his hand caress her neck and lower to the top of her breasts, which were straining against the material of her dress. His hand went lower to fully cup one breast, his thumb swishing back and forth, causing her to groan into his mouth. He let his hand move over the inward curve of her waist, and the outward curve of her hip. Then he gripped the material of her dress and pulled upward so that the gown's hem hitched up her legs.

He broke the contact of their lips. As he reached lower to caress her calf, he settled his mouth on the tops of her breasts. She gasped for air as sensation flooded her body. His touches were fanning the flames of desire, and she burned hotter than she ever had before. There was too much sensation, wave after wave building within her, and it seemed to pool in her breasts and between her legs.

That yearning, reaching feeling was beginning to be familiar to her, because every time they kissed or touched, it returned. As one of his hands slowly moved up her leg, he slipped his other hand, which he had been leaning on, underneath her back to undo her dress's ties. She arched her back, both pressing him tighter to her breasts and giving him more access to the ties running down her back. Once he had loosened them enough, he used both hands to tug on the material at her shoulders until only her chemise covered her chest. Crouching on his heels on the bed, he continued to pull the dress down past her hips and then her legs, until the gown was completely off, and he tossed it aside.

She propped herself up on her elbows as he did, watching as he exposed more and more of her chemise. He was wound tight as a spring, his muscles clenched and his eyes fervent. She could see that he was very aroused and appeared to fight for control. With a growl, he tore off his shirt and threw it to where her dress lay in a crumpled pile on the floor. He was back over her in an instant, his lips kissing her breasts through her chemise and his hands roaming all over her body again.

She realized her hands were doing the same. His skin was hot under her fingertips as she gripped his neck, his shoulders, his back. She let one of her hands move between them to trace the ridges of his chest then lower to his contoured stomach. At her touch, he intensified his kiss on her breast, laving and sucking the peaked tip through the material of her chemise. It drove her wild with need, and she tugged him up by the shoulders so their mouths could meet again.

He gave her mouth the same treatment, delving with his tongue and nibbling on her lower lip, while his hand moved back to her breast. He was letting more of his weight come on top of her, and she felt his hard shaft press hotly against her thigh. She raised one of her legs and wrapped it around him, drawing him more directly over her. She didn't know what was driving her or how she knew to do what she did, but she didn't question it, and instead let her desire guide her. Based on how urgent and instinctual his movements were, he too appeared to act without artifice or planning.

"I have to see you," he mumbled through the haze of passion.

She was unsure what he meant, for they were face to face, but then he began tugging on her chemise, trying to get the material off her shoulders. She paused at that, suddenly feeling exposed and shy despite the fire still coursing through her body.

Sensing her hesitation, he stilled his hands and placed a soft kiss on her lips. "You are so beautiful, Alwin. I want to see all of you," he said huskily.

She relaxed a little, letting their kiss deepen once more. Slowly, so as not to startle her again, he inched her chemise down over her shoulders then brushed her exposed skin with his fingertips. She shivered at his feather-light touch, and he continued to ease the chemise lower. It slipped over her breasts, then past her waist, her hips, and finally brushed her feet before he tossed it aside.

He inhaled sharply, causing her eyes to snap open. His eyes roved over her exposed body, a look of raw hunger in them she had never seen before. She felt a swelling in her chest at the look he was giving her. She had been told she was fair, but she didn't realize she could be the cause of so much desire, and in such a handsome and virile man as Robert.

She looked to him for confirmation. His eyes drank her in like a man dying of thirst. His hands and eyes roved over her smooth, creamy skin, her breasts, and her rosy nipples, which were taut from his touches and kisses. He smoothed his fingertips across her flat stomach, over her flared hips, and brushed the darker curls between her legs, which were slightly damp already. She inhaled sharply, and he gritted his teeth, not quite stifling a groan.

"I have to have you—now," he rasped. Without a second thought, he ripped off his kilt and positioned himself on top of her again.

She gasped at the feel of their naked skin pressed together, which seemed to fire both of their passions even more, but she tried to push him back a little. She had caught a quick glimpse of his naked form before he came back on top of her, and it caused her to hesitate again. He was so—big. She knew only the most basic facts about what happened between a man and a woman, and she was sure it wouldn't work between them. His hard length pressed against her leg. She knew it would never fit inside her.

That thought was like a slash of cold water over her enflamed body. She pushed against his shoulder harder this time and wriggled under him, trying to break the intoxicating contact. He seemed to barely register the change in her through the haze of his own desire for a moment, but when he did, he rolled slightly to the side and propped himself on his elbow again.

"We can't—" she said, panic edging her voice. What were they doing? How had they gotten so carried away? She couldn't give her innocence to him—not now. Didn't she still want to get an annulment? She was frightened by her own desire, by the way she had thrown every rational thought aside to satisfy her body's demands.

His eyes still burned with hunger. One of his hands rested on her breast, and the weight of it pressing on her nipple was distracting her even now.

"Why not, lass? We are married. We clearly want each other," he said.

"But…" she didn't know what to say, but felt terrified of going any further. Partly, she feared her own passion. She didn't know what she was capable of and didn't understand enough about intimacy to know what was going to happen. But she also sensed that to go further with Robert meant to admit the reality of her situation. She could not get an annulment or marry another, if they continued. She could not go home and would not go to Raef Warren. She feared the sense that doors were closing even as she lay here naked with him. But a voice somewhere inside whispered to her that something was opening with Robert as well, that she was walking through a doorway to a new and unknown life with him.

His fingers continued to stroke her breast, and his pale blue eyes blazed into hers. "Do you not long for release?"

She swallowed hard and nodded as his touch continued to build a yearning inside her, a striving to relieve the sweet ache.

"There are ways that we can experience release without you giving up your innocence," he said, seeming to read her mind. His lips burned a path from her ear down her neck and to her shoulder. "Let me give you pleasure."

After a long moment, she nodded again, unable to overcome her body's need with rational thought. His lips once again moved to her breast, but this time, her chemise no longer separated them. She moaned and arched into his mouth as he laved her nipple. His hand trailed down her stomach and to the top of the curls between her legs, pausing for a moment. Then he cupped her sex with his hand, pressing firmly. She felt her blood pulsing there and writhed for more—of what she didn't know. He ran a finger over the damp, swollen lips, then spread them and circled the pad of his finger over that bud of pure pleasure above her opening. She gasped and moaned again, her head swimming with pleasure. She buried her hands in his dark hair, clawing at him, holding his mouth in place on her breast as his fingers massaged between her legs.

"God, you're so hot and wet," he whispered, his lips brushing her nipple. He moved up to capture her mouth once again in a deep, penetrating kiss. His other hand found her breasts and continued to tease and caress them. He began moving his tongue along hers in the same rhythm that he was moving his fingers across her clitoris. She groaned and sighed as the pressure built to the breaking point. She began to move against his hand, longing for more, trying to increase the pace. But at the same time, his measured and unyielding rhythm was what was driving her insane with wanting. She felt herself climbing toward something, and all she knew was that she must reach it.

"That's it, lass," he whispered against her lips. His husky voice against her mouth made her hitch even higher. He pressed against her even more firmly, and that was enough to undo her. She felt as though she had climbed right up to the sky and was filled with a flood of warmth and light. Her body shook, and she let out a cry of pleasure as she found her release. She was sailing through pure ecstasy, a whole new realm of sensation she never knew existed. He kept up his caresses even as she was spiraling back down, causing her body to reverberate with lingering jolts of pleasure as she gasped and drifted to earth.

"Is it always like that?" she asked breathily several moments later. She still felt like she was in a daze. No one had ever told her it could be this way between a man and a woman. Of course she knew a man hungered after sexual pleasure, but she didn't know a woman could too.

His chuckle rumbled deep in his chest. "It can be, lass, with the right person."

She looked at him then. His eyes were still ravenous and heated, and his manhood was still pulsing rigidly against her thigh. She reached her hand out and placed it on his erect member delicately. Her touch was met with a sharp inhale from him.

"Can I do the same for you?" she asked, shyness mixing with the longing to make him experience the same thing he had just made her feel.

"Aye, lass," he said roughly. His hand wrapped around hers tightly and he moved it up and down his length. After only a stroke or two, he released his hand and let his head fall back against the bed. His brow was furrowed and his jaw clenched and unclenched, but she could tell from his heavy breathing and occasional moan that she was giving him pleasure.

He wove one of his hands through her now-loose hair and pulled her down to lay alongside him. Following the example he had set, she kissed the column of his neck as her hand continued to caress his hard shaft. She nibbled his ear and was rewarded with a heated groan and a muffled curse. She moved so that she was halfway over him, her breasts pushed against the hard planes of his chest, and pressed her lips to his, capturing another one of his moans in her mouth. Sensing his urgent need, she increased her pace. He quickly cupped his hand on top of hers and let out a groan of pleasure as he released his seed into his hand.

She lay still with her head nestled against his neck and listened as his heartbeat and breath gradually returned to normal. He sat up slowly and threw his legs over the side of the bed, then sauntered over to his desk, where a pitcher of water and wash basin sat. He wiped himself with a rag and then splashed water over his hands. She watched his back and buttocks as he went about it, in awe of the statue-like figure he cut. She was hypnotized by the way his muscles moved under his faintly tanned skin, bunching and stretching with each movement.

He turned and caught her staring, the light of desire clear in her gray eyes. "Did I leave you so unsatisfied, lass?" he asked, a hint of teasing in his voice.

Alwin missed his tone, though, and quickly lowered her eyes. "Oh, no, I was just—"

In two strides, he was on the bed, pinning her on her back with his large hands pressing her wrists into the mattress. "I suppose I'll just have to try again to please you." A predatory glint now lit his pale eyes.

Before she could respond, his lips came down on hers. In a matter of minutes, he had kissed, caressed, and stroked her back to the edge of release. This time as she climbed, she knew what she was climbing toward, making the heights that much sweeter when she reached them and spiraled back down.

As her breathing slowed for the second time that night, she threw her leg over his and nuzzled under his chin so her cheek rested on his chest. Sleepiness was threatening to overtake her, but she wanted to feel their naked bodies pressed together still. She had no idea what their actions meant, or what would come of them tomorrow, but she knew she needed to feel him near. She felt safe with him, she realized drowsily. And now she had to admit to herself that she also felt desire—both desire for him and desire from him. She would think it all over tomorrow and come up with a plan of action. For now, though, she let herself succumb to sleep.

Robert could feel her go limp in his arms, her breathing slow and steady. He brushed a few stray hairs from her face and pulled a blanket around them both. He doubted he would be granted such peaceful sleep tonight. He had thought they could give each other pleasure and that it wouldn't change anything, but he feared he had been sorely mistaken. He had plenty of experience with women, but something about Alwin was different.

The thought shook him to his core. He was completely intoxicated by her—the way she moved, her smell, her eyes, her spirit. He had thought that perhaps his lack of contact with other women had just been causing him to see what was not really there, or to magnify insignificant attributes into dazzling traits. He had told himself if he scratched the itch with Alwin, he would see, as he had with others, there was nothing so remarkable after all. But now, as the smell of her skin drifted to him and she made a little noise in her sleep, he felt something in his chest tug.

But what was wrong with that? As he had said to her, they were married, and they both wanted each other. It wasn't like he was ruining her honor—she was his wife! A part of him knew he was working to justify his nearly uncontrollable desire for her and the fact that he had acted on that desire. But he had wanted more than anything to give her pleasure, to see her experience ecstasy brought on by his touch. And she was a natural; he still couldn't believe how readily she had responded to him, how much passion stirred just under the surface. And when she had touched him—though inexperienced, her instinctive sensuality had heated him like no other.

Even as he lay in awe of the intimacy and fire they had just shared, he forced himself to return his mind to his responsibilities. He would damn well see his plan through, for thwarting Warren, and thus derailing a mounting war effort, was still his top priority. But his mind wrestled with the rest of it—his marriage to Alwin, her place at Roslin, what he would do once Warren and her father had been made to pay—into the early hours of the morning.

Chapter Twenty-Seven

Alwin stretched lazily and burrowed deeper under the down coverlet. She vowed she would never take sleeping in a bed for granted again. And what a bed she was in now. The down coverlet was finer than hers back in her father's manor, and the mattress was like sleeping on a cloud. Plus, the bed was so wide that she could lie on it in any direction and not be able to reach the edges. It was Robert-sized.

That thought brought her instantly back to reality. She blinked a few times and poked her head out from under the coverlet. Robert wasn't in bed, nor was he in the chamber. Suddenly, the events of last night came back to her, and she was swamped with a wave of thoughts and emotions. Her body heated at the memory of their shared pleasure, and she was filled with a strange mixture of guilt for what they had done and longing for more. What should she say to him? What did this mean in terms of her plan for an annulment? And how was she supposed to sort this all out without anyone to talk to?

It was far past time to acknowledge that she had

feelings for Robert. The problem was those feelings included lust, admiration, anger, confusion, and...hope. She still wasn't sure what her ideal solution to their tangled situation was, but she felt a stirring of hope that the future could be bright for her—for them.

Determined to be productive in some way today—whatever that meant—she threw back the coverlet and stood in the frigid air of the chamber. No fire burned in the brazier, and despite the thick rugs on the ground protecting her bare feet from the cold stones below, the air still held the note of winter. Scanning the room, she realized her dress and chemise from the night before, which Robert had thrown in a pile next to the bed, were nowhere in sight. Panic seized her, but then she caught sight of some clothes folded on the desk next to the armoire. Scampering over to them, she realized another clean chemise and gown of fine green material had been placed there. She suspected this was Stella's doing but didn't remember anyone entering the chamber. Then again, she also didn't remember Robert leaving, and he clearly had.

She slid into the chemise and gown, laced them awkwardly behind her, then quickly braided her hair and splashed some cold water from the pitcher on the desk onto her face. Walking to the window, she moved the furs and checked the sky. The scent of sea air met her nose. Patchy clouds hung low in the sky, and she could barely make out the sun's position. It looked to be about an hour after dawn; she had slept in. Longing to get something—anything—done, she let the furs fall back over the window and strode to the door purposefully. She pulled the heavy wooden door open, but once she was in the hallway, she began questioning her desire for action. She was not one to sit about fretting the day away, but perhaps she longed to be busy to distract herself from other thoughts and feelings. She glanced both ways down the hall, suddenly unsure.

Just then, Stella emerged from the stairwell leading down to the great hall. She carried a tray with steaming porridge and a mug of milk on it. Seeing Alwin in the hall, she smiled.

"Ah, mistress, I see you are up and about. I was just bringing you something to break your fast in case you didn't wish to come downstairs."

"That is very kind of you, Stella." Alwin considered retreating back into Robert's chamber for a moment but straightened her spine instead and said, "Actually, I think it would be best if you showed me around a bit. Perhaps we can start in the kitchen, so that I may dine on this fine breakfast?"

Stella bobbed a curtsy and nodded approvingly. "That sounds like a fine idea, my lady."

The older woman guided the way back down the stairs and across the great hall, which was empty now, to the kitchen. The room was warm, as a fire burned in the enormous hearth on one wall. Several servants bustled about, but Alwin recognized immediately that one woman was in charge. She was round and short but with an air of authority about her. Her cheeks were rosy, no doubt from decades of leaning over hot pots, and she wielded a wooden spoon as she directed the kitchen staff.

Stella cleared her throat, interrupting the cook's string of instructions. The cook whirled around and dipped into a curtsy at the sight of Alwin.

"Lady Alwin, this is our head cook, Nora."

Nora bobbed into another curtsy. "Pleased to meet you, my lady. I hope everything has been to your liking so far?"

"Yes, thank you, Nora. I must congratulate you on the feast last night. Everything was wonderful, and you had so little time to make it so!"

Nora turned even rosier under the praise and stammered out her thanks for her lady's kind words. Alwin had guessed right—the head cook would be an ally, just like Stella. Since her mother's death, she had been in charge of running her father's keep. She had become fairly good at reading people and creating camaraderie within the manor, a necessity since her father was so hard and distant toward her and everyone else.

Stella guided her to a stool in the corner of the toasty kitchen, and Alwin sat with the bowl of porridge in her hands, content to eat and watch the goings-on between the cook, head of servants, and the other servers. She gathered that for the most part a congenial, warm atmosphere surrounded Roslin and its people, which surprised her given Robert's exterior gruffness. Certainly the castle was a place of order, which she guessed was due to his influence. But she could tell the people felt calm, happy, and secure here.

When her porridge was done, Stella guided her around the rest of the keep. She saw well-stocked store rooms, a good sign since winter was well under way. The open courtyard where they had entered the castle was filled with people bustling about their work. The stables were clean and tidy, and the stable hands all blushed and nodded to her with downcast eyes. Stella also brought Alwin through each of the four towers, most of which were filled with sleeping chambers, servants' quarters, or strategic rooms for guards to survey the curtain wall and the land beyond. The fourth tower, however, took Alwin's breath away.

It was located in the northeast corner of the keep, closest to the ocean. As they wound their way up the spiral staircase, the sounds of crashing waves and seagulls echoed around the stone walls. Stella kept going up and up until they reached the very top of the stairs, where only one door stood. She pushed open the door, and Alwin gasped at the sight of the room.

It was an enormous solar, clearly meant for the Laird of the castle. The room's far walls were curved along the same contour of the tower, and windows, their furs pulled back to let in the morning light, lined the entire wall. A large wooden desk and finely uphol-stered chair stood out a bit from the wall. Thick rugs covered the floor, and several other chairs and benches were scattered across the room. Sharing the wall with the door there was a fireplace with a fire laid in it, ready to be lit. On the other side of the door's wall was a bookshelf filled with books, a rare luxury and sign of great wealth, especially this far north.

Fresh air and sunlight suffused the room, along with the fainter smells of candle wax and parchment. Alwin walked about the solar as if in a dream. She had often taken solace in her father's study, which he never allowed her to venture into. As a child, she had always loved the smell of books, even though she couldn't read then. Though her father had permitted her to be schooled in the keeping of ledgers, as it would be her duty as lady of a keep, he had seen no point in educating her further. Her mother had taught her to read in secret, claiming to be teaching her embroidery, but instead slipping the two of them off to the library for lessons. Something about this solar reminded her of that small, dusty library where she and her mother had whispered over the parchment pages so many years ago.

At the memory, tears stung her eyes.

"Is something wrong, mistress?" Stella said softly at her shoulder.

"Nay, nothing at all, Stella. I simply love this room," she said honestly.

Stella nodded, a little smile playing on her lips. "Our Laird loves it too, my lady. He spends whatever time he can steal from training, meetings, and missions up here."

"Where is he now?"

"Oh, I suspect he is out training with his men. He can never take too much time away from that."

Alwin didn't respond, for the thought of him training for battle with his men only reminded her of how she had come to be here and what he planned to do with her. She let her attention be drawn back to the room, which soothed her. Stella let her linger for several more minutes as she ran her fingertips lightly over the desk, the spines of the books, and the window ledges. Eventually, the older woman cleared her throat, and Alwin remembered herself.

"Please, continue with the tour, Stella. I'm sure there are other important things to see."

Alwin followed Stella back down the winding staircase and toward the great hall again. By now, preparations were underway for the midday meal, and servers moved briskly between the hall and the kitchen. Alwin caught the faint sound of Nora's voice giving orders and smiled. Everything seemed to run so smoothly here. She only hoped she wouldn't throw off the keep's apparent balance with her presence.

Stella walked them through the great hall and past the kitchen, through the courtyard and to the chapel, which was nestled between two of the great stone towers on the northwest side of the castle. They entered the chapel, and Alwin felt a familiar hush fall over her. This particular chapel was simple yet peaceful. A few candles flickered as they walked up the aisle toward the back of a robed figure hunched over the Bible in prayer. At the sound of their feet on the stone floor, the figure turned around, and Alwin saw that it must be Roslin's priest. The man was weathered but calm, and something about his plain robes and wrinkled face made Alwin instantly trust him.

"My lady, this is Father Frederick. Forgive me, but I must help Nora with the midday meal." With that, Stella gave a quick nod to each of them and bustled to the chapel door.

Alwin had a vague suspicion that Stella was plotting something, that she had intentionally saved the chapel for last and was now purposefully leaving her alone with the priest, but she decided the old servant had succeeded and there was no point in doing anything differently now.

"I am glad to meet you, Father," Alwin said politely but a bit rushed. She did in fact have something she wanted to discuss with him. He bowed but said nothing, seeming to sense that a weight was on her mind.

"As you know, Robert—the Laird—and I are married," she began a bit shakily.

"Yes, my child. I wish I could have been the one to perform the ceremony. I have been overseeing the flock here at Roslin for some years now and would have gotten much joy from seeing Robert wed," he said familiarly, a kind smile on his face.

She hesitated awkwardly, searching for the right words. "I must discuss something with you, but I hope you will understand," she said.

He waited patiently, his hands clasped in front of him.

Finally, she forced herself to spit it out. "I wish to discuss the possibility of an annulment."

Father Frederick's mouth fell open for a moment, and his eyes widened, but he quickly regained his calm comportment. "And why would you ask of such a thing, my child?"

"The circumstances under which Robert and I were wed were, well…"

A knowing look came into the priest's eyes. "My child, if you…partook of each other before the vows were spoken, then you should not worry yourself. You have done the right thing by being wed now, and surely—"

A choking cough from Alwin interrupted him. When she had gotten her sputtering under control, she said quickly, "Nay, that is not what happened. We have not—" This wasn't going well. She decided she'd better just get it out. "Father, Robert kidnapped me and tricked me into marrying him. He had the ceremony conducted in Gaelic and made his man Burke speak for me."

There. She had said it. But why did the priest now have a twinkle in his eye? "Yes, my child, I am aware of what happened. Robert confessed this morning. He has already received absolution and blessings."

Now it was her turn to widen her eyes and drop her mouth open.

Father Frederick went on. "These things happen, my child. This is the Highlands, after all. But I don't understand why you wish to seek an annulment. Robert didn't mention anything of the sort this morning, and I have seen you two together, first when you arrived, and then last night in the great hall. There seems to be real...regard between the two of you."

At her shocked expression, he hurried on. "And even if there wasn't any regard, the words have been spoken before God."

"But not by me!" she nearly shouted, finally snapping out of her stunned silence.

Father Frederick paused before responding, giving her a chance to draw in several breaths to try to calm herself.

Finally, he said quietly, "Do you know who my predecessor was here at Roslin?" A sinking feeling hit Alwin. "Father Paul resided over the flock during Robert's father's Lairdship, and he trained me. He knows Robert better than I do, and knows God better too, I'd wager," he said with a little smile. Letting his warmth fade, he took her hands in his and said seriously, "I *will* not go against Father Paul, and I *cannot* go against God. I am sorry, my child, but this marriage stands in the eyes of the church." He paused again, but giving her hands a little squeeze and letting the kindness flow in his eyes, added, "And I believe it stands in Robert's mind as well. Perhaps the two of you should discuss your future. I see no reason why this union cannot be a happy and prosperous one."

He let go of her hands and patted her shoulder. "Is there anything else, my child?"

"No, Father," she mumbled, too stunned by the priest's words and her own jumbled thoughts to respond further.

Without another word, she turned and walked stiffly out of the chapel. Outside, the sun seemed too bright and harsh, the air too sharp, the noises of the castle's daily activity too loud. Strangers' faces swam before her, and she was disoriented for a moment. She had to get out of here, get away from everyone and everything.

Chapter Twenty-Eight

She stumbled toward the great hall and thought for a moment of going back to Robert's chamber. But then the thought of his bed, where they had been so intimate the night before, only reminded her of their marriage and the wedding night consummation they had yet to complete. She turned without thinking and went toward a different tower. Her mind in tangles, she didn't pay attention to where she was going, only that she had started winding upward on one of the tower's staircases. Her thoughts were interrupted when she could go up no longer and found herself in front of a large wooden door. She was at the northeast tower solar. Pushing the door open, she slipped inside.

The light coming in through the windows was more muted now, as the sun had moved out of the east. She walked over to a window and leaned against the frame, gazing out at the seemingly endless sea before her. There was something mesmerizing and soothing about the repetitious crashing of the waves against the cliffs below the castle, the swell of the ocean, and the seagulls, turning and turning in endless spirals. She could hear their faint calls to each other mingling with the sound of swelling water.

She felt suddenly exhausted. She realized she had based all her plans on the assumption that she could undo this marriage she found herself in. She wasn't sure why, though, because she knew she didn't want to be wed to Raef Warren, or any other man for that matter. She also knew she could never return to her father's keep again; she had not felt at home there since her mother died, and now that she was married, she was no longer his concern.

She realized as she stared out at sea that what she had been holding on to was a memory of herself before she had met Robert. Things hadn't been easy then, but they had been simpler. She had entertained fantasies of escaping her father and finding a gentle, courtly love with an English knight, one of her choosing. But everything was so jumbled now, so much more complicated. She had never envisioned being kidnapped and held for ransom. She had also never imagined seeing the cruelty and callousness of an English nobleman, or for that matter the underlying kindness and honor in a rugged Highland warrior.

Yes, she had to admit that something was growing inside her: feelings of affection, perhaps even love, for Robert. Wary from years of being used for other men's gain, though, she realized she was holding something back from him—from herself. A part of her didn't want to admit that despite his deceit, she understood his reasons for doing what he did and actually felt grateful to have their lives bound together. Another part of her could acknowledge that her resistance was childish and stubborn, the less flattering side of her spiritedness. She knew he was a good man; she saw it in his protectiveness of her, the way he interacted with his men, and the harmony she sensed at Roslin. And, she thought as the heat rose up her neck and to her cheeks, they clearly desired each other. She had no idea it could be this way between a man and a woman, between a husband and a wife. Of course, their shared passion was no reason to stay with him—or at least shouldn't be the only reason. But then her mind circled back to his honor, his goodness, his kindness, his gruff command of his people—and her.

She didn't know how long she had been standing there gazing out at the sea, but she slowly became aware of her aching feet and back. The solar was now infused with the bluish light of evening. Her exhaustion suddenly overwhelmed her, and all she wanted to do was curl up and sleep, letting her mind cease its gnawing on these issues. The girl in her, which was awakened by this room's similarity to the beloved library of her childhood, longed to crawl into a small space and sleep hidden from view. She pulled out the upholstered chair a little and scooted her way underneath the desk, her back pressing against the desk's wooden panels, which blocked out the door and the rest of the room. From her nook on the floor, all she could see was the chair and one window. She watched as the sky continued to deepen into dark blue and then black before slipping into a slumber in a ball beneath the desk.

Chapter Twenty-Nine

Robert wiped the damp sleeve of his shirt over his brow. Despite the cold outside, he and his men had managed to work up a sweat during their training. With only a brief break for the midday meal, he had put them all through their paces for several hours. When the sun had finally set, he allowed them to break for the day, and now he sought Stella. He guessed the head servant had shown Alwin around Roslin and that she had a chance to get more accustomed to the place. Curiosity niggled at him about what she thought of Roslin. He took great pride in his holding and secretly hoped she was impressed. And curiosity wasn't the only thing pulling at him when his mind went to Alwin, as it had done without fail the entire day.

Entering the great hall, he saw no sign of either of the women, and so called out to Stella.

The old servant poked her head through the door leading to the kitchen. "What are you bellowing about, Laird?" she said curtly, clearly in the middle of something.

"Is Alwin with you?" he asked, a little too eagerly

for his pride to stand. His thoughts had been completely invaded by the lass. Her scent clung to his skin, and he couldn't stop the images of her naked body from swimming before him, or keep the little sounds and moans of pleasure she had made last night from echoing in his ears. And damn if he could forget the sensation of her hand on him, a bit timid at first, but then eager to bring him pleasure. She was innocent, and yet a deep current of passion and sensuality ran through her, which stirred him like nothing he had experienced before.

In truth, he had hoped giving himself and his men a thorough thrashing on the practice field would alleviate some of his pent-up energy. Yet even now, exhausted and sweaty as he was, he hungered for her more than ever. What was it about this woman? All he knew was that he had to have more of her. And judging by the smart smirk on Stella's face, his tone and question had given him away.

"She is not with me, Laird. Perhaps you should check your chamber?"

Robert turned without a word and bounded up the stairs toward his chamber. He yanked open the door, half expecting to catch her asleep across the bed in his shirt again, but all he found was a cold, dark, and empty room. He returned to the great hall and approached Stella, who was beginning to prepare the long tables for the evening meal. "She was not there. When did you last see her?"

Stella paused in her motions, hearing the shift in Robert's tone from annoyed to slightly concerned. She scratched her head and considered for a moment. "I left her with Father Frederick around midday today. I sensed perhaps she had something to discuss with him," she said, giving Robert a knowing look.

Of course the old head of servants would have pieced together a few things even without being told, Robert thought wryly. She had likely seen him head to the chapel first thing this morning.

Returning his thoughts to Alwin, he said, "I'll ask Father Frederick where she went after speaking with him."

Inside the chapel, Father Frederick explained to Robert that after a brief chat, Lady Alwin had left. He didn't say what they had discussed, but Robert would put money on it being about their marriage. He had confessed to the priest, anticipating the fact that Alwin would want to see him about an annulment. He wanted to be the one to explain things to Father Frederick, but also wanted to get a sense for how the priest would respond to the less-then-straightforward circumstances under which they were married. After the initial shock, the priest had given Robert his blessings on the union, confirming Robert's suspicions that the marriage would stand. If Alwin had been staking her hopes on an annulment, and Father Frederick had told her it would not happen, what would she do? How much did she want to escape this marriage?

Robert considered this uneasily. For some reason, the thought of her desperately trying to get away from him made him angry, and something else—scared. Would she have tried to escape the castle? It seemed unlikely, but the lass had tried to run away from him and his men before. She also had fortitude and a backbone of steel when it came to resisting being forced against her will. He had seen her fight tooth and nail against Warren when he had held her captive. Would she do the same to him?

Uneasiness filled him as he left the chapel. He crossed to the stables, but all the horses were accounted for and the stable lads hadn't seen Alwin. He next climbed the stairs that led from the inner courtyard to the curtain wall where guards patrolled, taking the steps two at a time. The guards had not seen her leave, though. Wracking his mind for what to do next, he turned and headed for the stairs back to the courtyard. Just then he spotted Stella coming from the great hall into the courtyard with a worried look on her face.

When he reached her, she said, "I asked the servants, but they haven't seen her since this morning, Laird."

She was frowning, and he guessed that she was responding to the worry that was quickly escalating within him.

"I'll check the chapel again," he said, frustration lining his voice.

Suddenly Stella's face cleared, and she grabbed his

arm before he could turn away. "The solar?" she asked.

"Why would she be there?" he said crossly. He was grateful for another place to look, but the solar was his private study, and he hadn't expected Alwin to even know of it yet.

"I showed it to her this morning on our tour, and she was quite taken with it."

Before she had even finished speaking, he was striding toward the northeast tower. Again, he took the stairs two at a time, anxious to find Alwin and get relief from the tightness in his chest. He didn't give himself time to ponder why the thought of her absence struck such fear in him. All he knew was that he had to find her, and not let her go.

He shoved open the door to the solar roughly, but all he found was another empty room. No candles were lit, and the furs were pulled back from the windows, revealing the darkness beyond. Was it his mind playing tricks on him, or did he catch a faint whiff of her scent lingering in the room? He exhaled and ran a hand through his hair in frustration. He strode over to the window, gazing out of it in hopes that something would occur to him that would lead him to Alwin.

Just as he was about to turn away, he heard a little sigh from behind and below him. He spun around, but all he saw was his desk, the chair slightly pulled out and askew.

Then he noticed it. A small slippered foot poked out from under his desk. He crouched down and through the darkness saw Alwin curled in a ball, fast asleep underneath the desk. Anger replaced his fear in an instant. The lass had frightened him half to death, all the while taking a cat nap in his private study. He shoved the chair aside, and the scraping noise it made as it slid off one of the rugs and onto the stone floor startled her awake. In a flash, he had grabbed her around the shoulders and hauled her out from under his desk.

"What are you doing? What were you thinking?" he nearly shouted in her face, giving her a shake by her shoulders.

Her eyes were wide and despite the shadowy room, he could clearly make out the disorientation and terror on her face. He tried to calm himself, taking a breath before he spoke again. "You had nearly the entire castle wondering where you were, to say nothing of Stella's and my search for you." Despite his efforts, his voice still came out harsher than he had intended.

She remained motionless, her mouth agape, that stunned look still on her face.

"Well? Speak, woman! Explain yourself, and it had better be good!"

Finally, she licked her lips to moisten them then raised a shaking hand and grazed over his cheek with her fingertips. "Is this a dream?" she asked, dazed.

Her tone and gesture broke through his haze of anger. He eased his grip on her shoulders and sighed.

"Nay, lass, this is not a dream. You scared me half to death. I thought you were…missing." He didn't want to admit now that he had feared she had tried to escape him.

"*I* scared *you*?" she said incredulously, clarity returning to her along with incredulity. "Heaven forbid you have to live through what *you* just did to *me*!"

Alwin questioned her huffy tone for a moment as she watched his icy blue eyes narrow, but then a most unexpected thing happened. He laughed. A deep rumble came from his chest, and his face split in a rakish grin. Without realizing it, she mirrored his smile, and the air seemed to become lighter around them.

When he regained his composure, he said, "I still wish to know what you were doing."

She squirmed under his gaze. "I was…thinking," she finally managed.

"Thinking? From midday to nightfall?" he said, raising an eyebrow.

"I have had much to think on," she said defensively.

"And what might that be?" he prodded. Just as she was about to assume the air of a lady, he took her chin in his hand so that she couldn't raise it. "Alwin, answer me."

"You can't order my compliance," she said, suddenly feeling guarded again.

"Oh, but I can. I am your husband."

Their playful moment evaporated instantly, and she felt herself growing warm with frustration. This wasn't going the way she had hoped. She had wanted to speak with him honestly about her thoughts and feelings, about their situation, and their future. But now that stubbornness of hers was surging inside her, demanding that she defy him.

"I apologize for inconveniencing you or anyone else," she said stiffly. "I will work harder in the future to remedy my shortcoming."

She had said the same thing to her father countless times, so it should have been easy to feed Robert the line and tack. Why did it rankle so much, then? She had secretly hoped that when she had left her father's keep she would be done with ever needing to tamp down her spirit with such hollow words.

Robert's eyes bore into her, and he seemed to sense that she had closed some internal door on him. But instead of chastising her further, he just continued to silently stare at her, waiting. She wasn't used to getting the opportunity to say more after her rote apology. Her frustration kept building until she couldn't stand his look anymore. Finally, she snapped.

"I was thinking, and I fell asleep."

He waited.

"Father Frederick told me I could not seek an annulment, so I came up here and looked at the sea for a while."

There was another long pause. He still wasn't

granting her any quarter.

She sighed. "I suppose I felt...overwhelmed at the thought of the finality of it all."

At her words, his face dropped into a frown.

She hurried on. "It's not that I want my old life with my father back. And I don't want to be with Raef Warren, either." She couldn't suppress a shudder of distain for both men. "I just never thought...I had hoped..." Feeling silly and young all of a sudden, she trailed off.

Softening, he said, "What did you hope?" He raised a hand and brushed a stray hair out of her face.

Suddenly tears were welling in her eyes, which shimmered in the darkness.

Just then, Stella emerged in the doorway. "Oh, thank goodness. You had the Laird in a fright, mistress," she said.

Blinking back her tears, she turned to the other woman. "I'm sorry, Stella. I just came up here to think, and I suppose I got tired. I fell asleep under the desk."

Stella chuckled and bobbed a curtsy then turned to head back down the stairs. Robert slipped Alwin's hand through his arm and guided them both toward the door.

"We will continue this conversation," he said in a low, serious tone that allowed for no argument as they began their descent down the spiraling stairs.

She only nodded, trying to swallow the lump that had formed in her throat.

Chapter Thirty

The evening meal that night was more subdued than the impromptu wedding feast had been the night before but was still merry and pleasant for the inhabitants of Roslin. Alwin sat quietly next to Robert at the high table, with Burke, always polite and friendly, on Robert's other side. Robert chatted casually with Burke but didn't say much to Alwin beyond offering her cuts of meat from their trencher. That was just fine with her. She felt refreshed after her nap in the solar, but her interaction with Robert had muddled things again. She was making peace with the idea of staying married to him and yet couldn't seem to have a conversation with him about it. Perhaps after the meal she would be able to speak with him alone. The real trick would be to find a way to avoid raising either one of their tempers.

When the server cleared their table, her nerves began to increase. Robert stood and held out his arm to her. She took it with a deep breath, steadying herself. He guided her toward his chamber—*their* chamber, she reminded herself—and when the heavy wooden door was closed behind them, she straightened her back and turned to face him.

"Robert, I wish to speak with you."

He didn't say anything but raised his eyebrow with a look of questioning.

"And I don't want to fight," she said in a rush. "I just want to inform you of a few things."

"Go ahead, lass," he said, a hint of amused skepticism in his voice.

She took a deep breath and barreled forward. "When we first met, I was on my way to marry another." Robert frowned, but she continued. "I was leaving behind my father's manor, a...less than happy place for me these past few years. I had hopes that in my new household I would make a place for myself, be valued for who I am, and have a happy union. Then you interrupted the plan."

"Lass, you know I did not know you were in that supply cart, and I damn well didn't get in the way of you having some sort of fairytale marriage with that bastard Raef Warren," Robert interjected heatedly.

She held up a hand to still him. "Of course. I didn't know it then, but now I am very grateful to not be married to that man." She couldn't quite repress a shudder at the memory of Warren's cruelty, cowardice, and disregard for her or other life. "Robert, listen to me. I am glad you took me away from him." She placed her raised hand on his cheek, and he swallowed, seeming to let her words and touch sink in.

"But then you took it upon yourself to have us wed," she said seriously, letting her hand drop. "You took away my choice, just as my father had, and just as Raef Warren would have if he had had the chance. You deceived me and used me for your own gain." She couldn't help the bitterness that was encroaching on her voice. It still hurt, and she wasn't ready to forgive him yet.

"Lass…" he said, his eyes suddenly shadowed with pain. "I wish I could take away the wrongness of my actions. You know I do not regret them, for I still believe it was the right thing for my people, but you must believe me that I regret the hurt it causes you."

She exhaled and nodded. She knew he spoke the truth. And she realized his actions were different from her father's or Warren's, for he sought both what was best for his people and also peace between their countries. Her father and Warren only sought personal advancement, and in Warren's case, war would be preferable to peace.

"As you know, I spoke with Father Frederick."

He nodded in response.

Her voice dropped off as she went on. "He would not grant my request, so it seems as though this arrangement is…permanent."

For some reason, her choice of words and the faint tone of distaste with which she said them made his chest tighten. He hardened his eyes, preparing to shield himself from potential pain. She hadn't noticed his sudden coldness, though, for she looked to be seriously struggling to say something.

Finally, she whispered, "As such, I would like…I would like to make this a good union."

He inhaled sharply. This whole time, he had thought she was putting distance between them and justifying it by reminding him of the wrongs he had done to her. But was she actually saying she wanted to be with him?

No, she hadn't gone that far—only that she wanted to make the best of the situation. For some reason, the thought of her wanting him, and not just in terms of the physical attraction that lay between them, had made his heart miss a beat.

"Will you say something?" she said, her voice sounding strained.

He cleared his throat. "Aye." But then he paused for a moment, thinking on his words. Finally, he said, "I am glad you accept the circumstances, and that you would like to make the best of them. I, too, would like to put the past behind us and move forward as husband and wife."

She nodded, but her eyes searched his, seeming to want something more. He didn't speak further, though, so she turned to the brazier, which had been lit just before they had entered the chamber by some thoughtful and prescient servant, most likely Stella. She rubbed her hands in front of the fire, feeling surprisingly let down. She had managed to speak with him without either one of them getting angry, and she had said what she had intended to. Why did she feel so unsettled, then? Perhaps a part of her had hoped that things would be made right between them, that there would be more ease in their interactions, more...affection?

She sighed and turned away from the fire, only to run right into Robert's chest. He had silently moved behind her and now stared into her eyes with a look of intensity. Raising his hand, he brushed a strand of light brown hair out of her face, a gesture that was beginning to feel familiar and intimate to her.

"Since we *are* husband and wife, I think we should start acting like it." A dark promise was suspended in his words.

Just as she realized that his intense gaze was filled with passion, his lips came down on hers. She gasped in surprise at the sudden fire in him, and he used the opportunity to slip his tongue into her mouth.

He invaded her senses, his clean, masculine scent filling her nose and lungs, his tongue caressing hers, his hands moving on her waist, pulling her against him. She felt her own desire kindling, but something else blossomed insider her as well: fear. She broke their kiss and put her hands on his chest, pushing him back a little. He complied, though his eyes told her he wasn't happy about it.

"What is it, lass?" he said huskily.

"I've never—I haven't—" She felt a blush rising to her cheeks that had nothing to do with the warm fire they stood in front of.

A soft smile came to his lips, and suddenly he looked more like a lover and less like a warrior. "I know, lass. But you liked what we did last night, didn't you?"

She nodded.

"It can be better than that," he said, hunger edging his voice, transforming him swiftly back to a warrior, a hunter.

"If we do this, we cannot go back," she whispered. She was still afraid, but anticipation mingled with it. She felt like she was standing on a precipice, about to jump over into the unknown, but she was jumping toward Robert, toward a future with him.

"Aye," was all he said.

She searched his face, his eyes. Silencing the hundred emotions jumbling inside her, she rose up on her tiptoes and kissed his lips softly.

It was all the acquiescence he needed.

Chapter Thirty-One

He wanted to make this last, to make it good for her, but her noises and movements were driving him crazy, and all he could think about was being inside her. He deepened their kiss, holding the back of her head as their tongues intermingled. She clutched his shirt between them, but he moved her arms around his neck so that their whole bodies could press together. His hands rubbed over her back then dropped to grip her bottom, pulling their hips even closer. He was already aroused and growing more so by each aching moment. She shifted her hips a little, and he groaned at the sensation it sent shooting through him. One of his hands traveled upward and cupped her breast. Electric heat passed between them at the contact, surprising him with how quickly her desire was building.

He tugged on the laces at the back of her dress until they were loose enough for him to shimmy her gown off her shoulders and down the rest of her body. While he was working on her dress, her hands went to the ties on his shirt. He could barely wait to feel her smooth, creamy skin against his. With that thought, he stilled her hands to yank his shirt over his head. She now stood in her chemise, and he in only his kilt. They rejoined their lips, and the feel of her bare arms on his naked torso sent his senses reeling and his desire soaring even more. Suddenly, he lifted her under the legs so that her thighs wrapped around his waist.

"Hold on, lass," he mumbled against her lips. In two strides, he had her back against the stone wall, his hands supporting her bottom, and his lips trailing down her neck.

The cold stones pressing into her back were in stark contrast to his blazing hot skin. She buried her fingers in his dark hair, half massaging his scalp, half desperately clinging to him as sensation washed over her. He kissed her collar bone then her chest above her chemise. Without moving his hands supporting her, he took the tie keeping her chemise closed in the front between his teeth and tugged. The tie came undone, revealing more of her creamy flesh to his lips. He nuzzled the material out of his way to expose one of her breasts. His lips and tongue teased the pink peak, drawing a moan from her. When he had thoroughly ravished one breast, he shifted and gave the other the same treatment. By the time he drew his mouth away, she was moaning, panting, and arched against him.

He stepped back from the wall, still clutching her, and rapidly strode to the bed. In a rush, he tumbled them both onto the mattress. He jerked to his knees and yanked off his belt and kilt, tossing them onto the floor. She stilled for a moment, her eyes traveling down his length. When they reached his manhood, which was fully erect now, they widened. He let her look, unashamed.

She had never truly looked at a naked man before Robert. She had caught glimpses here and there, but the most she had seen was the other night when she and Robert had been intimate. Even then, though, she had done more feeling than seeing. Now it was inescapable. He was there before her, gloriously naked, his erection swollen and standing out. She again had the creeping fear that what they were going to do was never going to work judging by his size. But before she could begin to fret on the thought, he was pulling up her chemise, and in seconds, she was naked too. She still felt shy but liked the raw look of desire filling his eyes as he drank her in.

In a flash, though, he closed the small distance between them and pulled her against him. She shuddered at the feeling of their skin pressed together. If it was possible, she felt even more raw, even more aroused than she had the night before when they had touched and kissed and brought pleasure to each other.

One of his hands slid down to the crux of her legs, and he teased her already-damp curls for a moment. Wanting more, she instinctually opened her legs slightly, earning a growl of hunger from him. He slipped a finger along her wet folds, causing her to shudder and moan. Then he let his finger brush inside to her most sensitive spot. She gasped as fire shot through her. That same achiness was building and building, centering where he pressed and caressed with his fingers.

He moved slightly lower, and slid one finger inside of her. She gasped again, suddenly feeling filled in a place that she had never realized felt empty.

"Christ, lass, you are so tight and wet," he whispered against her mouth. He began moving his finger, slowly easing it out and then entering her again, meanwhile using his thumb to brush higher against that electric spot. Her hands went wild on his back, his shoulders, his hair, trying to cling to him as she felt a similar pleasure that she had experienced the night before, but this time deeper. She began moving her hips along with his hand, desperate for contact as the pressure built and she felt herself climbing toward release again. Her body began to shudder, and she distantly heard herself call out his name as pleasure crashed into her.

Even as she was spiraling back down, he removed his hand from her and she felt him position himself over her. She opened her eyes, still in a haze of pleasure. His eyes were pinched with his efforts to control himself, and his whole body was tense as he moved between her legs. She felt something brush against the apex of her legs, and knew that they were about to cross the threshold. He looked her directly in the eyes then, searching for any sign of hesitation, but she gave him none. He began easing forward, the head of his manhood nudging her entrance. He moved farther so that he was just inside her. The sensation was strange—not painful, but new.

His shoulders began to shake as he worked to control his motion and his desire. Next to her ear, he whispered, "I'm sorry, lass." She wasn't sure what he was saying, but then he pushed forward all the way so that he was inside her to the hilt.

Pain tore through her, radiating from her core. She cried out and tried to push him back, but he didn't budge. He held still, waiting. Then he moved ever so slightly, pulling back and pushing in again. She tried to suppress a little sob of pain at the movement. A moment later, he moved again, and this time she thought the pain was slightly less. He moved again, and the pain began to mingle with something else. She felt the hurt mixing with a building pressure inside her, and with each of his movements, the pain subsided, and the pressure increased. Her body relaxed, and he began thrusting in and out of her with a slow, steady rhythm. Soon, she was near drowning in pleasure again, and she found herself moving in rhythm with him. He increased the pace, his patience seeming to wear thin. His jaw was clenched next to her face, and his shoulders were tight under her hands.

She was only vaguely registering this, though, for she was lost in a sea of sensation. He began to move even faster still, and the increase sent her over the edge to release. She called out as euphoria swept through her, shaking at the intensity and depth of her release. A second later, he groaned and thrust all the way inside her, shuddering and gasping as he too found release.

The moments stretched as they both drifted back. He rolled over onto his back, dragging her along with him so that she was nestled against his side. He stroked her hair for a moment, then whispered, "Lass?" but she had already drifted off into a deep and contented sleep.

Chapter Thirty-Two

Sometime well before dawn, Alwin stirred and slowly came awake. She was blanketed in the warmth and scent of Robert, who still held her wrapped in his arms. The events of the night—their talk, their touches, their pleasure—flooded back to her, but instead of feeling embarrassed or confused, she let the memories warm her even more than Robert's embrace.

She had struggled for what felt like a long time against Robert, against their connection, against their marriage. The decision to commit to this new path she found her life on had been difficult, but once she had decided, she couldn't imagine anything else feeling so—right. In fact, it was like they fit perfectly together. Obviously their bodies fit well, she thought, her lingering innocence causing her to blush a little at the images running through her mind. But she also liked his character, and sensed from him that he, too, respected her, cared for her, and enjoyed the way they challenged each other. Perhaps Father Frederick was right. Perhaps this could be a truly great union.

As she considered all this, she let her fingers lazily graze across his bare chest. His skin was smooth, and the muscles beneath were firm, even as he lay prone in sleep. She felt that she would never get enough of touching him, of having him touch her, and thankfully, they had their whole lives to do just that. She sighed contentedly at that thought.

"Have I not earned a few winks of rest, lass, or must you torture me with your touch at all hours of the night?"

She jumped as his tease rumbled through his chest, against which her ear was pressed.

"I thought you slept!" she squeaked in surprise.

At that, he chuckled and clasped her closer to him. "Being a light sleeper is a requirement of staying alive as a warrior," he said, the smile on his face tinting his voice as well.

She relaxed against him, smiling too. "And how did you learn such a skill? What was your training like? How long have you been a warrior?"

"Easy, lass! One question at a time!"

She sat up suddenly, and the cool night air of the chamber brushed her bare skin. She gazed down at his smiling, handsome face, but her brow wrinkled as she continued to consider him.

"I've just realized I know next to nothing about you," she finally said.

He raised an eyebrow at her. "I'd say we just 'knew' each other quite thoroughly, lass."

She swatted his shoulder lightly at his bawdy joke. "That's not what I meant, and you know it."

"I suppose since this arrangement is *permanent*, as you so affectionately put it, we should learn a bit more about each other," he said wryly.

Accepting his ribbing, she settled back down onto his chest and let him wind his arms back around her. "I'll begin. Do you have any other family? Father Frederick mentioned he was training here while your father was still Laird."

"Aye. My father was Laird of the Sinclairs until his death five years ago. That's when I became Laird, though, of course, I have trained for it my whole life." He paused, but she waited without prodding him. "He was a great man—both as a leader and as a father. He prepared all of us for our roles and responsibilities. He was stern and could be demanding, but we always knew it was because he loved us and wanted us to meet our full potential."

"'We'?"

"My parents had three sons. I am the oldest. Next came Garrick, then Daniel."

She laid a hand on his chest and propped her chin upon it to gaze at him. "Garrick? What an unusual name. Surely that isn't Gaelic?"

He smiled absently as he wound a lock of her hair around his finger. "No, it is Norse. It means warrior archer. I've never been sure if it was fate or just Garrick's insistence on living up to the name, but he has become just that."

"Where is he now?"

The briefest pause elapsed before he said "He serves Robert the Bruce."

She looked closer into his eyes, which held a hint of guardedness.

"What is it? What is the matter? Do you think—" and then realization hit her. "You think that because I'm English, I pose some kind of threat to your brother and the Rebel cause! But Robert, how could you imagine me a spy?"

"The very fact that you call us 'Rebels' is telling, lass," he said calmly.

"But I would never betray you or anyone you love! You must believe—"

Before she could finish her plea, his lips met hers and silenced her with a kiss. After several heartbeats, he finally broke their contact but met her eyes again.

"Aye, you're right, Alwin. Of course I trust you. I imagine we'll have some…smoothing out to do regarding our different nationalities, but I know you're no cold-hearted monster to betray your new family."

Family. The word made her heart swell. As an only child, her childhood had more often than not been lonely. And after her mother had died, she felt empty, isolated, with only her father's cold cruelty for family. Of course, she had made friends, and her old maid Betsy had been an immeasurable help. But now, she realized, she had a husband—and brothers! And perhaps one day, she and Robert would have children of their own...

"Say something, lass. Your face changes by the second."

"I'm just...I feel so..." Words failed her, so instead she flung her arms around Robert's neck and hugged him tight.

He returned the embrace and chuckled. But he let the jocund sound fade as he sensed the depth of her emotions. He wasn't sure what he had said that tapped something so powerful within her—his trust in her? His use of her given name? Something about family?—but he felt suddenly protective of her. He never wanted to hurt her again in any way and would kill anyone who did. Her hair spilled across his face, and he let himself inhale her intoxicating scent, of roses and skin, vowing to do right by her.

"And what of Daniel?" she said, clearly trying to even out the emotion in her voice and resume their previous conversation.

"He is with my mother's brother, who has a small holding to the west of here. My uncle William has been having some health trouble, and his eldest son is but eleven years old, too young to take over in his father's stead as Laird. Daniel is filling the gap, so to speak, helping to ensure our uncle's keep runs smoothly, and that, if it comes to it, little William will be ready to take over as Laird."

Before Alwin could ask, Robert anticipated her question. "My mother and William were very close. When she died giving birth to Daniel, William stayed with us for several years to help my father in the raising of us. You see, we three boys were all born within a year of each other. It was too much strain on my mother. My father blamed himself at first, but William was wonderful, reminding my father that my mother would live on in all of us. Daniel held that message especially close to his heart, and he sees it as a way of carrying out our mother's wishes to help William out now."

A quietness filled the room for several moments as Alwin considered all Robert had said, and Robert lingered over his memories. The sound of Alwin's yawn broke the silence, and Robert chuckled as she tried to stifle it.

"I've already stolen much sleep from you tonight, lass. Rest. No doubt you'll dream of three men, all breaking hearts with this handsome visage."

She swatted him again, but he merely pulled her snugly against him, and she acquiesced, relaxing into sleep.

Chapter Thirty-Three

Alwin stirred awake at the soft knock on the door. She stretched, warm and content, but found herself alone. The door inched open, and Stella's head popped through.

"Come in, Stella. From the look of the light, it's high time I was up," Alwin said, trying to clear the sleep and heated memories of last night from her mind. "Where is Robert?"

"The Laird is back to the training fields, my lady," Stella said, bustling about the chamber tidying things that didn't need it.

Alwin looked closer and saw the hint of a smile at the corners of Stella's mouth, though. Alwin didn't mind. She was grateful the head servant saw the Laird's happiness with his wife as a victory.

And she was happy with him as well. She let the warm feeling radiate through her whole body. What had she done to be so lucky? She didn't know how or why, but she and Robert seemed to have an innate connection. She was coming to trust him, and she already respected him. That would have been more than she would have gotten from a union with Raef Warren. But to have their marriage be blessed with such an...intense physical connection was remarkable. And he had been tender and funny and open with her in their conversation in the early hours of the morning. Perhaps her fantasy of a loving union would be possible after all...

She was suddenly eager to do all she could to bring her dream to reality, to have a marriage not only in name, but in heart and mind as well. But what could she do to ingratiate herself to him, to show him she cared for him? Several ideas began to formulate in her head. She threw back the covers as Stella came over to help her dress, feeling energized to have a task and a goal.

"Stella, are there any records about the Sinclair clan that I might look at?"

"Aye, mistress, the solar is filled with those kinds of documents," she said with a raised eyebrow.

Alwin brushed away her curious look with a smile. "Excellent. I'll be in the solar today, then, if anyone asks. And this time, I'll try to stay awake."

Alwin coughed as a cloud of dust rose from yet another of the Sinclair clan ledgers. She had already spent hours going through the solar's collection of books, which had been tedious, yet she could proudly say she knew more about the clan than when she had entered.

For one thing, she knew they needed a better system of keeping records. Much of her time had been spent sorting out the different recording styles of various authors, most of whom were either Lairds or the heads of staff from years gone by. Some filled pages and pages with stories of the clan's victories in battle, recipes, songs, and legendary tales of love lost and found, while others wrote only the births, deaths, and other major events in the clan's history. Each author's penmanship and abbreviation systems changed, and on several occasions, Alwin had had to put her face mere inches from the page to decipher what might as well have been chicken scratch.

She had managed to glean much, though. Apparently, the Sinclairs had both Saxon and Norse bloodlines. William St. Clair, a French relative of William the Conqueror, was given Roslin some centuries before, incorporating a French name and bloodline with the original inhabitants. Then a group of Norse Vikings had called Roslin home, and despite intermarriages between the French-Scots and the Norse, the Sinclairs bucked against outside control and regained self-reign. Nevertheless, Robert's ancestors were a mixed and rather violent lot. She could see the Saxon in him—his dark hair spoke of that. But the Norse was strong as well, in his icy eyes and enormous frame. She could only imagine what part of him came from the wild, fierce original inhabitants of this beautiful yet unforgiving land.

Setting down the heavy volume in her hands on

Robert's desk, she arched her back and circled her neck, trying to ease the aches from a morning spent bent pouring over books. Even as her body protested, though, her mind raced. This was better than any stolen moment in her father's old library. For one thing, it wasn't a secret that she was here, nor was she forbidden to learn, as her father had done. And she had a purpose beyond being pretty and proper. She was determined to learn all that she could about her husband's family—*her* family. Having a goal kindled her spirits, making her feel useful and productive. Why had her father insisted on taking such a feeling away from her? She guessed he hadn't wanted her to feel as powerful and driven as she did now. She would never come back under his control, though, she reminded herself. And, she thought suddenly, she would never raise a child like that.

The thought of a child—Robert's and her child—sent all thoughts of her father flying. That child would join this history, this string of ink on the page she had just been pouring over. And come to think of it, her name would also be recorded in these ledgers. She was part of this history, part of the clan, part of its future. The idea sent a wave of emotion through her. She had a home now, a place to be herself. And she refused to be just a name scrawled next to Robert's. She wanted to leave her mark.

A growl from her stomach brought her swiftly back to earth. She smiled ruefully at her own lofty musings and stood to descend to the great hall for the mid-day meal. She was only human, of course, but she promised to herself to return to the solar as soon as she had taken care of her bodily needs in order to keep feeding her mind.

Chapter Thirty-Four

It took several days hunched over in the solar, but Alwin had slipped the last of the dusty clan record books back in its place on the shelf that morning and couldn't wait to show off her new knowledge to Robert. His respect mattered to her. She nearly skipped toward the great hall for the midday meal, knowing she would get to share a quick bite with him, as she had in the past few days.

They had developed a pleasant routine—more than pleasant, she thought, heat creeping up to her cheeks. For the last several days, Robert had risen early to see to the most pressing needs of the keep and his clan, hearing complaints, solving disputes, and signing off on household maintenance requests. Meanwhile, she had gone to the solar for the morning light and to drink in all she could of the clan's history. They would meet in the great hall for the midday meal, where even over the simple vitals of bread, cheese, dried meat, and apples or dried fruit from the winter stores, they would talk, laugh, and brush hands under the table. Then Robert would head to the yard with his men to train, and Alwin would join Stella or Nora in some household task or other. By the evening meal, Robert would enter the hall sweaty and tired, but always found a hot meal laid out for him and his men, thanks to the coordination of the women running the keep.

Alwin took special pleasure in making sure the household ran smoothly and warmed under the praise of Robert and the others for their meal. But the real pleasures came later in the evening, when she and Robert would retire to their chamber. If she had ever had a doubt, she knew for certain now that whatever passion they shared wasn't a fluke and seemed to only build the more they explored each other. She was still a bit shy but was an eager student. Yes, she could get used to this.

With a smile still playing on her lips at that thought, she entered the great hall. Robert was already there, talking quietly with Burke. She took her seat next to him, and he turned to her, bringing her hand up to his mouth to brush a kiss against her knuckles. His eyes lingered on her, bringing another blush to her cheeks. Somehow he seemed to be thinking along the same lines as she so often did throughout the day. Now that she knew what was possible between married people—between lovers—she couldn't stop the images and memories from flitting to her, often at the most inconvenient times.

Luckily, the clear draw between the Laird and Lady of the castle only seemed to bring the clan more joy.

She had already caught Stella, Nora, and the other serving girls giggling at one of her momentary daydreams while working in the kitchen, and the men of the clan seemed to be slapping Robert on the back more than usual. Alwin didn't mind. She would enjoy the pleasure of being part of the clan's happiness.

"How go your studies?" Robert asked, her hand still raised to those enticing lips. He knew she was spending her mornings in the solar, but hadn't prodded her about why she was so interested in the clan records.

"Very well. In fact, I have finished my task and already have my sights set on a new one," she replied with a proud smile.

He nodded, brushing his lips once again against her knuckles before releasing her hand and turning back to Burke to continue their discussion about the increasing tensions between two families within the clan. From what Alwin could gather, an arranged marriage had fallen apart when two starry-eyed lovers had run away together. She repressed a smile. Though clan unity was important, and it was Robert's job to care for his people, she couldn't help feeling for the two youths.

When the meal was through, Robert rose and headed out to the yard for more combat training, but not before shooting Alwin a heated wink. Her mind wandered again to the promise in his sultry look, a promise she was sure he would deliver on later tonight. She shook the haze of desire from her, though. She had work to do. A particular task had been bothering her for several days now, and she finally felt ready to tackle it: the housekeeping ledgers.

As she had suspected on her first day at the Sinclair keep, the ledgers, while functional, were tangled due to Stella and Nora's different record-keeping styles. She couldn't blame the two women too much, though, since she suspected the underlying problem was the fact that Robert wasn't around enough to set a system and instruct his household staff to follow it. But now that she was the lady of the keep, she intended to create a smooth-running operation that would make life easier on both Robert and the staff. She smiled to herself, feeling proud that she was doing something to help the clan—her clan.

In the afternoons of these last few days, she had been assisting Nora and Stella, which had helped her understand the functions of this household, which, to her relief, were very similar to the kind of instruction she had received as part of her training to become the lady of a keep. She had also stolen a few more glances at the ledgers and was pleased to see that most things had been accounted for. Last winter, however, the castle had run dangerously low on dried meat, since someone had misrecorded or misread the ledger. Luckily, they could remedy the problem early enough in the winter before the deer had moved too far into the wooded area on the southern portion of the Sinclair lands. Alwin intended for there never to be a confusion like that again.

She found Stella and explained her intention while the older woman gazed upon her with approval. Stella gladly handed over the ledgers, which she kept in a small room in the interior of the castle, and even suggested that Alwin take them up to the solar where the light was better. With a spring in her step despite the increasingly stormy day brewing outside, Alwin made her way to the solar for the second time that day and plunked down in Robert's chair with a quill.

By the time the evening meal was ready, Alwin had already developed a system that incorporated both Stella's running financial accounting and Nora's date-specific records for food. She had even rewritten the last month's accounts using her new system just to make sure it would work. Now all that remained was instructing both women in the new system, though in all likelihood, it would be primarily Alwin making the decisions and keeping the records on household affairs.

The thought brought a pinch of apprehension to her as she wound her way back down the spiral staircase toward the great hall. She still felt nervous at the idea of taking over an entire household, but she reminded herself, unconsciously straightening her spine, she knew what she was doing, and she was smart, capable, and a quick learner even if she did make a mistake or two.

She surprised herself by realizing that she was no longer nervous at the prospect of staying here at the

Sinclair keep. In the short time she had been here, the clan had embraced her. There was a sense of wellbeing that suffused this place. The larders were full even at midwinter, the people were happy—and then there was whatever was developing between her and Robert. She didn't want to be overly naïve and call it love, but she was coming to trust in not only their passion for each other, but also the ever growing respect and consideration toward one another, and that led her to feel hopeful at the prospect of a happy union.

A girlish grin crept to her face, and she didn't mind. She glided into the great hall, her eyes searching for the ruggedly handsome face of her husband. She found it, but it was clouded with a deep frown. When his cold eyes met hers, a shiver of premonition rushed through her.

Chapter Thirty-Five

Robert wiped the sweat dripping down his face with the back of his bare forearm then returned his hand next to the other to grip his sword, poised and ready for Burke's attack. The two men circled each other slowly, waiting for an opening, but both were too well trained and too familiar with each other to give anything away easily.

"I thought you would have been a bit less timid to fight me, Burke. You seemed ready a week ago. What happened? Lose your bollocks?" Robert said, trying to get a rise out of him.

Burke didn't take the bait, and instead, just quirked his mouth. "Aye, well, we know where to find yours at least. I wonder where the Lady has stored—"

Robert's sword came crashing down on Burke's. Burke blocked, but just barely. Robert didn't care that he had fallen for Burke's teasing—aye, everyone in the clan could see plainly that he was smitten with his new bride. But he wouldn't let Burke go any further in his taunt in front of the rest of the men. He turned Burke's block into a bind, winding his sword up and over his opponent's and pushing both blades down toward the ground until both tips rested on the dirt of the yard. Robert moved forward lightning fast, thrusting his shoulder into Burke and knocking him off balance. The men surrounding them in a circle rumbled their approval. Burke stumbled back, but quickly regained his balance, grinning widely.

"Aren't you the one always bellowing at us to never reveal a weakness to our enemies?" Burke quipped.

Just as Robert was about to reply, a whistle from the top of the curtain wall overhead alerted the men below that a rider approached. Instantly, the playfulness in the yard evaporated, and Robert and Burke, opponents a moment before, were striding side by side up the stairs to the top of the wall. When they reached the top, the head watchman turned quickly to reassure them.

"A messenger, Laird."

"Open the gate to him, John, but keep a lookout."

"Aye, Laird."

As the singular rider drew near, the portcullis was raised. The road-weary man and horse entered the yard, and the rider flopped off the animal, clearly exhausted.

Robert approached and clasped arms with the messenger, then shouted over his shoulder, "Get the man some food and drink!"

"Thank you, sire. Lord Sinclair, I presume?"

Robert frowned. The man was English, and even

used the Anglicized title of Lord instead of Laird. He clearly hadn't spent much time delivering messages in Scotland.

"Aye, I am Laird here. You must have ridden hard from England to deliver your message," Robert said carefully.

"Yes, sire, from the Borderlands."

That was enough to confirm what Robert suspected. This was Raef Warren's messenger. His stomach turned to stone. He knew the missive in response to his ransom demand would come any day now, but now that it was here, he no longer relished its contents. He wasn't even sure what he wished to hear from Warren anymore. For some reason, Warren and his scheming had mattered less to Robert in these last several days.

"Come, let us discuss this further in private," he said to the messenger, guiding him inside the keep.

He knew Alwin was in his solar, so he led the messenger, along with Burke, into a small meeting room just off the great hall. After Stella discretely delivered a mug of ale and a platter of food and the door was securely shut behind her, Robert turned to the messenger with icy detachment.

"It is safe now. You can deliver the message."

The messenger slipped his hand underneath the dusty leather surcoat he wore, and after a moment of rummaging, extracted a sealed and folded parchment. Warren's seal. Robert broke it with more force than was necessary and unfolded it to reveal the short missive. Resisting the urge to crumple it in his hand, he instead passed it to Burke, who flicked his eyes over it quickly but didn't reveal his thoughts in front of the messenger.

"Thank you. Your duty is complete. You are welcome to stay the night and take any refreshment you require for yourself or your horse," Robert said to the messenger stiffly.

The messenger bowed and exited the small room, leaving Robert and Burke. Once the heavy wooden door was closed firmly, Robert swore. Burke's eyes were steady on him.

"Isn't this exactly what you wanted, Robert? For Warren to agree to a ransom?"

Robert raked his hand through his hair. "Aye, this is what I wanted when I wrote to him." He didn't bother saying that now he wasn't so sure he wanted the same thing anymore. Burke knew his mind and could see as plainly as anyone else that what was growing between him and Alwin was more than the typical politically advantageous arranged marriage. But the game he was playing was dangerous. He had known all along that inflaming Warren's pride and going for his coffers could be a double blow if it worked, but that was assuming he could keep Alwin safe and out of Warren's grasp. He had always relished the idea of depriving Warren of whatever it was that he wanted, but now it was more complicated. Now the thought of Alwin in Warren's hands—in his bed—made him sick and blind with rage.

And Warren was demanding just that.

He had written that he would require proof that his beloved betrothed was unharmed, and that therefore the exchange of money would only happen after Alwin had been delivered to his keep. Worse, the missive said that Warren had already informed Alwin's father, Lord Hewett, of his daughter's abduction, and Hewett had vowed not to pay out the dowry. The bastard! Robert was sure Warren was trying to find a way to both collect Alwin and not deliver the ransom money. Instead of a meeting face to face to facilitate the exchange, he would hide behind the walls of his stronghold like the coward he was, locking Alwin away with him. And he couldn't be sure whether or not Warren was lying about Hewett's knowledge and refusal to pay the dowry, but either way, Robert's plan was crumbling.

"Perhaps you can renegotiate the terms of the exchange," Burke said quietly.

"Perhaps." Or would there be a way to present Alwin to Warren and make the exchange, but pull her out of Warren's grasp somehow before he could touch her? Robert's mind churned, trying to come up with some alternative. He doubted Warren would budge on the details of the exchange, so his original idea to take the ransom money without delivering Alwin would no longer work. Warren had also been holding his castle in the Borderlands for several years, despite the battles swirling around him and several efforts by the Scots to retake it. It was unlikely that Robert, Burke, and a few of their best men could simply storm the castle and retrieve Alwin once she was delivered. And Warren had seen her, so a stand-in wouldn't work. What if…what if he simply gave up his pursuit of the ransom money?

Suddenly he felt a cold sinking inside him. How could he think of such a thing? His clan was counting on him, not only for the security that so much money would provide, but also because dealing such a blow to Warren would hinder his ability to incite more war. That would be money Warren couldn't use to provide supplies to English troops or fortifications on his keep. And he would lose face and standing with the nobility at court. He could no longer bend their ears about launching another campaign in Scotland if they were all laughing at him behind his back about his loss of a bride and the emptying of his coffers.

How could he let his selfish desire for one woman cloud his duty to his clan, to his country? He and Alwin had shared a few nights of passion, and he admired her character, but he had more to think about than just their regard for each other. He couldn't seek his own pleasure at the cost of his people's wellbeing.

Even as he told himself all this, though, a voice in his head screamed at him that he would be making the biggest mistake of his life to turn away from Alwin and whatever it was that was growing between them. He pushed this voice harshly aside. He had to do something to salvage his plans in the interest of his people.

"I am Laird," he said aloud, almost to reassure himself that he had not only the power to make his own decisions but also the responsibility to look after the best interests of his people.

Burke raised his brows, a look of worry on his face. "What are you planning, Robert?"

Without answering, Robert stepped around him and through the door toward the great hall. It was time for him to face up to his responsibility. Just as he reached the head table, he caught a glimpse of Alwin's radiant smile as she approached, though it slipped when her eyes met his. His heart clenched. He had to do this, even if it meant ruining them both. He would become the monster, close his heart against her so he could get through what he needed to do next.

Chapter Thirty-Six

Alwin approached Robert cautiously. When she reached him, she extended her hand toward his arm, longing to feel his strength, but she recoiled when she searched his eyes, finding only a detached iciness in their pale blue depths. He crossed his arms over his chest, seeming to build a wall between them.

"I have much to tell you about my day," she began hesitantly. "I think you will be pleased when you hear of it. I have been working to create a new system for the ledgers and—"

"Silence." His voice was low enough for only her to hear, even surrounded by clanspeople preparing for the evening meal, but it held such a jagged edge of ice that Alwin inhaled sharply.

"Robert, what is—"

He didn't let her finish. Instead, he wrapped a large hand around her arm and drew her toward the stairs leading to their chamber. Once inside, he released her arm, but loomed over her.

"When I give you an order, I expect you to follow it," he bit out.

She forgot her shock in the swell of anger his words and tone brought on. "I am not your subject or your serf to be ordered about. I am your wife!"

"You are my captive."

Her blood instantly went from heated with anger to chilled with dread. "Then what has the last fortnight been? I thought we agreed to make a *union*."

"That was a mistake. I kidnapped you for one reason, and one reason only."

All traces of the lover she had been getting to know, the honor-bound man, the caring leader, were gone from him. In front of her stood the terrifyingly determined, cold-hearted warrior she had met all those weeks before along the road. "What are you saying?" The feeling of dread building in the pit of her stomach told her she didn't want to know the answer.

"Warren has agreed to a ransom. Unfortunately, he insists that you be delivered to him before he will pay out. You will be transported tomorrow morning. We will do everything we can to extract you from his hold, but the exchange must happen first," he said flatly through gritted teeth.

It took her a moment to register the full weight of what he was saying. As she stood there with her mouth open, he turned his back on her, and she was left staring at the broad, muscled planes. Like a stone wall. He was sending her to Warren to collect the ransom money. She would be transported…like so many goods. Just as her father and Warren had done. He had said they would try to rescue her, but only after she was back in Warren's grasp. She meant nothing to him—or not nothing, but only money, a bargaining chip to get what he really wanted. And all the intimacy they had shared? The passion? The quiet conversations spoken in bed in the early hours of the morning about their families, their fears, their hopes?

"You coward." The words flew from her mouth, but she didn't regret them.

He spun on his heels to face her once again, but this time the flat detachment in his eyes was gone and in its place was a searing blue fire. "Coward, am I? Aye, I have been a coward to hide behind your skirts and seek my own pleasure instead of thinking of my clan. But no more—this liaison as been…entertaining, but we both knew it couldn't last."

"That's what this is to you? An entertaining liaison? You were the one who had us wed, and you were the one who denied me an annulment!"

"I acted in the best interest of my clan, which is exactly what I am doing now."

"Are you blind? You think a few extra coins are going to solve all your clan's problems? If you believe that, then you are a fool as well as a coward," she shouted in his face.

His jaw muscles flexed, and a long silence stretched between them. His next words came out icy cold. "I shouldn't expect a spoiled English lass to understand anything about responsibility, duty, or how to lead people who rely on you."

She felt her eyes widen, but she wouldn't back down from his insults. "Look around you, Robert. Your people are happy and thriving. There is enough food in the larders, enough coin in the coffers, the farmers are gearing up for spring planting, and the shepherds are awaiting a promising birthing season. The only thing this clan needs is for their Laird to be here more often."

His temper snapped at that. "How dare you try to tell me what's going on in my clan or what I should do as Laird? You are an outsider here."

She gasped, his barb finding its mark. Even if what he said was true and she was an unwelcome outsider, she still knew she was right about the state of his clan. "In case you haven't noticed, I have spent my time here trying to learn all I can about the clan's history and affairs. As I was trying to tell you before, I have been studying the ledgers that prove the stability of your people, and I have seen for myself that they are thriving. You are the only one who seems to think that your people are weak and broken."

Somewhere through the haze of his rage at Alwin's insults about his leadership and the sickening feeling he had at the thought of sending her to Warren, even if he could somehow find a way to get her back, he registered her comment about the ledgers. Part of him was surprised she had gotten so involved—that she cared enough to learn about his people. But the enraged part wanted to push her away further, to prove to himself that he was making the right decision in sending her away and collecting the ransom money. "What are you doing meddling with the ledgers? What gives you the right? Looking for weaknesses to exploit?"

She looked as if he had just slapped her. "I was trying to *help*. I naively believed that I would be staying here as mistress of the household, so I wanted to offer my skills and training for the betterment of all here."

"We don't need your help. We have always taken care of ourselves and don't need some Englishwoman meddling in our affairs," he said bitterly. He knew it was wrong to throw her nationality in her face—she hadn't chosen it, and he had already seen her show loyalty and caring toward his people, Englishwoman or no. But he couldn't seem to stop himself from poisoning things between them. It would make it easier to send her away. Perhaps if she hated him, if their union meant nothing, he wouldn't feel so guilty for risking handing her over to Warren. He had to push down his own feelings for her, silence the voice inside his head screaming at him that the risk in sending her away was too great. Even if he hated every damned second of it.

Her gray eyes blazed, and she looked ready to shout something in response, but then she stilled. He watched as the tension seemed to drain from her body, the fight leaving her, and her eyes turn flat and far off. Eventually, she spoke, but her voice was low and barely audible. "You had a choice to make, and you have made it." It was almost as if she spoke more to herself than to him, trying to resign herself to something.

"Aye, I have." Even as he could feel his knuckles going white from how hard he was clenching his hands, he refused to let himself reach out to her, comfort her, or listen to the part of him that knew he was wrong. This was the way it had to be. Since he wasn't going to get her dowry from her father, and Warren wouldn't pay out the ransom without securing her first, he had to send her away. He would find some way to get her back, but he didn't know how. He had to salvage what little he could from his original plan to spurn Warren and extract a price for the lass. He couldn't let his own feelings cloud his judgment. Alwin was just one woman.

The woman he was falling in love with. The thought sprung unbidden to his mind, but he harshly pushed it aside. What good did love do in times of war? How many others had already been sacrificed, and how many more would lose love, their homes, or their lives if he didn't do everything in his power to stop it? He was sure he was doing the right thing, but then why did it feel so wrong?

Alwin wouldn't meet his gaze. It was like a switch had flipped. One minute she had been yelling heatedly at him, and now she looked like a shell of herself, her spirit evaporated and only a passive husk left. He had accomplished what he had set out to do. He had poisoned her against him, and bent her into submitting to his will. A sick feeling was rising in the back of his throat.

"Prepare to depart in the morning," he managed gruffly, then stormed past her toward the door before he did something he would regret. The problem was, even without taking her into his arms and disavowing every cruelty he had inflicted on her, he was already swimming in regret. Drowning in it.

Chapter Thirty-Seven

As the chamber door slammed behind Robert, Alwin's composure cracked. She crumpled to the floor, no longer able to keep her spine straight and no longer caring. She had fought for so long against being controlled, against having her spirit crushed by those who saw her as only a pawn. But she couldn't fight anymore. She had thought she was strong, but perhaps she was just a fool. She had wanted to believe that things could be different with Robert, but she had been wrong. He was just like her father, and just like Raef Warren—power-hungry, greedy, and driven by ego. She was heartsick at constantly being used by such men. She didn't even have the energy to bring up the sobs that sat heavily in her chest. Instead, she just sat there in a pile on the floor of the chamber, the tears sliding silently down her cheeks.

The heady dream she had been drifting through with Robert seemed almost as if it had never happened. She had been so naïve, so willing to trust him, to allow herself to fall in love with him. She had never been in love before, but she knew this was it—or had been it.

And it wasn't just the blaze he lit in her, the way his touch could turn her fiery spirit into an all-consuming passion. It was the fact that she had been vulnerable with him, that he had honored and respected her vulnerability and showed her glimpses of his own. And she had come to respect him. He had been compassionate and protective of her, and of his clanspeople.

But she must have been wrong, for how could he care about her and still be willing to turn her over to Raef Warren? Even if he did manage to snatch her from Warren's clutches, what would Warren do with her while he had her? That day, which felt like ages ago, when Warren had attacked them and struck her face, Robert had vowed never to let the man touch or hurt her again. And now he would break that vow.

For some reason he was setting up this decision like it was between her or his clan, his happiness or his duty. Alwin saw it differently. His happiness *was* his clan's happiness. His duty was now *her* duty as well. She had tried to show him, had argued and shouted and pointed out all that she saw and thought, but he wouldn't listen. And she was too tired to fight him if he wasn't willing to fight for her. She had to take care of herself now.

Alwin wiped the sleeve of her dress across each cheek, forcing herself to pull her mind together. She would not be delivered to that monster Warren, no matter how briefly, and Robert wouldn't listen any longer. She had to take matters into her own hands. She had to escape.

Chapter Thirty-Eight

Robert barreled through the great hall on his way to the solar. He needed to quiet his mind, and the only place he could think to go was to the top of the northeast tower. Somehow the place always calmed him. As a lad, he had sat at his father's foot as he scrawled in a ledger or consulted a book. Though a warrior himself, his father had always reminded him that a Laird had to do more than fighting; he also had to shepherd his clan, learning their desires, hopes, and fears so that he could protect and care for them.

Robert cursed and shoved his hair back with his hand. How well had he been living up to his father's example about how to be a good Laird? Alwin's admonition that he was spending too much time away from his people was still wringing in his ears. But what could she know in such a short time with his clan?

The images of her eager and proud face at the midday meal every day for the last week came to him; she had been pouring over the clan history, trying to understand him and his people, and she had even said she had been working on the ledgers, which Stella had told him were a tangled mess more than once. He cursed again, the rising fear that Alwin had been right beginning to choke him—right about his responsibilities to stay with his people, about his recent failures as a Laird, about his blindness when it came to Warren...

He had already crossed the yard and was taking the stairs to the solar two at a time. He threw the door open and slammed it back closed, hoping the solitude would clear his mind and help him sort through his jumbled thoughts. Instead, he was hit with an instant wave of Alwin's scent—roses and warmth. She had been spending so much time up here that her presence lingered even now. That was the last thing he needed to clear his head. Her soulful blue-gray eyes swam before him, her rosy mouth turned up in a playful smile. He could clearly picture those same eyes cloudy yet blazing with passion. Then the image was replaced with the hollow, flat look she had given him moments before. What had he done?

He tried to shake the regret from him. He had done what was necessary. If he had hurt her, then so be it, but he had to do this. He stomped to the desk and tossed himself into the chair, searching for a clean sheet of parchment for a missive to Warren, confirming their exchange. He would just have to sort out the details of how to extract her from his keep later. The prospect of such a rescue attempt seemed ridiculous even to him, though.

His eyes fell on the bookshelf on the opposite wall.

Dust coated some of the volumes, but several were clean. Those would be the ones Alwin had inadvertently dusted when she had drawn them off the shelf and pored over the pages, probably swirling a strand of her honey brown hair around a finger distractedly. Christ, he would drive himself insane!

Suddenly he heard the door being pushed open, and in the next instant, Stella walked through. She started when she saw that he was in the room.

"Apologies, Laird. I was just coming to collect the household ledgers. I believe Lady Alwin has been working on them, and I think she may have left them up here."

She spoke calmly, but Robert was sure he was glaring at her. He glanced around the desk, noticing the leather-bound volume perched on the corner. Without saying anything, he picked it up and extended it to her. She tucked it under her arm before turning to go.

Before she made it all the way out the door, though, she stopped and turned back. "The mistress has us all practicing a new system of record keeping. Somehow, she thinks she can teach a couple of old bats like me and Nora a new way of doing things." She chuckled then paused before going on. "The more I think on it, though, the more I see that it will be for the better. You know I can be stubborn, but perhaps it is time for a change. And truth be told, though I am stuck in my ways, the lass's new system will actually be better for the clan." She stood in the doorway for a moment longer before returning down the stairs quietly.

Robert stared after her. There was no way the old woman could have overheard what he and Alwin had spoken of. Perhaps it was all written on his face. Stella had been there for his birth, had raised him after his mother had died, and reminded him of the lessons his father had taught him in the first few years of his Lairdship. If he couldn't or wouldn't listen to himself, he knew he'd damn well better listen to Stella.

There had to be another way besides pushing Alwin away, turning her over to Warren, collecting the ransom money, and then attempting some futile rescue attempt. Why was he more willing to give up the woman he was falling in love with than give up the hunt to thwart Warren?

He had been at the chase for too long, and had become blinded by his desire for vengeance. The realization caused the air to rush from his lungs, and he sat down heavily on the corner of the desk. Was he really thinking only of his clan while on all the countless raids in the Borderlands? Surely his efforts had helped, but he was more than a soldier or a raider—he was Laird of the clan Sinclair. He had let himself become caught up in the hunt, in the pleasure of inflicting wounds on his enemy, and forgot his larger responsibility to be a leader to his people.

And now he would take away his clan's lady, his wife, in pursuit of money. Could Alwin be right? Was he any better than Warren?

Aye, he still believed he sought the best interests of his clan, whereas Warren thought of no one but himself. He would die for his clan, but, he realized, they would be better served by a living and present Laird.

He was being a blind fool. He would talk it all over with Burke. Together they would come up with a plan, but first he had to find Alwin and tell her that he was wrong, that he would never give her up, that he—that he loved her.

The thought shook him, but only because he knew it was true. He sprinted down the stairs, needing to see her, needing to make things right again, if he could.

That slowed him. What if he had truly broken her spirit with his harshness and controlling manipulations? What if she could never forgive him? He cursed himself again for his blindness, determined that he would find a way to show her how he felt, what she meant to him, and that he would never let her go again.

His long strides turned into a trot once he was down the spiraling tower stairs and into the yard. He had to find her, to explain everything, to kiss away the stony detachment his callousness had brought on.

Then he heard the scream, and he was running at a dead sprint.

Chapter Thirty-Nine

She would need a horse, for starters. There was no way Alwin would be able to escape Roslin and Robert on foot. First she would have to gather some food, though she knew she wouldn't be able to take enough for the entire journey to Iona. The tiny island on the western coast was the best destination she could muster at the moment. She was certainly not returning to her father's manor—he would either disown her to put as much distance between himself and his presumably ruined daughter or marry her off quickly and quietly to the first man (probably some widower old enough to be her grandfather) who would take her given her status as a kidnapped and disgraced woman. She hadn't even considered seeking out Raef Warren for protection. He was more likely to beat her into submission or lock her away from public view, based on what she knew of the man. And she couldn't stay here.

Tears welled in her eyes again, but she pushed the pain aside. She had to be strong. Just because she had fallen in love—yes, she could admit it to herself now—

with a man who had turned out to be like all the others, that didn't mean she would crumble into nothingness under his cruelty. She would not let him use her, and she would not let him break her. She would rather live as a nun on a remote island in western Scotland.

She had slipped an extra dress and chemise into a satchel she found in Robert's armoire, then spun her cloak, which had been hanging there as well, over her shoulders. Now she just had to make her way to the stables after stopping in the kitchen for supplies.

She eased the heavy wooden door to Robert's chamber open, wincing as one of the hinges squeaked. No one was within earshot, apparently, because the stairway remained quiet. She crept downward, winding her way toward the great hall. Luckily, the evening meal had already been served and cleared away, and she hoped she could pass through unnoticed.

At the bottom of the stairs, she paused and peeked around the stone archway into the great hall. She breathed a sigh of relief—it was completely empty. Trying to calm her nerves, she forced herself to walk at a moderate pace through the open expanse. Bolting through the hall like a scared cat would surely draw unwanted attention.

She made as direct a line as possible toward the back corner of the hall, where a swinging door led to the kitchen. Just before reaching the door, she again paused to listen. Her stomach clenched. At least two voices could be heard on the other side. It was likely just a couple of the scullery maids cleaning up after the evening meal. Alwin was tempted to throw out her plan to gather some food before sneaking to the stables but realized through the fog of terror at the thought of being discovered that it would be dangerous to head out without any supplies, especially this early in spring. Besides, she reminded herself, trying to soothe her nerves, the maids still knew her as the mistress of the castle. They wouldn't question or try to detain her.

On a shaky breath, she set her shoulders back and plastered a smile on her face, pushing the swinging door inward.

Her heart sank even as her pulse ticked up. Instead of two scullery maids, Stella and Nora turned and smiled at her entrance.

"My lady! What brings you into the kitchens at this hour?" Stella said, her eyes quickly scanning Alwin, resting ever so briefly on her heavy cloak.

"Oh, I was hoping to steal a leftover heel of bread before catching some fresh air," Alwin replied, her voice as breezy as she could muster.

Nora smiled knowingly at Alwin, her eyes glittering. "I understand perfectly, my lady. The Laird has been…ahem…raising your appetite in the evenings."

Alwin felt her cheeks flame and her ears burn with a deep blush. "Y-yes, I find that I am more hungry than normal." Thinking fast, she added, "In fact, he and I are both famished. Perhaps I should take a light meal up to our chamber?"

"I'll fix you right up, my lady. We can't have our Laird and Lady going hungry, not when the Sinclairs can finally call ourselves one of the most prosperous clans in all the Highlands. And especially not considering that someday soon, God willing, we might have a new heir." Nora continued to chatter excitedly as she moved about the kitchen, grabbing a loaf of bread baked that morning, a wedge of cheese, and a generous handful of expensive dried figs from the Holy Land.

Alwin was careful to keep the smile on her face, despite how difficult it was to listen to the woman go on about how bright their future was, how she and Robert were known about the castle to be wooing and making love, and how they all hoped an heir would come soon.

Stella stayed quiet but kept a sharp eye on Alwin, making her itch. She was sure the head of servants knew something was afoot. Alwin put on her most serene air, though, and refused to grow jittery under Stella's watchful gaze.

Before Alwin could crack, Nora blessedly handed her a tray heaping with food. Knowing she would have to load up her satchel somewhere else, she took the tray gratefully and smiled at both women.

"Thank you so much. I'll just drop this off in the chamber and take a stroll in the yard. Good night."

Each woman gave her a bobbing curtsy, Nora smiling back at her and Stella with a slightly furrowed brow. Alwin didn't dare try to smooth things over or explain anymore, fearing getting caught in a lie or betraying herself with a nervous gesture or quaver in her voice.

Instead, she pushed through the swinging door back into the great hall as if she were going back up the staircase that led to Robert's chamber. But instead of crossing the hall again, she stepped to the side and into a dimly lit hallway leading to one of the smaller meeting rooms off the hall. Crouching, she hurriedly stuffed all the food into her satchel, not even bothering to wrap the cheese or try to protect her extra gown from crumbs. She left the tray in the dark hallway; by the time it was found, her absence from the castle would have already been noticed anyway.

All she had to do now was make her way to the stables, find a horse, and get out of the castle's thick curtain wall somehow without being noticed. Straightening her spine against the long odds of her escape plan working, she moved silently toward the yard. Knowing that there would be guards on the curtain wall, looking not only out toward the surrounding landscape but also inside the wall for troublemakers, Alwin skirted the yard, staying in the darkest corners and away from the light of the near-full moon overhead.

She knew the stables would be quiet at this hour, but when she reached them, she peered in through an open-framed window before reaching for the door just in case a lad hadn't finished mucking out one of the stalls. Finding that all was quiet within, she eased the latch on the wooden door and slipped inside.

It was dim but warm within, the smell of fresh hay and horses mingling pleasantly with the leather of the tack and saddles lining the walls. Her eyes instantly went to Dash, who, though shadowed, clearly stood several hands above the other horses in their stalls. She discarded the idea of riding him, though, remembering that he only responded to his master. Next to Dash's stall, however, there was a smaller but spry looking horse, whose white coat seemed to glow bluish in the low light. Alwin slowly approached, holding out her hand, entirely focused on the animal in front of her.

The white horse, whose nose she was almost touching, suddenly reared. It was the only warning she had. Then a hand clamped down over her mouth.

Chapter Forty

Alwin tried to scream, but only a muffled noise came out behind the man's hand over her mouth. She thrashed violently, throwing her elbows backward, but before she could make contact, the man's other arm snaked around her torso, pinning her arms to her sides. She tried to kick him with her legs and landed a few blows to his shins. She heard an English voice behind her curse, then she was slammed front-first into the back wall of the stable. Her head impacted with wood, and her vision blurred. She could feel her knees give out under her as her head swam, but a voice screamed inside to resist the darkness that was creeping over her consciousness.

The vise-like grip around her arms vanished for a moment, and she thought she would be freed, but then she felt the cold sharpness of a blade pressed against her throat.

"Warren said you'd fight back, but I don't mind playing a bit before I slice this pretty little throat of yours," her attacker whispered into her ear.

He inhaled in her hair, and she thought she would

be sick. Whoever this man was, he was going to rape her then murder her. And Warren had sent him. Terror clenched her. She was pinned against the stable wall, her face pressed into the wood, her head swimming, a knife at her throat, and her attacker's hand still clamped over her mouth. He was already using his body to trap her against the wall, but now she felt his hips press into her bottom, his erection jutting against her.

"You'll be a good girl and stay quiet, won't you?" he whispered as he continued to press against her. His breath was hot and foul.

Those words made something inside her snap—or rather click into place. This man was not only going to rape and murder her, but he expected her to behave, to bend to his will, to stay quiet and docile while he forced and killed her. Despite her best efforts throughout her life to please others, it was never enough—she was never enough. She was done trying, done caring. All she knew now was that she had to fight.

Without thinking, she sunk her teeth as hard as she could into the hand that sealed her mouth. At the same moment, she jerked her elbow back into the soft stomach of her attacker. He grunted in surprise and pain, and her blow to his middle caused him to instinctively draw his arms in, freeing her mouth and moving the blade away from her neck.

Before he could recover, she turned and dove headfirst into Dash's stall, flinging herself behind his hooves without regard for the danger of being trampled by the huge warhorse. She scrambled further back, around Dash's legs and into the very back of the stall. She could hear her attacker quietly cursing. His shadowy figure loomed in front of the stall.

"You'll pay for that, bitch!" He raised the knife, and it caught a moonbeam from one of the open windows along the stable's walls.

"Dash!" she screamed at the top of her lungs, fear shooting her voice up.

The powerful horse had stood alert until then, amazingly not trampling her underneath his hooves when she had thrown herself underneath him. Now he gave a loud snort and took a step toward the open end of the stall, where the man stood. Muttering something about a dumb animal, the man backed up to avoid Dash's powerful chest, then tried to angle his way around into the stall, but Dash took a sidestep in front of him. Losing patience, the man swung the knife toward the horse, making contact with Dash's shoulder. The warhorse shrieked, not in pain but in rage. He had been in enough battles to respond on instinct. He reared and brought his huge hooves down toward the man who was attacking him.

Realizing what he had just instigated, the man flung himself out of the way, but not before one of Dash's hooves clipped him on the shoulder. He screamed in pain, his arm hanging limp at his side as he landed in the hay on the stable floor. Just then, the door to the stable flew open and even in the weak half-light of the moon, Alwin knew it was Robert. His warrior's frame filled the doorway, his fists clenched at his sides. He was illuminated from behind in the cold blue light, but his eyes seeming to glow like ice.

Cursing again, the man on the stable floor fumbled with his good hand for the knife, which he apparently dropped in the hay. A strangled cry came out of Alwin's throat as she tried to warn Robert, but couldn't find words. But he didn't need her warning. He moved like lightning, darting across the distance between himself and the man.

Just as the man raised the knife from the hay, Robert's boot struck his hand, sending the knife spinning into the shadows. Robert launched himself at the other man, sending them both tumbling backward. From behind Dash in the stall, Alwin could hear the two men struggle but couldn't make out what was happening as they twisted and turned in the straw. She knew Robert didn't carry a weapon on him within the safety of his own castle walls. Fearing her attacker would kill Robert and then her, she screamed again at the top of her lungs for help, praying that someone would hear.

Just then she made out Robert on top of her attacker on the floor of the stable. He had his large, strong hands wrapped around the other man's neck and was squeezing mercilessly despite the man's flailing. The man on his back began to gurgle, and his thrashing slowed, growing weaker. She could see the contours of

Robert's powerful arms in the moonlight, his muscles flexed and exposed past the rolled-up sleeves of his plain white shirt. He squeezed even harder, and the man beneath him finally went limp, but Robert kept his grip locked on his throat for what seemed like ages, his jaw clenched and his eyes like she had never seen them—filled with pure rage, burning blue fire at his enemy.

Suddenly the stable door flew open again, and the stable was flooded with light. Alwin blinked and threw up a hand to shield her eyes. Through her squint, she saw Burke, a lantern in one hand and his sword in the other. Behind him, she could make out at least a dozen more soldiers outside in the yard.

Taking in the scene, Burke cursed. He thrust the lantern at one of the men behind him and darted to Robert's side but turned in a slow circle, both hands on his sword, scanning the stable for potential threats. When he saw no other attackers, Burke lowered his sword and put his hand on Robert's shoulder.

Blind with rage and still in the haze of battle, Robert jerked up and took a swing at Burke. Burke barely managed to duck under the powerful right hook flying at his head.

"Robert, it's me! It's Burke! All is well! It is over!"

Robert stood panting, the haze beginning to lift as his eyes adjusted and he took in his friend in front of him. Before he seemed to fully grasp where he was and what was happening around him, his eyes flew to

Alwin in the back of Dash's stall.

A sob escaped her lips as she realized she was finally safe. Before her wobbling knees could give way on her, Robert pushed past Dash, who still stood halfway in his stall, and rushed to her, slamming his body into hers in an embrace.

"Are you all right, love? Please, God!"

He raised a shaky hand toward her right temple, and she realized that something warm and sticky was matting her hair and running down her cheek into the collar of her cloak.

She lifted her fingertips to her scalp and drew them back with a sharp inhale of pain. Her fingertips were bright red with her own blood. "I...I hit my head..." she said in a daze.

Before she could form any more words, he scooped her up and carried her into the middle of the stable. He unceremoniously sat down in a pile of straw, still cradling her.

"Did he do this to you? Did he hurt you anywhere else?"

She almost didn't recognize his voice, it was so strained and rough. She shook her head then winced in pain. A deep throb was spreading inside her skull to accompany the sharp pain of the bloodied area on her scalp. "He tried, but he could only manage this," she said, somehow managing to raise a weak smile.

Robert's face darkened, apparently not appreciating her attempt at humor. She noticed that he, too, had injuries. A bruise looked to be forming on one of his cheekbones, and a trickle of blood dripped from a cut on his lip, but he didn't seem to be aware of either. Burke interjected before she could ask him if he was all right, though.

"Robert, what happened here?"

Robert reluctantly pulled his eyes from Alwin to scan the room. His gaze fell on the motionless body of Alwin's attacker. She couldn't suppress a gasp that rose to her lips at the sight of the dead man, his eyes bulging from his skull and his tongue lolling from his slack jaw.

"The messenger!" The shock in Robert's voice caused Alwin to lean into him even further.

Burke strode to the body, then, recognition dawning, exhaled sharply.

"He attacked me and said he would—he would kill me," Alwin choked out. "He said Raef Warren had sent him."

Burke and Robert exchanged a dark look, and Robert's arms tightened around Alwin protectively.

"A clever plan, and very like Warren," Burke said, keeping his eyes locked on Robert. "He likely never planned to go through with the ransom exchange at all, and instead thought to...eliminate the source of any further embarrassment for him. The missive he sent regarding Lady Alwin's ransom probably only served to create the opportunity for this attack."

Robert's jaw ticked, but he didn't attempt to rise and held Alwin firmly on his lap. "We will discuss this further later, Burke," Robert said in a dark tone.

Burke gave a nod, turning to the door. "George, you and the others are in charge of making sure this vermin gets a burial suited to one who would attack our Laird and Lady," he said to the man holding the lantern and the other soldiers crowded behind him. "One of the stable lads can see to Dash. It looks only to be a scratch. I'll send Stella to your chamber to have her see to both of you," he said over his shoulder to Robert and Alwin.

Without releasing her, Robert stood and followed Burke into the yard, where several of the castle's residents had crowded to see what all the commotion was about. Taking a deep breath, Robert said loudly, "There has been an attack tonight. The castle was infiltrated by an assassin posing as a messenger. He was sent to kill your Lady."

The gasp of surprise from the crowd quickly turned into a collective growl of anger. Tears stung Alwin's eyes. She couldn't believe how these people had taken her in as one of their own so quickly and had already grown protective of her. *They are following their Laird's example*, a voice whispered inside her. He was still cradling her to his chest as if she weighed nothing, warming and shielding her with his powerful arms.

"The assassin failed, however, and is dead, due in no small part to your Lady's bravery," he said in an unwavering voice.

Those gathered heartily rumbled their approval.

Without waiting further, Robert strode through the crowd, which parted respectfully for them, toward his chamber.

The chamber door was already open, and a swarm of servants moved in and out by the time they arrived. Inside, Stella was shouting orders and directing the hustling servants. When she caught sight of the two of them entering, her brow settled into an even deeper frown.

"Bring her over to the bed, Laird. Gently now."

Alwin's head spun as Robert lowered her onto the bed, worry clouding his eyes.

"I'm all right," she said, trying to push up onto her elbows. The room spun and she squeezed her eyes shut.

"Get me water and a cloth. And get all these damned people out of the way!" Robert barked at Stella.

Alwin heard the older woman *tsk* quietly, but then she gave the orders, and soon, Alwin felt a cool damp cloth being pressed to her temple where the sharp pain seemed to radiate from.

"It looks worse than it is, Robert," Burke's voice floated from somewhere nearby. "Head wounds always bleed a lot, but with rest she should be fine."

Robert didn't reply, but the gentle pressure on her temple vanished briefly, and she heard him exhale with relief, then return the cloth to her head. She felt as if her limbs were sinking into the bed, heavy as lead. She fought against the swimming darkness but felt herself losing to its swirling pull.

"It's all right now, lass. You're safe. And I'm never letting you go again." His husky whisper close to her ear was the last thing she heard before the darkness pulled her under.

Chapter Forty-One

For what must have been the millionth time, Robert dragged his hand through his hair and turned to walk the six paces back across his chamber. He had started pacing after Alwin had been asleep for eight hours. First, he had done it out of impatience for her to wake and prove to him that she would be all right. Then, after about a day and a half, he had counted his paces to occupy his mind and keep himself from going mad with worry. Now, he paced because he felt completely useless and helpless in the face of her continued slumber.

If—no, *when*—she woke, he would be there at her side, albeit bedraggled and exhausted. He had barely managed to swallow a few bites of food that Stella had forced on him, which tasted like dust and did nothing to relieve his anxiety. He had also caught a few intermittent winks of sleep in a chair he had pulled up to the bedside where Alwin lay, pale but still breathing steadily. He had reassured himself that such a blow wouldn't kill her, but as the days had stretched on, he began to fear that perhaps when she did awaken, her mind wouldn't be right.

A few days before Warren's messenger had attacked, the village healer had been called away to help deliver a child for a peasant family living on the very edges of Sinclair land. Apparently there had been complications, for she had still not returned. Stella, who had stepped in for the healer many times before, stayed calm and level-headed as always, but even her steadfast reassurances that all would be well had done little to ease his mind or still his feet from pacing.

Making the turn at the door, he began his six paces back toward the bed. Glancing down, he cursed a few choice words in frustration. A faint line from the door to the side of the bed was visible in the finely woven rug, revealing the path he had worn with his pacing. The cost was nothing to him now, but Stella would likely chide him for the dozenth time for his useless worrying. He must be strong, Stella had told him repeatedly, for both Alwin and the clan. For some reason, though, Robert no longer felt that he could be strong without Alwin.

"Does Father Frederick know you have such a foul mouth?"

Before he knew what he was doing, Robert had flown to the bed and fallen on his knees at its side. Before him, he saw what he had longed for, dreamed of for these nightmarish four days. Alwin's gray-blue eyes fluttered open, locking on his. They looked just like the winter sky of the Highlands after a storm. A small furrow appeared in her brow, and he took her hand.

"What is it, love? Are you in pain? Tell me what I can do."

"The light," she said, her voice a bit scratchy from disuse.

Instantly, he was at the window, closing the shutters then pulling the furs to block out as much light as possible. Then he resumed his kneel beside the bed, his large hand engulfing her delicate one.

"How long was I…"

A dry cough interrupted her, and he reached for a cup of water on the table next to the bed. As gently as he could, he lifted her head slightly and tipped the cup toward her lips. She took a few tentative sips then gulped greedily, draining the cup.

"Four days," he replied as he refilled the cup and offered her more. When she had drained it again, he lowered her back to the bed, then asked tentatively, "Do you remember what happened?"

She creased her brow again, her eyes drifting around the room. "I was going to the stables, then—" She inhaled sharply. "Then that man attacked me. And Dash—Is Dash all right?"

Her concern for the animal made something ache inside him. He raised her hand to his mouth and pressed a soft kiss to her knuckles. "Aye, lass, Dash is just fine. He's practically healed already. If anything, he is getting spoiled rotten. I have sent a stable lad to feed him extra oats and an apple every day for protecting you."

The corner of her mouth inched up as her eyes followed his lips. "And then you were there, and you...killed that man." She swallowed, dropping her eyes.

Robert clenched his jaw. "Aye. He was an assassin sent by Warren. He acted as a messenger to get into the castle but apparently aimed to kill you." The reality of the man's attempt, and Warren's actions behind it, had sunk in, but he feared the way she seemed horrified that he had killed another with his bare hands. He wouldn't apologize for it, though; he had done worse in battle and would tear anyone who threatened her limb from limb with his teeth if he had to.

Seeming to read his mind, Alwin gave his hand a little squeeze. "Robert, I hope you do not think that I judge you. That man meant to violate me and slit my throat. I don't know how to thank you."

His eyes flew to hers, seeking confirmation of the truth of her reassurance. Her large stormy eyes met his unflinchingly, her soft gaze filled with something that made his heart clench.

"You don't need to thank me. It is I who owe you. I must beg your forgiveness for my..." He forced the words out past his shame. "For my unconscionable treatment of you. I was a blind fool. I let my desire for revenge cloud my judgment, and you had to pay the price for it. You were right, Alwin. I see now that my clan needs me here, not off raiding and seeking vengeance against Warren or the English. And I have wronged you by denying your choice in all this. I have acted like a blockheaded barbarian, which I am sure you think I am. I hope that perhaps with time you can someday come to trust me again. I swear I will never let harm come to you again, and I will never be the one to hurt you."

He kept his eyes locked on her face as he spoke, looking for some sign to tell him if he could ever hope to regain her trust—her heart. She belied nothing, though, and a laden silence stretched between them. Finally, she spoke, keeping her voice carefully flat.

"I have been told my entire life that I am too spirited, too stubborn, too quick to speak my mind. My father tried to break me, and I would bet my life that Raef Warren would have done worse. And then you attempted to do the same. You all took away my choices, my freedom. You all put yourselves and your money, your battles, and your revenge, before me."

She paused, closing her eyes for a moment, whether in pain or thought Robert couldn't tell. He held his breath, his jaw clenched, waiting for what he feared most to hear from her.

"The difference with you, though, is that I fell in love with you."

Robert's heart surged at her words, then twisted painfully at the look in her cloudy eyes. Though he longed to tell her that he loved her too, he let her go on without interjecting.

"I fell in love with you because I thought of you as honorable. I thought you to be compassionate and protective of those in need. And I thought you to be a good leader, putting your people first, doing what was best for them rather than for yourself." Another long pause stretched. "Was I wrong?"

He swallowed the tightness in his throat, brought on by the power and insight of her words. Her opinion of him meant everything to him.

"Nay, love, you weren't wrong. I have…strayed in my duty to my people and shamed myself and my family name, but I am the man you fell in love with—or at least, I will always strive to be so in your eyes."

She held her gaze steady on his face, seeming to read him. Deciding something, she gave a little nod and the corner of her mouth turned up.

"Then perhaps we can continue to try to make the best of this…unusual union?"

He barely stopped himself from scooping her off the bed and into his arms, but at the last moment reminded himself of her injury. Instead, he cupped her cheek in his palm, trying to soak in every exquisite slope and angle of her face, the look in her eyes that penetrated him to the soul.

"I love you, lass." He almost didn't recognize his own voice, edged with raw emotion.

Instead of a slight upturn to her mouth, this time he was hit full on with a radiant beaming smile.

"I love you, too."

With his eyes riveted on her warm smile, he realized he would do anything to make her happy. And he knew then that the pain and rage he had fed toward his enemies would no longer rule him. The light Alwin had brought into his life had chased away the shadows, reminding him of who he was and who he was meant to be. He leaned forward and captured her lips in a soft kiss.

Suddenly, a thought popped into his head. "Alwin, why were you in the stables to begin with?"

Her smile slipped, and she seemed to look everywhere but at him. Calming herself with a deep breath, she said steadily, "I was planning another escape."

He raised an eyebrow at her, but she plowed forward, seeming to gain momentum and courage as she went. "I couldn't just sit idly by while you planned to give me over to Warren, could I? I was going to steal a horse and head to Iona to take vows as a nun."

At that, he nearly chuckled, but it came out as more of a guffaw.

"What would you have had me do, wait for you to realize what a complete fool you were being?" she asked indignantly.

"Peace, lass, peace! I heartily commend you for seeing clearly what I so obviously did not. I was merely surprised at the idea of you being a nun." He gave her a wicked look that he hoped conveyed his meaning.

It worked. She blushed from neck to ears. This

time when his lips met hers, the sweetness was gone, and in its place was a dark promise of pleasure to come.

"Oh, my lady, you're awake!"

Robert jerked back from their intimate kiss at the sound of Stella's surprised voice in the doorway.

Stella turned a glare on him. "I hope the Laird has not been accosting you when you need your rest, mistress."

"Actually, I feel as though I've had plenty of rest, Stella. I would be much obliged for something to eat, though." As if to concur with her words, her stomach growled.

Stella hurried over with the tray she had been carrying. "This was going to be for you, Laird, but I'm sure you wouldn't mind sharing."

The older woman set the tray on the desk nearby then brought over a bowl of steaming porridge with milk. Robert reluctantly let go of his hold on Alwin's hand and cheek in order to prop another pillow under her so she could eat. She winced the first time her head shifted, but then raised it on her own and turned her neck this way and that.

"Don't push yourself, lass. That was quite the blow to your head," he soothed.

"I am not made of glass, Robert. I should hope all that sleeping helped me heal, and now I want to start getting back to normal," she said firmly.

He almost retorted that she wasn't strong enough but stopped himself. He felt a surge of protectiveness for her, but he had to let her make her own decisions. "Aye, you're right, love," he said softly. "But promise me you'll go easy on yourself—for my sake."

That seemed to please her, for she gave him another little smile.

Breaking between their gaze, Stella leaned in and began spoon-feeding Alwin the porridge. "Unlike the Laird, who seems to have fallen under your spell, mistress, I'll hear no arguments about your care for the next week. You will remain in bed with the windows covered and absolutely no shenanigans." She gave Robert another sharp look. "Of any kind."

As Stella turned to deposit the porridge bowl on the desk and retrieve a pitcher of water, Robert locked eyes with Alwin once again.

"We'll see about that," she whispered, an impish gleam in her eye.

He knew without a doubt then that she would be right as rain in no time—and so would he.

Chapter Forty-Two

Alwin's week of forced convalescence flew by relatively quickly, in part thanks to the dozens of stolen kisses she shared with Robert. He was also her co-conspirator when it came to helping her walk around the chamber, then up and down the spiraling stairs that led from the chamber to the great hall. They were careful to keep their activities from Stella, which was difficult because she always seemed to be just around the corner with another bowl of porridge or broth and more admonitions on the importance of bed rest.

A few days after she awoke, the village healer returned to the castle. Apparently the birthing she was seeing to had gone smoothly, but her wagon had broken a wheel on the journey back, forcing her to wait for repairs. After examining her, the healer declared that Alwin was well on her way toward being completely healed, with only a little residual swelling around the temple.

By the end of the week, Alwin was itching to get some fresh air and move her legs more—and perhaps see what Robert's kisses promised in their increasingly heated intensity. Stella had managed to shoo him out of the chamber earlier in the morning, telling him it was high time he did something useful instead of getting in her way with all his hovering over his wife. He was likely back with his men in the yard, training with them.

After a luxurious bath, Alwin felt more refreshed than ever. She hummed a tune as she got dressed. Stella had insisted that she wear stout wool stockings underneath the fine blue gown she had laid out, despite the surprisingly mild spring air floating in through the open window. She couldn't be annoyed with the older woman for her extra care, even though there was nothing she desired more than to have the sea- and grass-scented air brushing her bare ankles.

It was nearly time for the midday meal, and she could hardly contain her excitement to dine with the clan in a chair rather than in bed. But before she could settle into a meal with Robert and the others, she had a stop to make.

Her bright blue skirts swinging, Alwin strode through the great hall and into the kitchen, where the staff was making their final preparations to serve the light and simple meal. Looking past the serving girls' heads, Alwin spotted Nora directing the action in the middle of the room. Alwin cleared her throat in an attempt to gain the head cook's attention but got more of a reaction than she had planned. Suddenly all eyes were on her, but instead of questioning looks or even displeasure at the sight of the English mistress, she was hit with a wall of broad smiles and several well-wishes.

Nora's voice managed to sound stern, even though she was smiling around the corners of her mouth as well. "All right, that's enough girls. Don't overwhelm the mistress with your noise!"

One by one, the serving girls passed Alwin, each with a tray in hand, bobbing a curtsy to her as they went. As they filed out, Nora sighed and rested a hand on her ample hip, tired but smiling.

"Nora, I cannot comprehend how you manage to keep things running so smoothly in here with such a large castle to feed," Alwin said sweetly.

"Och, mistress, you're too kind. Truth be known, though, I have become too old to do this work all on my own. I thought I should tell you I've been training Bess this last week so that she can help out more in the years to come."

"Of course! And how is Bess taking to it?"

"Quite well indeed, mistress. In fact, just yesterday, I introduced her to the new system of ledger keeping you devised. She's already taken to it, but it's no surprise considering how much clearer it all is. Stella and I are both ever so grateful to you, mistress, for making it so much easier."

Alwin smiled brightly. This was the real reason she was visiting the kitchens. She longed to know if the cook and the head of servants had adapted to and stuck with her new notation system. "I'm so glad to hear it. Thank you, Nora."

With a light step and an even lighter heart, Alwin headed back to the great hall. Robert and his men were just beginning to file in, sweaty but laughing among themselves after their first training session with their Laird since the attack by the messenger. Robert had told Alwin when she had still been on bed rest that he had briefed his men on increased security measures, and that several of them had been angry or ashamed that their castle, under their proud protection, had been infiltrated by an assassin. Robert had assured them, however, that they hadn't failed. They were even glad for the extra grueling training, as it gave them the opportunity to identify and weed out any potential weaknesses in their defenses.

"You look pleased with yourself, wife," Robert said with a smile as he settled himself in the chair next to hers. She was always surprised by his smile, as it transformed is ruggedly handsome face into a mischievous boy's. Lately, though, she was seeing more of that smile, and thought contentedly that she could get used to it.

"I am. I have just heard from Nora that the changes I have made to the castle's record keeping are going smoothly. You see, Nora and Stella were each doing it differently, and—"

She stopped in mid-sentence when she saw his smile slip and his face harden ever so slightly. "What is it?"

"Are you sure making changes now is wise?" he said levelly.

She felt her heart plummet, then her temper flared. "Do you still doubt my loyalty? You think because I'm English that I will somehow betray you and your clan? Or is it that you are so resistant to change that you won't even hear out a good idea when it's staring you in the face?"

"Nay, lass, hear me out!" he said on a chuckle, throwing his arms up in surrender.

She was so confused by his rapidly changing demeanor that she merely stared at him.

"I only meant to ask if you were sure that you were up to the task on your first full day upright in nearly two weeks!"

"Oh," she said in a small voice. Then she felt a smile creeping over her mouth. "Sorry. I suppose I'll have to work on not jumping to the conclusion that you are behaving like—" She didn't want to finish and risk shattering the delicate trust they had been building over the last several days.

He grasped her chin in one of his large, warm hands, not letting her lower her eyes in embarrassment. "That I was behaving like a fool, just as I was not long ago? It's all right, lass. You have every right to doubt me still. It will take time." Releasing her chin, he ran a hand through his dark hair and exhaled, leaning back in his chair. "Truth be told, I'll have to keep working on all this too. I've been away so much that I've nearly forgotten how to run my own castle or how to compromise and adapt to change for that matter. But we'll practice together."

Confusion filled her once again. "What do you mean, *together*?"

He took her hand in his and gave her a serious look. "I mean my raiding days are behind me."

She gasped, but he continued.

"Of course, if King Robert the Bruce calls upon me to serve him in battle, I won't refuse. But it's time for me to see to the needs of my people. I thought I was doing what was best for them by plundering in the Borderlands, but perhaps they would be better served by me here, where I can get to know them again and look after the castle more closely. What is it, lass?"

Tears were blurring her vision, but she smiled through them. "I'm glad," she said simply, and before her tears got the better of her, she flung her arms around Robert's neck and pulled him to her.

After a moment, Robert withdrew from her embrace, but cupped her cheek and tilted her face toward his. His pale blue eyes bore into her, searing her with heat. Her eyes dropped to his lips, which were curved slightly. Her own lips tingled in expectation as his mouth moved toward hers. When their lips connected, warmth seeped through her, chasing away the tears of joy and replacing them with a longing. Robert tilted his head to the side, deepening the kiss, shooting tingling anticipation through her limbs, and especially in certain areas—

Burke coughed surreptitiously from his seat on Robert's left side. Startled and a little embarrassed, Alwin jumped and pulled back from her intimate kiss with Robert, which happened to be taking place in front of everyone gathered in the great hall for the midday meal. Robert turned and raised an eyebrow at his second in command, trying to give him a fierce glare. Alwin thought that for the briefest moment an expression that had the faint appearance of a boy caught with his hand in the sweets pantry flitted across his rugged face.

"I fear we are disturbing Burke's meal, wife," Robert said wryly. He pushed back from the table and stood, taking Alwin's hand in his and pulling her to stand alongside him.

"Forgive us, Burke. We will leave you in peace to sate your appetite," then on a whisper to Alwin that was loud enough for Burke to hear, "while we sate ours."

"Robert!" Alwin gasped and swatted his shoulder.

Without acknowledging her shock or Burke's muffled laughter, Robert pulled her around their table and through the filled tables toward the stairs leading to their chamber, confident and proud as the leader she knew he was.

He increased their pace until they were nearly running up the stairs. By the time they reached their chamber door, she was panting and laughing, one hand still captured in his, the other wrapped around her middle.

"No more, I beg of you! I am spent!" she gasped through her giggles.

"Oh, but lass, I have so much more planned for you," he said darkly.

In one smooth motion, he managed to toss her over his shoulder and sweep into the chamber, closing the door behind him with his boot. She shrieked in shock and delight, slapping his back.

"Robert, it's the middle of the day! The sun is shining, and I think the entire clan knows what we are about! We cannot!"

He strode to the bed, undeterred by her playful swats and the astonishment in her voice.

"Clearly I have not been a good enough lover to you, lass. If I had, you would know that pleasure can and should be enjoyed at all hours of the day, and you would be as hungry for this as I am." He tossed her on the bed, a predatory gleam in his eyes.

"I am...hungry," she said, feeling a blush rise to her cheeks but refusing to back down from his unspoken challenge.

He made a satisfied masculine growl in the back of his throat then raised one knee and placed it on the bed, bringing himself a few inches closer to her. Picking up on the game, she scooted back a little to the far side of the bed. His eyes gleamed fiercely, a wicked smile curving his mouth up. He raised his other knee to the bed, and she inched back again, keeping distance between them. Suddenly he lunged at her, but she moved quick enough to avoid his embrace. She shot to the foot of the bed and leapt off then turned to stare triumphantly back at him sprawled across the bed.

Bending an elbow, he propped his head up with his hand and sighed dramatically. "Will I ever capture you, lass?"

"Perhaps," she said mischievously. "If I let you."

Like lightening, he leapt from the bed and wrapped his steely arms around her, crushing her against his stone-hard body. She gasped but smiled, loving the feeling of his strength, her body melting against his. She looked up into his eyes and saw that all the traces of their game had been replaces with hard need.

"Will you let me now, lass?" he said huskily.

As an answer, she reached up and wove her hands through his loose dark hair then pulled his face toward hers. Ever so lightly, she brushed her lips against his. He groaned, and she felt his chest rumble against her breasts, which were crushed against him. She pulled him even closer, deepening their kiss. Then she tentatively touched her tongue to his lips and he seemed to snap. Their tongues intermingled, stroking and twisting. He raised a hand to her hair and gripped, slightly pulling a handful of her loose strands, but instead of pain, she felt a tingling pleasure shoot from her scalp. His other hand dropped lower to grip her bottom, pressing her hips against his already hard manhood. The aching need that was now familiar was building between her legs, and she pressed back into him.

Pivoting, he spun them both around so her back was to the bed then slowly walked them toward it, until the backs of her legs bumped the mattress. But he didn't stop moving forward, and she was forced to sit down on the edge of the bed. Breaking their kiss, he went to his knees before her. She leaned back, resting her weight on her hands, watching him. He lowered his hands to skim down her skirts and to the hem of her dress then slipped under it, grazing his warm palms against her stockinged lower legs. Even through the thick wool stockings, the heat and sensation of his touch caused her to gasp. His hands went higher, and his fingertips brushed the backs of her knees. She nearly kicked him, the sensation somewhere between a tickle and an erotic caress. She squirmed and bit her lower lip to try to keep from either giggling or moaning, she wasn't sure which.

His touch lost all traces of play, however, as he continued to inch upward. His fingers found the exposed skin of her upper thigh at the top of her stockings, and a bolt of pleasure surged through her. He shifted both hands to one leg and unhurriedly untied and began rolling down her stocking, letting his fingers caress all the newly exposed skin as he moved downward.

She realized she was panting, her eyes locked on

him as he moved achingly slowly. Finally, he had the stocking down to her ankle and past her foot. But then he started all over on her other leg, and the feathery-hot sensations shooting through her seemed to hitch impossibly higher. As he pulled the second stocking free of her foot, she sighed, unsure if she could have taken much more. But then he did something even more shocking.

He pushed her skirts, including her chemise, up and up, exposing all of her legs, all the way to her waist. Then he lowered his mouth to her naked flesh, first pressing a kiss to her inner thigh, then going even higher.

Her eyes widened. "What are you doing?" Her voice sounded breathier than she had anticipated, but her shock was still audible.

He looked up and speared her with his hard, passion-filled eyes. "I want to taste you and make you come," he replied roughly.

Unable to form words, either to protest or inquire what exactly he meant, she merely stared at him, her lips parted. Not waiting for her to reply, he lowered his head again and placed a kiss directly on the junction of her legs.

Her shock instantly transformed as jagged bolts of pleasure caused her to moan. He repeated his kiss, then deepened it so that his tongue caressed the most intimate and throbbing part of her. Her head fell back as wave upon wave of heated sensation washed over her entire body. Her arms, quivering under her, gave way, and she sagged back onto the bed. Just when she thought his caresses and swirls of the tongue would drive her mad with ecstasy, she felt a nudge of pressure at her opening, then his finger slipped inside her, filling her and causing the wild aching to hitch up yet another notch. She called out his name and begged him not to stop, twisting her hands in the bed linens. He growled in response and matched the caresses of his tongue to the thrusts of his finger, going deeper, faster.

She climbed higher and higher until suddenly she felt as if her whole body exploded. She cried out as she soared at the top of pleasure then slowly returned to earth, residual jolts rippling through her now limp limbs. She was vaguely aware of Robert rising from his knees between her legs and ripping off his simple white shirt. Then he was on the bed next to her, and the haze of pleasure began to clear when she saw—both in his hungry eyes and in the prominent bulge under his kilt—that he still longed to join her in release.

"I didn't know that was possible," she said, luxuriating in contentment. Then a thought occurred to her. "Can I do that...to you?"

He cursed, but there was no anger in it, only pained longing. "Aye, lass, but I can't promise I'll last long."

She gave him a quizzical look but quirked a smile. "I think I could get used to the idea of you being at my mercy as I was just at yours."

He snorted but didn't want to waste any more time in verbal parlance. His needy cock throbbed at just the mention of her sweet mouth on it. Instead, he twisted her shoulders slightly so he could work on the ties running down the back of her dress. She pulled her honey-brown hair out of the way, exposing her creamy, slim neck. He couldn't help himself; he leaned in and gave her a little nip with his teeth on the soft spot where her neck joined her shoulder. Her breath hitched, but before he could administer any more nibbles, she had twisted back around to face him, her dress loose enough now to slide enticingly down her shoulders.

As he tugged down her dress, chemise and all, her hands went to his belt buckle, quickly unfastening it. The material of his kilt no longer bound, it slid from him. Just as the air hit his aching and hard member, he managed to pull Alwin's dress down enough to free her breasts. The combination had him groaning. He drank her in, longing to rub his slightly bristled chin against those creamy curves, to lick and suck and tease each of the pink tips, to feel her come again, but this time with him inside her.

She didn't let him, though, for her hand wrapped around his cock, and he instinctively jerked with pleasure. In two torturous strokes she already had him clenching his teeth and praying that he didn't finish right at that moment. Placing her other hand on his shoulder, she gave him a little push backward so he lay flat on the bed, completely naked. She took the briefest moment to scoot her dress past her hips and kick it off the side of the bed, then her hand was back on him, stroking. She leaned over him in a crouch, her hair cascading all around him like a waterfall.

Then she did what he ached for—ever so slowly, she lowered herself down the length of his body, trailing kisses down his neck, his chest, his stomach, then paused. He raised his head to look down at her, her lips hovering tantalizingly over his enlarged cock. With the slightest hint of uncertainty, she leaned forward and placed a kiss on the head of his shaft. Heat jolted from her lips through his cock and bollocks, and he moaned. That seemed to encourage her, for her lips opened slightly and she took him partway into her mouth. This time he groaned even louder, and his hips uncontrollably twitched.

"That's it, lass," he rasped.

She took him in farther, her tongue swirling as his had on her clit. She pulled back a little, only to sink down with her mouth once more. He cursed, thinking he might go blind trying to last. She was a quick study. She gained in confidence, her mouth pulling him in as her breasts rubbed against his upper thighs. He couldn't take any more.

Suddenly he sat bolt upright and gripped her shoulders, pulling her mouth from his cock, which felt like it would explode at any moment.

Startled, she said, "Did I do something wrong?"

"Nay, lass," he grated. "But I can't last a second longer if you keep that up, and I want to share this with you."

Her surprise shifted instantly to pleasure, an eager look spreading across her face. Releasing her shoulders, he lay back on the bed once more. "I want you on top of me."

A look of confusion flitted through her eyes, but when she glanced down at his upright cock, he saw it replaced with understanding. She swung a lean leg over his hip so that she was straddling him, her hands on either side of his head and her perfect breasts nearly in his face.

Taking her hips in his hands he glided into her with a groan. She too gasped and arched her back, jutting her breasts closer. He stretched his neck to capture a nipple in his mouth and was rewarded with another, deeper moan from her. He lifted her hips a few inches, then guided them back down so that she was fully settled onto his cock. After only a few strokes, she seemed to gather what to do, and took over, setting her own provocatively slow pace. He gritted his teeth, willing himself to resist the urge to thrust into her hard and fast. Though he wanted his release, he wanted her to join him, and he was even more turned on by her slowly building passion.

He let his head fall back and take in the sight of her. Her rosy lips were slightly parted, and her cheeks were flushed with desire. Her hair once again cascaded all around him, surrounding him with her scent—roses and warmth. Glancing lower, he took in the sight of her pert breasts bouncing in rhythm to their thrusts. Christ, he wasn't going to last any longer.

Gripping her hips, he increased their pace and pulled her harder down onto him so that he was inside her to the hilt. Her breath hitched at the sudden shift, and he could feel her start to tighten and spasm. That was the last straw. He exploded into a thousand pieces of pure light and ecstasy, bellowing his pleasure as he thrust once more into her. His voice mingled with hers as she too found her release and cried out her pleasure. They both hovered in bliss for several more moments, rocking together as they drifted back down.

Spent, she slumped over him, and he turned slightly so he could wrap an arm around her as she draped herself across his chest.

"Do you feel differently about making love in daylight hours now?"

She gave a breathy chuckle. "I could get used to this."

His chest rumbled with his own laughter. "I'll make sure that you do."

Epilogue

June, 1307

Alwin twisted her arm behind her and tugged on the laces of her dress for what seemed like the hundredth time just since this morning. She would have to ask Stella to help her loosen them a few more inches. She knew she was being silly, but she didn't want to ask the castle weavers to make her a new dress for her changing figure just yet. Part of her liked the way her dresses hugged her new curves—one new curve in particular.

A smile crept to her lips just at the thought of it: Robert's babe growing inside her. She was not only the Lady of the Sinclair clan and the mistress of Roslin castle, but she was going to be the mother of the next Sinclair heir. And she and Robert would raise their son or daughter to know love, acceptance, and happiness. She would give her child the joyful childhood she never had, and she knew Robert would be a devoted and loving father. He was already mooning over her like she was made of the finest glass from Murano— both treasured and fragile. She wasn't allowing him to be *too* delicate with her, though. The memory of their bed-rattling lovemaking earlier that morning sent a tingling thrill through her blood.

She practically sailed from their chamber through the great hall and the yard, nearly skipping to the northeast tower and up the stairs to the solar. Humming to herself, she threw open the solar door, only to halt dead in her tracks, the tune dying on her lips.

Three huge warriors turned to stare at her. One of them was her husband, but he looked fiercer than normal, his face shrouded in a scowl and his eyes intense. Burke, standing next to him, was transformed as well. Normally gallant and chivalrous in Alwin's presence, he looked more like a battle-hardened warrior at the moment. Unlike Robert, who wore the same plain white shirt with the sleeves rolled up and clan kilt that he always donned around the castle, Burke had on a leather vest studded with metal, and a huge sword was strapped to his back. He, too, bore a look of strained concentration.

If the appearance of Burke and her husband had startled her, the third man in the solar downright made her knees knock. He was just as tall and broadly muscled as Robert, which few men were. Like Burke, he wore an armored leather vest over a linen shirt, but both the shirt and his Sinclair-colored kilt were soiled with dirt, grime, and—was that blood?

He, too, had a large sword strapped to him, but it was on his hip, for across his back was slung a bow and quiver full of arrows. His hair, dark brown rather than black like Robert's, was pulled back and tied at the nape of his muscular neck, and his hard jawline was covered in at least a week's worth of stubble. When her eyes met his, she nearly took a step backward before she reminded herself that she was the lady of this keep. Their steely gray cut her like a knife. He was strikingly similar to Robert in appearance, but a far dirtier, deadlier, and meaner version, based on the glare he was shooting at her.

"Look at my wife that way much longer, brother, and you may find yourself a few teeth shorter than when you arrived," Robert said, clearly taking notice.

"Brother?" Alwin had looked forward to meeting Robert's siblings but hadn't anticipated it to be quite so terrifying.

Before Robert could explain, his brother strode toward her with the deadly grace of a true warrior. She had to resist the urge for a second time to back up, feeling as though just being near so hardened a killer would be dangerous. He surprised her, though, when he halted and gave her a sweeping bow.

"Lady Alwin. My brother has bent my ear with tales of your grace and beauty, but clearly his words fail to capture reality."

Too stunned to reply for a moment, Alwin remembered herself in time to drop a quick curtsy to her new brother-in-law.

"You are too kind…?"

"Garrick, my lady. The middle one."

"Ah yes," Alwin brightened, "the warrior archer."

Garrick raised a dark eyebrow at her, but Robert only chuckled.

"You forgot to convey how fearless your new bride is, Robert," Garrick said over his shoulder dryly.

Alwin looked between the two men. Through his smile, Robert said, "We always teased Garrick about his Norse name and his insistence to live up to it. Don't mind him, love, he looks rougher than he is."

"Perhaps we should test that theory on the practice yard, *older* brother," Garrick said with a dangerous smile.

Alwin's eyes widened at Garrick's barely-masked challenge and insult, but Robert roared with laughter and clapped his brother on the back.

"Aye, it's good to have you home, brother!"

Burke and Garrick were smiling too, so Alwin breathed easy. Perhaps this was how siblings treated each other. Or men anyway.

When Robert's rumbling laugher had died down, the three men's faces sobered.

"We should continue our conversation but perhaps more privately," Garrick said softly.

Alwin knew he was referring to her intrusion. Before she could excuse herself, though, Robert interjected.

"Nay, Alwin can stay. This involves her too, and she should have a say."

Burke and Garrick both looked uneasy, but Robert's authoritative voice brokered no argument. For her part, she wasn't sure based on the atmosphere in the room when she had entered that she wanted to become involved in whatever they were discussing, but she was touched that Robert wanted her to have a voice. He loved her decisiveness, her stubbornness, and her willingness to form and share her opinions, not only about how the household should be run, but also regarding the increased activity by the English in the Lowlands, and the rumors of Robert the Bruce's plan to make a move against them. He listened to her, respected her views—it was better than the girlish fairytales she thought she could never have. Theirs was a true partnership.

"As you wish, Robert, but it doesn't seem right to upset a woman in her…condition," Garrick said with a glance at her middle.

Now it was Alwin's turn to raise an eyebrow at him. "For your information, sir, I am not made of glass. I am quite capable of carrying on a conversation, I assure you."

Her words came out tarter than she had intended, but to her surprise, Garrick cracked a half-smile and nodded in acquiescence.

"Nevertheless, why don't you take a seat, love? We discuss warfare," Robert said gently.

Alwin walked around to the other side of the desk that the three men had been leaning over and plopped down in the chair, only mildly defeated by Robert's overprotectiveness.

Robert cleared his throat. "As I was saying, we can't know for sure where Hewett's allegiance lies, or if he has funded Warren's cause with Alwin's dowry money."

Though prepared to discuss the complex intricacies of politics and the threat of war looming over them all, Alwin had not been ready for such a direct statement about her father. She sat upright, suddenly alert.

"About a month ago, I sent him a missive letting him know that our bairn was on the way, partly out of courtesy, since I didn't exactly ask his permission before our marriage. But I was also curious to see if he would reveal anything about a lingering alliance between him and Warren," Robert continued to Garrick, who nodded, grim-faced.

"I haven't received word back, but that doesn't tell us much. Perhaps he is too ashamed to acknowledge that he'll have a Scottish barbarian for a grandchild and has simply cut Alwin from his life."

Alwin cringed slightly at his words, because they were all too likely. She had tried not to get her hopes up that her father might respond to the missive about their child, but some part of her still hoped he would set aside his greed and embrace his only daughter. As the days and then weeks stretched, she had slowly given up that small hope.

"It is also possible he wants nothing to do with

Warren now that their marriage arrangement has fallen apart. But we can't discount the chance that he has aligned with Warren to promote and fund another war effort. Hewett would be a wealthy and strategic if not militarily powerful ally for the English cause. We simply can't know where he stands without gathering more intelligence." Robert dragged a hand through his hair in frustration.

Alwin knew that part of him wanted to be out there on the front lines, but that he didn't want to risk leaving his clan—and his wife and child—unprotected and leaderless.

"And we still don't know what Warren plans," Burke said grimly. "We have heard word that he has blathered to anyone who will listen that his wife was stolen by a Highland barbarian, and that his messenger, who was sent to negotiate a ransom, was murdered in cold blood."

"With King Robert's defeat of the English forces at Loudoun Hill last month, there seems to be more talk of all-out war from everyone except Longshanks, who is rumored to be ill," Garrick added. "It wouldn't surprise me in the least if Warren was trying to drum up more conflict, especially if Edward is on his way out. A shakeup at court could mean more room for Warren to make an even greater name for himself and expand his power."

"And where does Robert the Bruce stand in all of this? Does he court war as well? If so, it will be hard on our people," Alwin said.

Garrick gave her a steely stare, and Robert, seeing it, spoke quietly to him. "It's all right, brother. She is with us."

Garrick grunted and finally broke his hard gaze at her. "Aye, brother. It's just not every day that I hear concern about 'our' cause and people from an English mouth."

"The English accent grows on you," Robert replied, eyes twinkling.

"Are you sure you're not just growing soft, brother?"

For a second time, Robert didn't take the bait, only shot a smile at Alwin. "Perhaps one day you'll understand," he said to Garrick, then gave Alwin a wink.

"If you lovesick bairns are quite through," Garrick said dryly, "I can speak to King Robert's perspective. He knows a head-to-head confrontation with the English would be suicide for the Scots. They outnumber us, but their disadvantage comes in the form of a war of attrition. The English fight stiffly, in rows and with full armor. Because there are so many of them, they move slowly, and they don't know this landscape very well. If they launch a full-scale war against us, we will let them come, but they will be met with constant harassment, stealth assaults, skimming of their supplies, and surprise attacks when they're least ready. The Bruce knows this will be hard on the people, as all war is, but he believes that by refusing to meet the

English on their terms, we can harrow them into retreat and show them whose country this is."

"And you agree with the Bruce?" Robert asked, all playfulness gone.

"Aye. I would be at his side now as he plans his next move if he hadn't granted your request for me to return to Roslin."

This was news to Alwin. "Why did you send for him, Robert?"

"Because now that I have resumed my responsibilities to the clan here, I need someone I can trust to carry on my work in the Borderlands, and I trust no one more that Burke and Garrick," he replied, exchanging heavy looks with each man.

Garrick tensed despite the compliment. "As I told you before, I work alone. I don't want your man getting in my way and—"

"And I won't leave your side, Robert. You need me here as an extra set of eyes and ears, especially now that you are more...preoccupied." Burke said the last word carefully, but everyone in the room knew that Robert had been more distracted with Alwin carrying their child.

"Enough." Robert's stern and authoritative tone reminded Alwin that he was a Laird and had been raised to be so since he was born. "This is only for one mission. King Robert only agreed for you to be out of his service for a few months. He only granted my request because I have fought against Longshanks for so many years. He also likely understands well that this mission will help his cause. In addition to gathering whatever information you can, you are to do anything you can to interfere with England's building war effort." He gave them each another hard look. "Including pursuing and dispatching of Warren."

Alwin stifled a gasp behind her hand. Of course, it came as no surprise to her that Robert would want Warren killed once and for all. She knew how much he longed to be the one to finally put an end to his scheming and get vengeance for all that the power-hungry Englishman had inflicted on his land and his people. What surprised her was that he was apparently giving over his desire for revenge.

Seeming to read her thoughts, he turned to her and said softly, "I still want to see him dead. He brought war to my doorstep, killed my people, razed my land, and dared to attempt to harm you." This last he said through gritted teeth. "But I am not so vain anymore to insist that it be me who brings him to justice, just so long as he can no longer threaten us."

"I relish the opportunity, brother," Garrick interjected heatedly, "but as I said, I work alone. I have done the same kind of work for the Bruce and never needed a babysitter before."

Before Burke could add his objection, Robert held up his hand. "It is already decided. Both of you will leave on the morrow for the Borderlands. I expect you to be able to move quickly and quietly, considering there are only two of you. Once you approach Warren's holding, make sure you are less conspicuous; otherwise you'll stand out like sore thumbs with your weaponry and warhorses. You are to stay no longer than a week, collecting as much intelligence as you can. If you happen to stumble upon any important missives, shipments, or supplies, well—" Robert gave a predatory half-smile "—all the better. But you are to return after a week in the Borderlands—*together*."

Burke scowled, and Garrick crossed his muscular arms in front of his chest, looking like he wanted to challenge Robert once again, but he said nothing.

Trying to break the tension in the room, Alwin stood and took a deep breath. "Well, if that's all decided, we should prepare a fine evening meal for tonight to see the two of you off. I'll go speak with Nora."

"And perhaps each of you would like to prepare for your journey," Robert said, pointedly ending further discussion.

The two unhappy warriors strode out of the solar, Alwin following behind them. But before she could reach the doorway, Robert had snaked an arm around her middle, just above the still-slight swell of her belly. He spun her around, and to her surprise, planted a passionate kiss on her lips.

When he finally released her and she could breathe again, she said, "What was that for?"

"Oh, nothing. I just had to make sure you were real. Sometimes I can't believe I am not only married to the most beautiful woman in all of England or Scotland, but also that she is smarter and braver and more spirited than I."

She swatted his shoulder in play annoyance but beamed at his compliment. "I am glad you agree I am smarter, because I have some ideas about how we could improve upon the organization of some of the rooms in the main southwest tower."

He groaned and rolled his eyes, but before she could swat him again, he kissed her heartily once more, then said, "Go on, love, tell me all about it. We have nothing but time."

The End

Thank you!

Thank you for taking the time to read *Highlander's Ransom*! Consider sharing your enjoyment of this book (or any of my other books) with fellow readers by leaving a review on sites like Amazon and Goodreads.

I love connecting with readers! For book updates, news on future projects, pictures, and more, visit my website at www.EmmaPrinceBooks.com.

You also can join me on Twitter at:
@EmmaPrinceBooks.

Or keep up on Facebook at:
facebook.com/EmmaPrinceBooks.

Teasers for the Sinclair Brothers Trilogy

Garrick and Jossalyn's story unfolds in **HIGHLANDER'S REDEMPTION,** Book Two of the Sinclair Brothers Trilogy. Available now on Amazon!

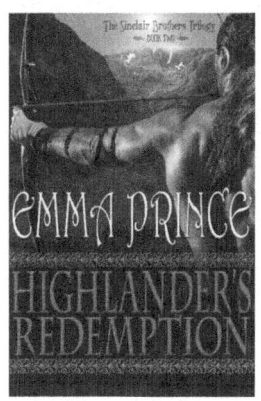

He is on a mission…

Garrick Sinclair, an expert archer and Robert the Bruce's best mercenary, is sent on a covert operation to the Borderlands by his older brother, Laird Robert Sinclair. He never expects to meet the most beautiful woman he's ever seen—who turns out to be the sister of Raef Warren, his family's mortal enemy. Though he knows he shouldn't want her—and doesn't deserve her—can he resist the passion that ignites between them?

She longs for freedom…

Jossalyn Warren is desperate to escape her cruel brother and put her healing skills to use, and perhaps the handsome stranger with a dangerous look about him will be her ticket to a new life. She never imagines that she will be spirited away to Robert the Bruce's secret camp in the Highlands, yet more shocking is the lust the dark warrior stirs in her. But can she heal the invisible scars of a man who believes that he's no hero?

Burke's story continues in **HIGHLANDER'S RETURN**, a Sinclair Brothers Trilogy BONUS novella. Available now on Amazon!

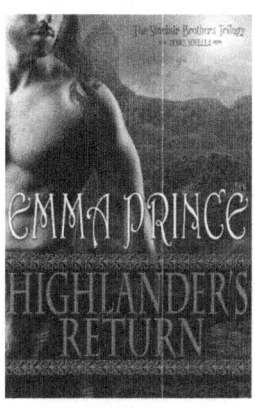

First love's flame extinguished...

Burke Sinclair and Meredith Sutherland want nothing more than to be married, but ancient clan hostilities tear them apart. When Meredith is forced to marry another to appease her father and secure an alliance, the young lovers think all is lost.

Only to be reignited...

Ten long years of a stifling marriage nearly crush Meredith's spirit. But when her unfeeling husband dies and Burke, now a grown man and a hardened warrior, suddenly reappears in her life, the two may get a second chance at first love—if old blood feuds don't rip them apart once and for all.

Follow the thrilling conclusion of the Sinclair Brothers Trilogy with **HIGHLANDER'S RECKONING**. Available now on Amazon!

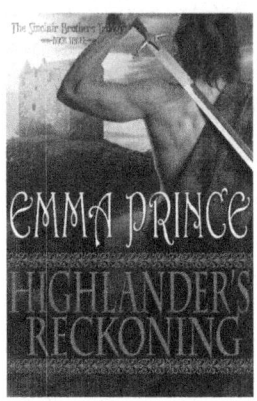

He is forced to marry…

Daniel Sinclair is charged by Robert the Bruce to secure the King's ancestral holding in the Lowlands—and marry the daughter of the castle's keeper to secure a shaky alliance. But the lass's spirit matches her fiery hair, and Daniel quickly realizes that the King's "reward" is more than he bargained for.

She won't submit without a fight…

To protect her secret—and illegal—love of falconry, Rona Kennedy must keep her new husband at arm's length, no matter how much his commanding presence and sinfully handsome face make her knees tremble. But when an all-out war with Raef Warren, the Sinclair clan's greatest enemy, finally erupts, will their growing love be destroyed forever?

Teaser for Enthralled (Viking Lore, Book 1)

Step into the lush, daring world of the Vikings with **Enthralled (Viking Lore, Book 1)**!

He is bound by honor…

Eirik is eager to plunder the treasures of the fabled lands to the west in order to secure the future of his village. The one thing he swears never to do is claim possession over another human being. But when he journeys across the North Sea to raid the holy houses of Northumbria, he encounters a dark-haired beauty, Laurel, who stirs him like no other. When his cruel cousin tries to take Laurel for himself, Eirik breaks his oath in an attempt to protect her. He claims her as his thrall. But can he claim her heart, or will Laurel fall prey to the devious schemes of his enemies?

She has the heart of a warrior...

Life as an orphan at Whitby Abbey hasn't been easy, but Laurel refuses to be bested by the backbreaking work and lecherous advances she must endure. When Viking raiders storm the abbey and take her captive, her strength may finally fail her—especially when she must face her fear of water at every turn. But under Eirik's gentle protection, she discovers a deeper bravery within herself—and a yearning for her golden-haired captor that she shouldn't harbor. Torn between securing her freedom or giving herself to her Viking master, will fate decide for her—and rip them apart forever?

About the Author

Emma Prince is the Bestselling and Amazon All-Star Author of steamy historical romances jam-packed with adventure, conflict, and of course love!

Emma grew up in drizzly Seattle, but traded her rain boots for sunglasses when she and her husband moved to the eastern slopes of the Sierra Nevada. Emma spent several years in academia, both as a graduate student and an instructor of college-level English and Humanities courses. She always savored her "fun books"—normally historical romances—on breaks or vacations. But as she began looking for the next chapter in her life, she wondered if perhaps her passion could turn into a career. Ever since then, she's been reading and writing books that celebrate happily ever afters!

Visit Emma's website, www.EmmaPrinceBooks.com, for updates on new books, future projects, her newsletter sign-up, book extras, and more!

You can follow Emma on Twitter at:
@EmmaPrinceBooks

Or join her on Facebook at:
facebook.com/EmmaPrinceBooks

Made in the USA
Monee, IL
23 August 2021